FOLLY

Recent Titles by Stella Cameron
from Severn House

SHADOWS
SECOND TO NONE
NO STRANGER
ALL SMILES

The Alex Duggins series
FOLLY

FOLLY

Stella Cameron

Severn House Large Print
London & New York

This first large print edition published 2015
in Great Britain and the USA by
SEVERN HOUSE PUBLISHERS LTD of
19 Cedar Road, Sutton, Surrey, England, SM2 5DA.
First world regular print edition published 2015 by
Severn House Publishers Ltd., London and New York.

British Library Cataloguing in Publication Data

Cameron, Stella author.
    Folly. – (The Alex Duggins series)
    1. Cotswold Hills (England)–Fiction. 2. Murder–
Investigation–Fiction. 3. Detective and mystery stories.
4. Large type books.
    I. Title II. Series
    813.5'4-dc23

    ISBN-13: 9780727872715

Severn House Publishers support the Forest Stewardship Council™
[FSC™], the leading international forest certification organisation. All
our titles that are printed on FSC certified paper carry the FSC logo.

Typeset by Palimpsest Book Production Ltd.,
Falkirk, Stirlingshire, Scotland.
Printed and bound in Great Britain by
T J International, Padstow, Cornwall.

Acknowledgements

When you make a leap without a safety net you're in dangerous territory. My leap into *Folly*, introducing Alex Duggins, her series, and the world of mystery it inhabits, was taken both as a seasoned writer and with a small army of fabulous supporters. This move was never a risk. Once a writer, always a writer, but still I needed courage and a fresh dose of self-belief. The former I had, the latter I might never have gained without the following people and props:

Thank you Jayne Ann Krentz and Mary Daheim for saying, 'You can do it.' Thank you Matt Cameron for being my sounding board when I wavered. Thank you Patricia Smith for being the best editor in the world and for working with me.

Thank you Gloucestershire, the Cotswold Hills and your amazingly generous people for answering many more questions than you might have answered with such willing interest and care.

Thank you Terri Farrell for loaning Bogie-the-beautiful to me and to this story.

Thank you Linda Hankins, DVM, Curt Girouard, DVM and the Danville Small Animal Clinic for advice and encouragement.

Thank you Cissy Hartley and Writerspace.com for the years of support.

Thank you Sheri Brooks and Dave de Heer for having my back every step of the way.

Thanks always to Dietrich Nelson & Associates, dnelson@dnaepr.com, for the years of support, but most of all for the friendship.

And this may get whacky, but . . . thank you to the following for being scrumptious enough to flavor my stories:

Trebor-Bassetts Sherbert Lemons (Detective Inspector O'Neil is grateful, too).

Spring Breweries and in particular their Ambler Ale.

Tesco's Digestive Biscuits and the many brands of similar goodies that have always been part of 'tea time'.

Marks and Spencer's Battenburg Cake.

All the Cotswold tea shops I love – they are too numerous to single out, as are the pubs. One day I'll write that list!

And last, but really first, Jerry Cameron, my fellow companion and patient sufferer along the often rough road of being a writer's husband; you are the best, my love.

Author's Note

Alex Duggins is not the girl next door. At first glance she could be – but only until you come to know her better. Pub owner, graphic artist and animal lover, Alex returned to her little home town of Folly-on-Weir in search of a chance to regroup following her divorce. Surely she could find peace in the idyllic Cotswold Hills where she grew up.

Wrong, but you'll learn much more about Alex's trials and triumphs, and her close calls with disaster, as you read *Folly*.

A year ago, when I had written this, the first book in what I already knew would be a series, I brought the book out in a narrow print-on-demand program. This was my trial balloon as, after publishing many books with American settings, I moved into writing British mysteries.

How thrilled I was when Severn House came to me with a plan to publish the Alex Duggins series to a wide audience. Nothing warms an author's heart more than having a good publisher who 'gets it.' And better yet, really loves it!

Prologue

How long had it taken to change a life forever? A minute, ninety seconds – while he listened, barely understanding, as two men destroyed his own young innocence, and allowed another child to die?

Nothing was ever the same after that day. All the days and years that followed had led to this night of hope and fear.

'Come on, boy, catch up,' Dominic called. 'We'll freeze if we don't keep moving.'

The only reason he could see the dog at all in the darkness was that his dark gray fur showed up against a thickening carpet of snow underfoot, and the falling flakes that grew heavier with each moment.

Brother Dominic stopped and watched Bogie approach like a trotting miniature show horse in slow motion, lifting each foot as if it burned.

'OK, we'll keep each other a bit warmer.' He swept up his little gray buddy and tucked him inside an old tweed coat. 'Now, we've got to get a move on. This is a borrowed coat and we need to give it back to Percy.'

Talking to his dog was an indulgence Dominic reserved for when they were alone. He smiled at the thought. They were rarely as alone as they were in the middle of this night, on this hill in the Cotswold Hills that were so spectacular in

1

daylight, yet so pitiless when every step was an act of faith.

He had pulled the hood on his habit up to cover his head and ward off some of the cold. The old, brown cloth was already soaked and starting to freeze.

Silence seemed absolute. Except when a gust of wind sent frigid, leafless branches raking together.

Not a single vehicle had passed on the narrow road that forked away from the tiny village below and rose to traverse the hill. There was a scatter of farms and houses up here, all with feeder tracks from the road. But any people out there were probably tucked up and sleeping by now.

You couldn't see any buildings from the road.

Bogie scrabbled closer and pressed his wet nose to Dominic's neck.

The wind picked up, drove straight at him, and he leaned against it to push his way on. The snow drove into his face and crammed inside his collar.

He crossed his hands over the dog and pushed his bare hands beneath his arms.

This had to be done.

Old wrongs must be put right, lies dispelled quickly, for the sake of peace, his own but more importantly, the others involved. His challenge was to bring secrets into the light without harming the innocent.

His faith should make him unafraid for himself but he was, after all, still human. And his first attempt at reaching out in friendship had gone so badly.

Below lay the village of Folly-on-Weir but he

saw only a few pinpricks glowing from windows.

A light bobbed up the hill, getting quite close, he thought, and stopped. It looked like a lantern rising and falling in a walker's hand.

Gone.

Ahead he saw the deeper shade of dark where some woods spread along the side of the road.

As hard as he stared, he didn't see the jiggling light again. Company would be welcome but he shouldn't expect any.

The walk since the last place he'd found to sleep had been long and often difficult.

A voice carried on the wind. Dominic stood still again and strained to hear, but it must have been his thoughts playing tricks.

'Help!'

There was nothing imaginary this time. It came from the direction of the woods and Bogie, straining around to see and growling faintly, got rid of any doubt that they had heard something.

'. . . hurt!'

Without another second of hesitation, Dominic struck off the road and headed for the woods. The uneven ground was treacherous, tripping him repeatedly, but he blundered on, his pulse pounding at his temples.

The stiff, wet hood fell down around his neck.

Once among the tree trunks, his pace slowed. He had to put Bogie down again and grab at branches as he went.

'Oh, thank God,' a man cried out. 'I see you, keep coming. Over here.'

Dominic speeded up, not caring what he might

3

walk into, and almost yelled with relief when he saw a crouching figure.

When only feet separated them, the man rose and held his torch so that Brother Dominic could see him better, see how he prepared to attack.

He knew it was too late now but he had to try reason. 'Why are you here?' he asked.

'I'm making sure you can't do more harm,' the other said. 'Because I won't have you spoiling everything, *Brother.* You should have stayed away, damn you.'

One

Privacy and peace.

Early the previous year, Alex Bailey-Jones had come home from London to the Cotswold Hills, to Folly-on-Weir, to bury herself in familiar surroundings and to become too busy to live in the past.

So far she wasn't doing so badly, even if she did catch some curious stares from those she had once happily left behind.

Snow covered the frozen leaves and twigs that crackled beneath her feet. The canopy of tree limbs overhead was bare.

The snowfall had dwindled to a fine, icy swirl. She blinked and turned her head aside.

The woods stood on a knoll overlooking the village below. Up here in the surrounding hills there were homes and farms, each one distant enough from the others not to be overlooked.

On the highest point to the west stood what locals called The Tooth – the jagged remains of Tinley Tower, the folly from which the village got part of its name.

The world felt still.

Gray skies slumped on gray-white fields, and on the hills beyond the village. Thin smoke straggled from chimneys and lights through small leaded windows were signs morning came early in Folly-on-Weir. These and the inevitable dog walkers on the village green, a couple of hardy, dedicated souls who threw balls into the snapping air. Their joyful companions were clearly unperturbed by the cold while they dashed back and forth beside the long pond.

Her breath puffed white vapor into the air and she swallowed against a lump in her throat. Gratitude and sadness were strange but familiar companions. This was her future, this place and whatever she made of her life here. It was the only future she wanted from now on and making it count felt like her big chance at healing the past. Thirty-three was a fine age, a great age to hope for a fresh start.

To the left of the main village, obscured by a ridge, lay another smaller, shabbier section known as Underhill. With her single mother, Alex had grown up there, although she'd gone to school in Folly-on-Weir while Lily Duggins worked at the only pub, as she still did.

Despite the dismal morning, honeyed shades of stone showed up warm and inviting on the buildings lining the commons. Corner Cottage, with its thatched roof and single second-story gable caught Alex's eye as it inevitably always did. Some years earlier she had finally been able to buy the little home for her mother, and Lily's quiet pleasure made them both happy.

Emerging from the edge of the woods, Alex looked back between the trunks of old beeches and the snow-etched bark of younger trees and saplings. The hard lines of jagged brambles and sticks of undergrowth stood out against the bluish haze like snapped, fragile black bones. Too bad it had taken shock and loss to open her eyes to these small beauties everywhere she looked.

She saw another shade, gray, fleeting and fleeing. There and gone. A breath lodged in her throat.

Something had moved.

Probably a rabbit or a pigeon – perhaps a stoat. There had been reported sightings.

Squinting into the eye-watering brightness cast by the snow, Alex saw the shadow move again. It seemed to rise for an instant, then fall away, out of sight.

Pricking, a thousand tiny points buzzed from between her shoulder blades, up her neck and into the hair at the base of her scalp. Her own primal warning of menace.

She tied a green woolen scarf tighter around the neck of her heavy black coat and pulled the hood further forward over her short hair before turning downhill again. Time to get on. No time to get hung up on imagined wraiths.

The Black Dog Inn sat to her right and a little back from the village green with a lantern-strung forecourt in front where people ate and drank for a good part of the year. The multicolored lights were on now as they were every morning, a welcoming twinkle no matter the weather.

Very faintly, she smelled wood smoke.

Most mornings Alex walked down the hill to work, but she drove her Land Rover along the narrow road between village and hill dwellers a couple of times a week – when she needed to visit nearby Bourton-on-the-Water, Broadway or somewhere further afield.

She owned The Black Dog now; in fact, it had

been when she'd heard Will and Cathy Cummings, the former owners, might have to sell up to clear their debts that she'd decided to come back from London and step in. Now the Cummings managed the place and continued to live on the premises. And Lily, who used to be the Cummings' barmaid, was in charge of the seven guest rooms and reservations for the small restaurant. Receipts were picking up well enough. These things took time but they were going in the right direction.

A good arrangement.

Wasn't it? There were times when Alex noticed quick looks from the Cummings, at her or at one another, that belied the friendliness they showed her openly. Apart from her failed marriage, she was the local success story, the girl from nothing who had made her name as a graphic artist at the head of a department in her husband's prestigious advertising firm. After they married Mike had made her his equal partner in every way. But money and success did different things to different people, and without her knowing it was happening, his search for new thrills had poisoned what she and Mike had. There could be no mending the rift, no matter how much Mike had wanted to try.

Alex couldn't always shake the feeling that there were those in Folly who would have enjoyed seeing her creep home, penniless and defeated. Some folks didn't hold with people who got above themselves . . .

She still looked at the pub with a twinge of amazement to think that it was hers. The walk down the hill each day gave her a great view of the place and a lot of satisfaction.

The ground was steep here and Alex took short running steps, driving in the heels of her short boots to keep a solid footing.

An unexpected and icy wind caught her by surprise. Her lips and nose reacted immediately and she put a gloved hand over the lower half of her face.

A moan that built to an agonized wail startled her. She jumped sickeningly hard and, with a pounding heart and her stomach twisting, looked in all directions.

It came again. Pain or desperation – or both. And whoever cried out was in the woods, above Alex now and to her left.

She fingered the mobile phone in her pocket. *I think I heard someone yell – they could be in trouble.* Constable Frye would come in a hurry and he'd be kind enough, but she'd feel a fool having him search for a sound.

The next thing she heard was whimpering and this time she spun around and started back into the trees. Why hadn't she considered she might be hearing a trapped animal?

Instinct took her to the left. A renewed howl made sure she knew she was going in the right direction. A brief picture of the vicious metal teeth of a gin trap came and went. Those things scared her badly but she knew how to release one of them.

Uphill she saw no other living being. She rarely did at this time of day. Gasping, her mouth open, she leaned into the slope and tried to speed up – and caught her foot under a root.

The fall was spectacular but painless enough,

except for the snow and debris that crammed under her hood and into her curly black hair – and her eyes, nose and mouth.

Another time, she would have laughed at herself, but not this morning. First she had to smack her gloves clean, then dig her face and hair out of the mess.

The howling grew steady, an otherworldly, keening knell filled with desolation.

Alex got to her feet, stumbled again in her haste but kept going. She glanced around for any sign of Tony Harrison on his way back from his daily hike into the hills with his dog. Tony worked on livestock at the surrounding farms but his small animal surgery was in the village. He was her closest neighbor on the hill and lived in a red brick house, out of keeping with the local stone buildings, and surrounded by beautiful gardens. She frequently encountered the tall, quiet man on her way to the village. Where was the local vet when you needed him?

Rocketing at her from between the trees came a dog, not big, maybe twelve or fourteen pounds and with unidentified fragments stuck in his woolly, mostly gray fur. He saw Alex, yapped hoarsely and shot away again, his black-tipped ears flapping.

The signal was clear. *Follow me*. Hot and sweating, then cold enough to shiver, Alex broke into a shambling run, keeping her eyes on the path the dog had taken. She strained, listening for more sounds, either from the dog or perhaps another animal who had been with him.

She tried not to think about stories of dogs howling when their owners were injured – or

10

dead. But one of the visions she hated flitted, semi-transparent, before her. For one dreadful instant she saw that brightly lit corridor, felt the rush of whispering people . . . looked into an open grave. Such a small grave. And the wail she heard as a remembered echo was her own.

Alex felt dampness on her cheeks and wiped it away. Silly, silly – how silly to get that image again. It used to be part of an aura she got before a panic attack but she was grateful she so rarely sank all the way into that dark place any more.

Another single howl sounded, much closer this time.

Mounds of shrouded debris made the going hard. Alex resorted to using her hands for balance, gripping anything she could find even though the icy stems slipped through her fingers. Her breath billowed in short, steamy bursts and her throat made raw noises. She couldn't give in to panic.

Steady, moaning yelps had replaced the dog's howling, and when she finally saw him he sat, staring toward her, woolly ears pinned to the sides of his head.

'OK,' she said, trying to soothe him. 'It's OK. Are you hurt? Poor boy. Good boy.' As she got closer, she held a gloved hand toward the dog.

'That lumpy, cold stuff can't feel good on your bottom,' she said. He perched on a heap of snow with rocks and twigs sticking out. 'Silly boy. Come on, I'll find out where you belong.'

He didn't move except to twitch his ears a little away from his gray head. Soft brown eyes stared at her, implored her?

Alex stopped walking – and talking.

Raising his head, the little animal let out another howl.

Red stained the snow behind him. A shocking, rusty scarlet she gradually realized was a huge patch. The more she glanced around and back, the more marking Alex could make out. And some pieces of what stuck through the snow were not rocks but tweed fabric.

Scrambling, desperate, she scrabbled around, pushing snow out of the way, pulling at the material and hearing herself sob.

Let it just be a discarded coat or something. Don't let it be a person. She felt faint.

Her right hand closed around something solid. Stiff and solid. A man's bloodied right hand. The ring finger stuck out at a ghastly angle and must be dislocated or broken.

She couldn't stop to phone for help. Seconds might be all she had to help him. Lying face down, he was too heavy to move even a fraction. All she could do was brush at his face.

Blood-tinged short, almost shaved, graying dark hair.

'Wake up,' Alex said. 'Please wake up. You'll freeze to death if you stay here. Please wake up. Get up!' She started to shake him by the shoulder but stopped, afraid she would hurt him even more.

His thin, fine-boned face was partially visible, covered with patches of blood and mud and bits of debris. Blood even sealed his eyes shut, and she could see more dark red beneath him. Snow had covered some of the congealed blood – there was so much blood. Pulse. That was the first thing. Brown woolen material bunched around the man's neck and she pulled it away at one side to reveal his throat.

Rocking back on her knees, Alex barely registered that the dog was growling. A dart, like some of those kept at the pub for casual dart players, the yellow flight and brass barrel bloodied, leaned crazily from a hole and a jagged tear that must have punctured the carotid artery.

She would never wake the man up.

Two

Thanks to the docs James and Tony Harrison, who showed up on the hill in the wake of Constable Frye and half an hour before the heavy artillery from the police, Alex had been released from the cold and horrifying woods to the warmth of the Black Dog.

Doc James was Tony's father and the local GP.

The reprieve from questions wouldn't last long but she intended to make the best of whatever thinking time she could get. The two Harrisons had threatened a Detective Inspector Dan O'Reilly with Alex's impending collapse from shock and probable essential sedation (answering no questions at all for days) if he didn't get her driven down the hill.

As the police car, with its yellow and blue checkerboard motif, had arrived at the pub and drawn around into the yard behind the building, Alex had seen a row of faces at the front windows of the public bar.

13

Once inside, her mother had been waiting to give her the rundown about the way the news had spread through the locals, but when Alex made herself appear behind the bar, she was still jumpy and wished she could hide.

Hiding, Lily Duggins had assured her, was something they didn't do.

Bloody Saturday morning, as some wag had already dubbed this horrible day, gave the locals too much time to hang around in the Black Dog asking questions and coming up with answers based on nothing but conjecture.

'There you are, Alex,' Major Stroud, long-time retired and a fixture in the pub, announced loudly the instant she appeared. 'About time, too, old thing. You can't pretend nothing's happened forever, y'know. Best way to put silly rumors to rest is with the truth. Tell us all about it.' His nose looked more bulbous and purplish than usual and his small, watery eyes skewered Alex.

Will Cummings, busy changing over beer barrels, gave Alex a sympathetic look. His wife wasn't so calm. Tight-lipped, Cathy Cummings drew beers as fast as she could and slapped glasses under the pours to measure spirits. A slight, blonde woman, her thin face showed how strained she felt. Highly strung, everyone dubbed her, but to Alex she seemed to be overreacting today. Something horrible had taken place but Cathy wouldn't help by going to pieces. Cathy was a little younger than Will, or so Alex thought, probably early fifties to his late fifties or so. She had noticed how he often treated her like a teenager rather than an adult. He was paternal toward her.

14

'This lot were all milling around outside,' Will said. 'I let 'em in early rather than have anyone freeze out there.'

Usually they opened around ten and it was the coffee and biscuits group until just before noon.

Alex smelled the coffee and freshly baked sugar biscuits, but for most customers a death on the hill was obviously an excuse for a wee, or not-so-wee dram of something to calm the nerves.

Barely contained excitement, only slightly dampened by the serious reaction the customers knew was expected of them, brought the noise level to a buzzing pitch.

Alex rubbed her still-cold palms down the sides of her jeans. Her brain didn't want to track with her eyes and she couldn't think of anything to say. She supposed she really was shocked but couldn't bring herself to pour a brandy.

Will did it for her, setting a full shot glass on the wooden sill beneath the upturned bottles of spirits. Stocky, balding and affable, he was the perfect pub manager. 'This'll hit the spot,' he said to Alex.

She nodded and took a sip; the heat felt good going down. The police who arrived in response to Constable Frye's phone calls had kept her up on the hill for an hour, shivering and watching the clinical official activity around the body, inter-mittently peppered with questions or left alone to stare at the efficient activity at the death scene. She could have kissed both of the Harrisons when they had come to her rescue. What they had told the detective wasn't far from the truth. She wouldn't have been surprised if she had passed out or thrown up – or both.

Warmth from the fire, and from bodies pressed into the space around the bar, felt good to Alex. The smells of beer and piping hot meat pies were comfortingly familiar.

'I say, Alex,' Major Stroud boomed. Foam speckled a mustache rolled out along his upper lip like iron-gray Velcro. 'We're all on your side, y'know. Not one of us thinks you were more than an unlucky witness, but you do need to bring the rest of us up to date. Was there as much blood as they say?'

Cathy Cummings gripped the edge of the bar, her eyes filled with tears.

The brandy had already started to calm Alex down. She rubbed Cathy's back and shook her head at the major. 'You don't know. Maybe my formerly secret hobby is knocking people off in the woods.'

Someone laughed – big Kev Winslet – and a communal snicker went up.

'I shouldn't joke,' Alex said, embarrassed. 'Some of us get shaken up and then we're silly at the most inappropriate times. Sorry about that. There's nothing for me to tell, Major' – the police had been sure she knew to keep her mouth shut – 'we'll hear what the authorities want us to hear soon enough.'

Going to work beside Cathy, Alex served customers and kept pork pies, Cornish pasties and sausage rolls – standard pub fare – popping in and out of the microwave at a great rate. She forked pickled onions and Scotch eggs from giant jars filled with vinegar and pickling spices. But she repeatedly needed to pull her attention back to what she was doing, trying not to see images

16

of the man with the terrible wound in his neck, or to think how he had bled out on the frozen ground, alone except for a little dog.

Goosebumps shot up her arms.

'I say,' Major Stroud said. 'Aren't you going to tell us at least something about it? Man or woman, that much at least? How was the killing done?'

Alex shook her head. 'We'll all know more than we want to before long. I was told not to discuss anything. The police will be stopping by with questions soon enough, not that I can think anyone here knows anything.'

There, that was already more than she needed to report. Alex shut her mouth firmly.

'I should think so,' old Mary Burke said from her chair beside her younger sister Harriet's. 'Gossiping never did anyone any good.' Although Mary had been known to spill a few beans on occasion. The sisters, both retired teachers, ran a tea shop that also offered books and handcrafts for sale.

Through an archway into the small restaurant, Alex could see her mother at the reception desk. Lily met her daughter's eyes and smiled encouragement, then went back to poring over the reservation book and behaving as if nothing unusual had happened. Quietly turned out as long as Alex could remember, Lily was professional in her black dress, and in her manner. A handsome woman, statuesque beside Alex, with a light hand when it came to make-up, Lily knew how to manage any situation.

'I expect they called Doc Harrison up there,' someone said.

'Would that be James or Tony Harrison?' Major

17

Stroud said, and looked put out at the laughter that followed.

Kev Winslet, who worked as gamekeeper on the Derwinter estate, said, 'Doc James, I expect, unless Doc Tony is treatin' humans now.' He joined in the mirth.

Tony Harrison had, so it was told, disappointed his father by choosing veterinary medicine rather than joining the senior Harrison's practice. When they'd both been teenagers, Tony and Alex had become friends, two of a kind, both quiet and determined people. Tony was several years older and had left for university before Alex got a scholarship to prestigious Slade Art College in London.

Up on the hill that morning, both James and Tony Harrison had shown their quiet brand of compassion.

'Alex,' Mary Burke's sturdy voice demanded. 'Can we get some service, please?'

Mary was one of Alex's favorite people, as was Harriet, who sat with her at a table near the Inglenook fireplace. Flames reflected a glow on the women's weathered faces and white hair, and bounced off the polished horse brasses hung along the gnarled oak mantel.

'Coming,' Alex said, forcing a smile, but as if he knew he'd been mentioned, Tony Harrison chose that exact moment to walk in with the gray and black dog from the woods in his arms. Tony's waxed green Barbour coat was open so he could hold the animal against the warmth of his body and wrap some of the coat over him. His rubber Hunters squeaked on the wooden floor and left muddy footprints behind.

That quieted the uproar.

'Just passing through,' Tony said. 'I've got to get this chap to the surgery and check him over. Thought I'd ask if anyone remembers seeing him before.'

Mumbles followed and a few pressed in for a closer look. Reverend Restrick from tiny St Aldwyn's church, rose from a settle with its back to the rest of the bar and came around to scratch the dog under the chin. A large man with a sweet smile, he said, 'Someone's missing you, aren't they, little fellow?'

'He's well fed,' Tony said, 'although he's probably very hungry at the moment. Name on his collar is Bogie. He's not a stray.'

No one had any information but Alex lifted the flap in the bar and went to offer her hand to the dog. 'Hello, Bogie. Poor boy.' A doggy tongue tentatively met the end of her fingers but an incessant, faint squeaking came from Bogie's throat and the animal trembled violently.

Alex looked at Tony. 'I'm glad you've got him. He—'

'Yes, I know,' the vet said, cutting her off with a warning glance. 'I'll make sure he's OK. I'd better crack on. Give me a call if you hear anyone's looking for him.'

Tony's kind, dark blue eyes reminded Alex that he had always taken the side of any underdog kid, including herself, and what a good friend he'd been until he left home.

'Does he belong to the murder victim?' Major Stroud demanded, jutting his considerable jaw toward Tony. 'Or should I say, *did* he?'

19

Tony gazed from Alex's raised eyebrows to the major's pugnacious expression and said, 'What murder victim?'

Three

Within the hour, two detectives arrived. Alex had already talked to both of them at the death scene, where they'd identified themselves as coming from Gloucester. Murder squad detectives, she was sure, which seemed unreal.

The darts cupboard wasn't locked; a point Detective Inspector Dan O'Reilly had been quick to criticize soon after he got there.

O'Reilly came to the pub in an unmarked car with a Detective Sergeant Bill Lamb and asked for the pub to be cleared until he said otherwise.

People shuffled out, grumbling, while Lily took the Burke sisters and a number of the regulars, including Major Stroud and Reverend Restrick, into the comfy private bar still called the snug in the old-fashioned way. They settled into worn tapestry easy chairs around dark oak tables. Silence lasted only long enough for the door to close behind Lily.

'Thanks, Mum,' Alex said, smiling and inclining her head to the snug where low voices were already very busy.

Lily said, 'Don't you worry. It's a terrible thing but people will lose interest soon enough.' A little gray streaked through hair which was as dark and curly as Alex's own. They both had the oval, greenish eyes Alex had been teased about as a girl when other children accused her of being a witch. Lily continued, 'We don't want to put any regular customers' noses out of joint, though. They'll be happy enough in the snug. This is one of those times I'm glad we're among the few pubs that kept one. I'll be at the desk. Bad news travels fast. We've got a line-up for the restaurant – curiosity fills tables, I suppose. They're rushed off their feet in the kitchen.'

The Cummings had already left for their rooms. Reluctantly, feeling unsure of herself, Alex returned to the pub, where boxes of darts were being removed from their cupboard and dropped into plastic bags by a man in a blue jumpsuit that rustled like paper with every move. Very tall and thin, his head brushed the swags of dried hops that decorated exposed beams. He left without a word and with several yellowing hops stuck in his dark hair.

The detectives indicated a table and they all sat down. Both men were well dressed. Nothing said 'detective' about this detail. Alex had the thought that O'Reilly's dark gray suit probably hadn't hung on any rack.

'Did you know him?' he asked her without preamble.

'The dead man?' Drawing away from the table a little, Alex went on: 'No. I never saw him before, or I don't think I did. With all the . . .' She looked away and muttered, 'I didn't get a really good look at his face. Poor man. No one should die like that.' A flash of anger surprised her. 'No one should interfere with another life. It's sick and evil.'

'Why aren't those darts kept locked away?' O'Reilly continued, ignoring her comments and repeating his earlier remark while the detective sergeant made notes. 'Or are they normally?'

'Never,' Alex told him. 'The cupboard is high on the wall and children don't come in the bar alone anyway. With the scoreboard over it, most people wouldn't know there *was* a cupboard.' Chalked-up scores remained on the blackboard from a recent match. 'The darts we keep here are for anyone who wants a casual game. Serious players bring their own sets. Do you know if it was one of our darts—?'

O'Reilly cut her off. 'The Black Dog has a darts team, does it?'

'Runner-up league champions,' Alex said. 'We're proud of them.'

'We'll have a list of their names later, right?' O'Reilly said. His Irish accent was pleasing in a low, quite soft voice. He had dark, thoughtful eyes and the hands he rested on the table were long-fingered and expressive. Alex realized he was the kind of man who inspired trust.

'Would you go through the details of what happened this morning, please?' This was the detective sergeant. 'Would you start with leaving home?'

'I didn't find him till I'd already walked through the woods and turned back again.'

'Sometimes it helps to start at the beginning and see if everything is exactly as you think you remember it. Little details can pop up. You live where?' He sounded unthreatening.

'Lime Tree Lodge. In the Dimple. That's what we've always called it around here. Right on the other side of the big hill, like a shallow oval valley. I do have a room here, of course. Just in case.'

Alex heard her voice chattering about stuff no one wanted to know and cleared her throat. Composing herself, she rubbed the space between her eyebrows.

Lamb wrote as if he were taking lecture notes and falling behind. 'Why did you decide to walk this morning?' he asked without looking at her. The top of his head showed off straight, thick sandy hair that was short enough to stand up all over – but tidily. 'Miss Bailey-Jones?' he prompted.

'Ms,' she corrected him automatically. 'I walk as many mornings as I can – most mornings.'

'Even in the snow?' Blue eyes, oddly innocent, suggested she couldn't expect him to believe her.

Flustered, Alex said, 'The snow had almost stopped. I wished it hadn't. I love walking in a snowfall. Let me get you both something to drink.'

'We're on duty,' Lamb said promptly.

'I meant coffee,' Alex said, and felt a bit smug.

Both men shook their heads, no, and muttered thanks.

'You own this place?' O'Reilly asked. He dug a crumpled white paper bag from his jacket pocket. It was obviously lumpy with the sweets inside.

'I've already said I do.'

The man smiled slightly. A good face, lived-in

in a nice way with laugh lines among signs of a lot of frowning. A crooked scar on his jaw didn't look very old. He offered the bag to Alex and the sergeant. When they both refused he fumbled inside, dislodged a sticky, yellow sherbet lemon and held it between his fingers.

'So you left Lime Tree Lodge at what time?' he asked.

'Just before seven. We usually open at ten but people were waiting outside today so we let them in early. Will and Cathy Cummings manage the place well – they live in – but there's a lot to do before we open and I like to be here. It's not that they need me, but I'm hands-on. I don't stay late.'

Both men stared at her until she began to think she'd said more than necessary again.

'Is there a Mr Bailey-Jones?' Lamb asked.

Thinking about Mike still brought back the sadness. 'We're divorced.'

'I see,' Lamb said. 'Do you always go through the woods? Seems a pretty lonely part of the route.'

'The whole route is lonely. Quiet is a better word. This isn't a bustling kind of place.'

O'Reilly sucked the sherbet powder from the middle of his sweet and Alex's mouth watered just imagining the tartness.

'The Cummings live here?' Lamb said.

Alex hoped they wouldn't want the same information twice on every topic. 'They do.'

Lamb made another note and underlined it twice.

'You said you went back into the woods because you heard a dog howl.'

'Yes.' That had to be three or four times.

'Not very cautious, are you?' O'Reilly tucked what was left of the sherbet lemon into a cheek. He tended to stare rather than look at you, and the sensation unsettled Alex. 'All alone up there with an animal who could have been dangerous and you trotted back to do . . . what?'

A vague sickness started in the pit of her stomach. 'I wanted to see if an animal was hurt and needed help.'

'You said you saw the dog running around.' Lamb and his boss traded off questions.

'I said I thought I saw an animal move. But at first I wondered if it was a bird, even.'

Lamb's guileless eyes settled on her face. 'But you talked about a dog howling. Why would you think it was a bird?'

'I said,' she told him slowly and clearly, 'that I thought I saw something move and didn't know what it was for sure. I carried on walking, heard a howl that sounded like a dog, started thinking about traps, and went back.'

'Traps?' Lamb appeared bemused.

'In case there was another animal caught in a trap and the one I saw move was howling for help.' And she was sinking into the weeds. 'They'll do that if they run together. Like packs – they look out for each other. Or for all I knew it could have been the one I saw that was caught . . . Oh, I don't know. I did what I did. Some of us are more interested in animals than people on occasion. I love animals.' She looked at her hands, then back at O'Reilly.

He gave her a nice enough smile. 'We'll come back to that.'

A third man came into the bar with a brown envelope in hand. 'They've done the best they can with these,' he said. 'Better be a bit careful how you show them, though.' He shrugged.

'Thanks.' O'Reilly took the envelope and slid out several photographs. He held them up so that she couldn't see them and Lamb got up to look over his shoulder.

'There's a woman out there,' the third man tilted his head, indicating the door leading into the pub. 'She saw the envelope and asked if I had photos of the victim. I didn't say one way or the other but she just about lost her wool, throwing her arms about and saying she needs to see whoever's in charge – and the victim. That's what she said – she wants to see the victim.'

O'Reilly frowned. 'We'll have to ask you to wait in another room, Ms Bailey-Jones. Please don't leave. Send the other one in, Madden.'

'Who is it?' Alex asked, unable to stop herself.

Lamb muttered, 'Doesn't matter if she knows.'

'Right you are,' the man, Madden, said. 'She says she's one of the managers here. Cathy Cummings.'

Four

By six, with Cathy Cummings in bed and sedated by Dr James Harrison, Alex was more than grateful to see the evening staff arrive, and she sent Will off to be with his wife.

She had no idea what had transpired between Cathy and O'Reilly but the result had left the woman sobbing in her husband's arms.

Lamb and O'Reilly spent a couple more hours questioning Alex then left, letting her know they'd be back when they needed to talk again.

Once she could, Alex left the bar, still wishing she could ask why Cathy had wanted to see the dead man. So far she hadn't worked out any way to get more information, but she would.

'Are you staying with Lily tonight?'

Alex jumped and turned sharply to see Tony Harrison, Bogie in his arms again, sitting on a wooden settle in the pub vestibule. She blinked, too tired and confused to say anything, but still glad to see a friendly face.

Tony got up and smiled. He hadn't changed a lot over the years. His dark blond hair was still curly and a bit too long because he wasn't the type to fuss, but perhaps the lines beside his mouth were deeper. She realized how much she needed familiar faces and old friends around her today.

'No,' she said. 'I'm not staying with Mum. Why would I?'

He looked at his toes. 'No reason. I heard you had some unexpected drama when the police were here. I'd have come earlier to see if I could do anything but my day's been busy.'

A couple from Underhill, Frank and Gladys Lymer, stomped into the foyer, both flapping their arms across their bodies. 'All right, then?' Frank said to Alex. 'Cold enough to freeze a . . . damn cold,' he finished.

Gladys, bundled in a gray, fake fur coat, rolled her eyes and hustled her husband into the pub.

'It's nice of you to be concerned,' Alex said to Tony, noticing for the first time that his own dog, a blonde border terrier called Katie, had squeezed herself under the settle and looked up at her boss with doleful brown eyes. Alex grinned. 'Is Katie pouting? She's not used to sharing you.'

'Just tired like the rest of us,' he said. 'And a bit wary, too. That's natural. When are you going home? You don't have your Rover.'

'No. I wasn't thinking when . . .' Funny, he must have checked the yard for her vehicle. 'I'll get a lift back from my mum.'

'That's why I came in. I can go anytime you're ready. No need to put your mother out.'

She started to refuse but stopped herself. Why sound silly and ungrateful with someone she'd known since she was a kid? Besides, he must have heard about Cathy's meltdown from someone, likely his dad, who would probably know something about the reason.

And it felt good to feel someone had actually thought about how she was doing.

'Thank you. That's so nice of you.' And if she were a better person she'd be ashamed of planning to winkle information out of him. 'I'll get my things.'

Tony had parked his own Land Rover in front and they walked out side by side with Katie between them.

Katie climbed happily into one of the kennels in the back but Bogie started to whine pitiably when Tony went to put him into another one.

28

'Let me hold him,' Alex said. 'He'll probably like that better.'

Tony opened the passenger door for her to get in and put Bogie on her lap. The dog huddled so close she had difficulty buckling her seatbelt.

'I'm surprised he isn't fighting to get away from us,' Alex said when Tony sat beside her and started the engine. She rubbed the dog's short, wiry curls and got a tentative lick on the back of her hand.

'Animals aren't so different from people. You never know how they'll react to shock.'

She looked at him and thought about Cathy Cummings.

A new idea struck her. 'Why didn't the police want to examine Bogie? He might have had blood . . .'

'He did. I saw to the examination myself – and took samples.'

'But . . .' But what? But wasn't that weird when, for all the police knew, Tony Harrison could be a suspect? Instantly, her skin felt too small for her scalp.

'But, what?' He had driven on to the narrow road between cottages and the green and headed for the track that wound up into the hills. 'I've done the same sort of thing before.'

It was dark enough that although she could see the glitter of what snow was left on the green, the pond in the center was invisible. 'What a nasty day this has been.'

Tony grunted. 'I don't get the feeling the police are any further forward, do you?' He looked at her. His face was angular and looked grim in the dashboard light.

'No.' In fact, she had no idea what they might have found out. 'I don't suppose they would tell us if they were.' She was with an old friend. Why couldn't she relax with him?

'The dead man didn't have a wallet or any identification on him.'

'They told you that?'

'No.' He smiled at her and looked completely different, warmer, more like the boy she'd known. 'I was there when they were checking.'

'They asked if I knew him,' Alex said, jolted as they turned uphill. 'I didn't get a good look at him really.'

The dog trembled and she felt his wet nose on her neck. Automatically she rubbed her cheek on the top of his head.

Tony seemed lost in thought.

'Did they . . . was he turned over while you were there? Did you see his face?'

'I saw a lot of blood, but yes. Whoever did the number with the dart wanted to be sure the victim didn't rise up and walk again.' Tony shook his head. 'Stabbed the thing in and tore at the artery, I should think.'

Alex shuddered. 'I don't think I want to know about that.' She rubbed her fingers tightly together. 'Could he have taken his own life?'

'I said I didn't know him but there's something that keeps prodding at me.' He registered what Alex had asked and puffed up his cheeks. 'Damned if I know about suicide. Seems an extreme way to pull it off. But almost anything's possible.'

Tony slipped into a lower gear. The ground was

30

icy and from the starless sky Alex thought they might have more snow before the night was out.

She waited for him to continue.

When he didn't, she said, 'What kind of something keeps prodding at you?'

Again he fell silent and when she glanced at him, his eyes were narrowed, his features set in grim lines once more.

'What, Tony?' she pressed.

'Nothing. I keep expecting to hear the police already know who he was.'

But there had been something else, something significant, or he wouldn't have mentioned it.

'Stop.' Alex said it sharply and without thinking. 'Pull over and let's talk this through.'

'It's slippery. Best to keep going.'

'So you don't know how to slow down and stop . . . no, don't stop, keep going. I'm not myself and I'm jumpy. Sorry. We're almost at my place.'

Tony had slowed down but he drove on and they didn't speak until they had climbed the hill, passed on the far side of the woods and dropped into the Dimple.

Stone gateposts, each with an unlikely griffon on top, guarded an open iron gate in front of Lime Tree Lodge. The gateposts were probably the most distinctive feature about the property. Two stories of pale yellow stone, a solid but unimaginative box of a house, had sold itself to Alex because she knew how much she could do with the inside, and the small grounds were pretty.

Tony idled outside the gate. 'Hope I haven't offended you somehow.'

31

'Is there someone waiting for you at home?'

He turned his head slowly toward her and cleared his throat at the same time. 'Not unless squatters arrived during the day. Why?'

Fortunately, realizing how funny the question sounded, she laughed before she could blush. 'I was going to invite you and the dogs in for a drink. Didn't want to impose if you've got something on, is all.'

His conflicted thoughts were almost audible as he steered carefully down her driveway. 'That would be great if you're sure you're OK with the dogs coming in.'

'Hah. You'd have to choose between the dogs or me, hmm? And the dogs would win.'

This time he was the one who laughed.

Motion sensors turned on lights at the front of the house. Tony got out of the Land Rover and Katie erupted from her kennel the moment she was freed. When Alex opened the front door the dog bustled inside, her big nose sniffing overtime. Alex continued to carry Bogie, who struggled to stay close to her whenever she tried to set him down.

'Come into the sitting room,' Alex told Tony. 'Put that coat somewhere. You'll need it to warm you up when you go back outside.'

'Yes, Mother.'

'I'm nobody's mother.' She sounded like a shrew. *Damn, lighten up.* 'But thanks for the compliment. It's the take care bit in me; it pops out very occasionally.'

She didn't miss the very direct look he gave her before taking one of her sleeves to help her from her own coat and waiting for her to get a fresh grip on Bogie before pulling it all the way off and laying it over a chair.

His own coat followed.

'Coffee or something stronger?' she asked, drawing heavy draperies over the windows.

'Stronger.' He tilted his head toward a brass tray with two cut glass decanters and some glasses. They were meant more for decoration than use.

'Left is Scotch, right is sherry,' Alex told him, sitting on an overstuffed couch covered in a rough fabric of stylistic roses and leaves. 'I'll have Scotch,' she added, seeing him reach for the sherry.

Tony smiled to himself and poured equal measures in two glasses.

'This place was falling down before you bought it,' he said, tucking a glass into the hand she freed from Bogie. 'It might be a good idea to let him sit on your lap for just a couple more minutes, then put him down.'

'He's frightened.'

'I know.'

Alex took hold of two shaky front legs, pried them free and settled the dog on her lap. 'There's no need for him to get down altogether,' she said. 'Sit down, please.'

'The house is warm,' he said, and sat across from her in a green tapestry chair.

'I had heating put in. It cost so much to do it, I won't be able to afford to run it if the business goes pear shaped on me. But I shouldn't complain. I think some people were actually glad to see me come home and start pulling the Black Dog back to where it was. It always used to be a destination pub and it's getting there again. It brings money into the village.

'Will and Cathy Cummings have helped a lot. And it doesn't hurt that Will could help so much with the electrical stuff and some of the plumbing, or that every contractor around is a friend of his and gave me deals.'

'Your business will be a complete success,' Tony said, in a way that brooked no argument.

Alex hoped he was right.

They fell into a silence that grew long enough to be uncomfortable. Bogie sighed every few moments but started to fall asleep.

'It smells nice in here,' Tony said. 'Like roses – like you.' He instantly looked mildly aghast, then chuckled. 'A bit of latent Lothario coming out in me. I just meant I like the scent.'

'Thank you.'

'I'd better get this down and leave you to your dinner.'

'If there was dinner waiting in the kitchen I'd be inviting you to eat with me.' Alex gave a short laugh, cleared her throat and straightened her shoulders. 'I think we should talk – if you've got a few minutes.'

'I've got all night.'

They both burst out laughing. Tony fell back in his seat, shaking his head from side to side.

Alex took a deep breath to control the giggles and said, 'The police wanted to know if I'd seen anything unusual lying around. When I asked if they meant a weapon, they didn't sneer at me so I give them kudos for that. They did remind me they already have the weapon. They didn't give

34

me any hints about what they were looking for. Did they ask you?'

Tony got up, went to his coat and worked a big paper bag out of the back game pocket. He opened it and offered her a rather mangled roll of some kind. 'They're cheese and tomato,' he said. 'Not so fresh any more but they'd fill a hole.'

Rather than be rude, she eased one out and watched Tony take the other. 'Didn't have time for lunch,' he said. 'I'm starving.'

'Me, too.'

They munched and amazingly the dogs didn't beg.

More silence.

'Did they ask you if you'd seen anything in particular that you remembered?' Alex said around a piece of cheese.

He nodded and his eyes slid away. Gradually he looked distant, deep in thought.

'What?' Alex said.

He chewed his way through a mouthful of roll, swallowed and chased the food with Scotch. 'I don't think I should say.'

'Tell me.'

'I think it's going to be hard to get to the bottom of a murder in a place like this. Think about it. It's remote but everyone knows everyone else. Have you heard anyone say they saw anything? Anything at all?'

Alex scooted forward. 'If we call, will the police tell us if they have any suspects, anyone helping them with their enquiries, as they say? We could pretend to be the press.'

His expressive brows went up again. 'I don't

think that's a good idea. It was the asking about anything we might have found that got me thinking. Are they wondering about a serial killer? Have there already been more deaths? Do they already know there's something missing from the victim? Maybe they're wondering about trophies, you know, what serial killers . . .'

'I know how they collect things from their victims,' Alex said quickly. She glanced at the windows and was glad she had drawn the drapes. She felt safer when she was closed in. 'What a horrible thought. A sickening thought. Everyone around here should be very careful.'

'But the police didn't warn anyone about that, did they?' Tony asked. 'Surely they would have if that's what they were worried about.'

She nodded, yes, and felt a little comforted. 'They always try not to panic people, though, don't they?' The butterflies in her stomach took off again.

Frowning, Tony bounced the knuckles of one hand against his teeth.

'Don't they do that?' Alex pressed. 'Say if people should be really careful?'

'I don't know. Maybe they assume everyone knows to be cautious. Gave me a shock when I saw he was some sort of religious.'

Alex stared at him.

When he looked at her, he frowned. 'You realized that?' She got a very navy blue stare.

'No. I was pretty shocked and disoriented. A priest?'

'Monk, more likely. With an old tweed coat over his habit.'

36

She recalled the brown fabric around his neck. 'Then they can find out who he is,' Alex said, suddenly excited. 'His order will know he's missing. And can't they identify the habit?'

'We'll see. The police seemed as surprised as I was. He had on sandals and thin socks, poor bloke. His feet must have been frozen.'

'All of him was frozen,' Alex said, not quite under her breath. 'This only gets worse. If they don't get a break quickly they often never do, isn't that what they say?'

'I don't think you can make generalizations like that,' Tony said.

'You didn't go for your walk with Katie this morning,' she said, without thinking how it might sound. 'I mean, I didn't see you this morning.'

'We went really early. I had a busy day planned.'

His expression changed subtly and she could tell he was thinking she had wondered about him, about whether he could have been in the woods before she got there.

'I didn't stab a man with a dart,' he said quietly.

Alex was in full, pulsing blush mode when the doorbell rang. She jumped up, still holding Bogie. 'Who could that be?' she whispered. 'At this time of night?'

Five

The bell rang for a second time and Tony waited for Alex to react.

Rooted. That was the best description. She didn't seem able to move her feet.

'I didn't see the lights come on,' Tony said after the bell rang again. 'Your curtains are heavy. Let me get the door.' He didn't mention that his Rover was in front and there were lights on in the house so there was no point in pretending not to be at home.

'No. I should. But thanks.' She glanced around. 'Stay in here.'

The stunned expression on her face was probably because she had just accused him of murder. More or less. And now she was asking him to hide himself. Their eyes met. She feared gossip about the two of them. Her widened eyes reflected her embarrassment.

'I'll go,' she said rapidly. 'You're a really decent man, Tony. You're trying to be a friend to me and – and I don't know how to react to that any more.'

Her footsteps rushed along the hall toward the front of the house.

Quickly, Tony reached for his coat and tipped it behind a couch. Then he sat back in his chair, legs crossed, the hand holding a glass of Scotch resting on his knee.

He'd make a picture of a man comfortable in his surroundings – and familiar with them.

The Devil made me do it.

Sometimes a fellow wasn't flattered by being called a really decent man. Like, *not a bad cut of meat,* or, *passable merlot but not memorable.*

Geez, he should pick up that coat and look as if he was leaving.

Voices came from the area of the front door and he stayed where he was, listening.

'Heather and Leonard Derwinter,' a familiar voice – Leonard's – said.

'Of course,' Alex said, very formal and more than a bit surprised. 'Are you having car problems?'

She must have seen the Derwinters, self-acclaimed lords of the manor and owners of a good part of the village in fact, many times. They turned up at the Black Dog, usually late in the evening and usually with several of their arrogant lot, but of course, Alex was the daughter of a former barmaid there. Tony doubted they even knew she owned the business now.

'We feel so guilty.' Heather's well-modulated tones were quite clear. 'It shouldn't take something so horrible to remind us that you're a neighbor . . . and alone, for goodness' sake. We don't want to intrude but we do want you to understand that we are here for you. Say the word, and whatever you need . . .' She let the sentence trail off.

'How kind,' Alex said.

Tony spent many hours at the Derwinter estate. He'd started taking care of the livestock there when the old man was still alive and the son had continued using Tony after Cornelius Derwinter died.

'We really do want to know you better,' Heather said. 'Don't we, Leonard?'

'Mm, absolutely, darling.'

'Would you like to come in?' Alex asked, reluctance loading each word. If she had said, *I don't*

39

want you to come in it would have been in the same tone.

'Well—'

'We'd love to.' Heather cut Leonard off. 'Alex – may we call you Alex – Alex, we simply can't believe you had such a horrid experience, and on our property.'

Tony closed his eyes for an instant and suppressed an urge to laugh. There was an almost irresistible tone-deafness to Heather. Almost. She never considered that using every opportunity to mention 'our property' could be a bit crass. Neither did she ever stop to consider that there might be an inch or two of this corner of Gloucestershire that *didn't* belong to the Derwinters. This house, for instance – or the Black Dog. Or his own home, among others.

He heard Bogie give a single annoyed bark as the Derwinters must have crossed the threshold and smiled again. Dogs very quickly became territorial.

'Sweet little dog,' Heather said.

'What is it exactly?' This was Leonard.

'A Bogie,' Alex said clearly and with an edge of frost. 'This is Bogie and he's one of a kind.'

Tony grinned again. She wasn't the quiet kid he'd once known.

She came through the door first and the expression on her face when she saw his relaxed attitude was comical. Her mouth opened but she didn't make a sound. He thought she looked rather lovely like that. Funny he'd never noticed how pretty she was until he'd been away at university and come home for the holidays. By that time he was already deeply involved with another student.

Life had matured Alex, made her sharper and less sunny, but he'd found her casually curly dark hair and green eyes good to look at from the moment she'd returned to Folly-on-Weir. He liked her. He didn't like thinking about whatever disappointments she had left behind in London.

'You know Tony Harrison,' she said to the Derwinters.

'*Tony*.' Heather hailed him like a very close friend. That was before her blonde bob swished from side to side when she looked from him to the rest of the room, to Alex's glass on a table, to the glass in his hand. 'Look, Leonard, it's Tony of all people.'

'So it is,' Leonard said with a smile that turned down at the corners. 'Look, sorry to interrupt. We're on our way home so we decided to stop and offer Alex our support. Glad she's got you to lean on.'

'That doesn't mean a girl can't use more than one broad shoulder,' Heather said before Tony had a chance to respond. Pink had risen over her high cheekbones. 'I can't rest until I know everything, Alex. And until I make sure you have our home and mobile numbers.' She peeled off a gray tweed hacking jacket, showing off a fabulous figure in a tight red sweater, and sat down on the couch Alex had used. She patted the seat beside her and Alex obliged, even managed a relaxed and serene manner.

'There,' Heather said. 'Now tell us everything.'

Heather was a beautiful woman, and at least a

41

generation younger than her husband. Her features were delicate and pert but she was athletically built, all sleek lines intended for the expensively tailored riding outfits she usually favored. Despite hours spent outdoors, her skin remained translucently pale.

'I'm sorry,' Alex said as if she didn't understand. 'Tony and I have known each other since we were children. He was kind enough to give me a lift home.'

'Leonard,' Heather said as if Alex hadn't spoken, 'you've got one of our cards with all the numbers on it. Put it on the mantel, there's a love.'

Her husband followed instructions. He was a good-looking man, sleek with olive skin and dark brown hair and eyes. Tall and all muscle. Probably more than ten years older than Tony, as a boy he had scarcely known who he was. They did have the same prep school in common but Leonard was long graduated by the time Tony got there.

'We should leave these people to their evening,' Leonard said, turning back from the fireplace.

'Is it true the dead person was shot?' Heather asked Alex. 'And there was a frightful amount of blood?'

'No,' Alex said, then caught Tony's stare and rolled her eyes. She clearly wasn't accustomed to dissembling. 'They didn't tell me anything. The police, that is.'

'What sort of things do they ask when something like that happens?'

Leonard took up Heather's jacket. 'I believe the police prefer you not to give out details, my dear.'

She flapped a hand. 'That doesn't mean us,

Leonard. Do you know that . . . well, I shouldn't mention names, but I was told it was a man wearing some sort of habit.'

'I wasn't aware of that,' Alex said, managing to look surprised even as she lied.

'Yes, probably a priest, I suppose?' Heather said, the question hanging there, a not-too-subtle prod for information. Her nose wrinkled as if a priest were something foreign to her. 'Apparently he probably killed himself, or so I was told.'

'The police didn't say anything like that to me,' Tony said, 'but anything's possible.'

'Of course,' Heather said, turning her full attention on him. 'You were there, too, weren't you? How did the man die?'

'Apparently we'll be told with everyone else, after the post-mortem. Even then, they won't give details that could compromise their case.' She was irritating him severely.

'But you were *there*. You must have some opinion.'

'My father's the GP,' he said, hoping he'd be forgiven for using his dad to shift attention. 'I just wandered around in the background. There was obviously nothing I could do.'

'Let's get on,' Leonard said. Tony appreciated the man's decency. 'These people have had a hard day.'

'I'll be up to look at the little filly tomorrow,' Tony said, standing to move things along.

With an obviously disappointed Heather in tow, Leonard led the way out of Lime Tree Lodge.

Once the front door closed behind the Derwinters, Alex said, 'I might as well just ask. Do

43

you know why Cathy Cummings said she wanted to see the body then went to pieces? Was it something the detective said that made her collapse?'

'You get points for controlling your curiosity so long,' Tony said. 'We both know we're not supposed to discuss this.'

'And we know we will. And the police know everyone around will discuss theories. As long as we don't give away information others can't know, I don't see the harm. I'm worried about Cathy.'

He believed her. She was the type who cared about other people. The two of them hadn't exchanged more than a few words since her return to Folly, until tonight, but he was drawn to her frankness. What the hell, he wondered, had Bailey-Jones done to ruin the marriage? Fleetingly, Tony decided it had to be Bailey-Jones's fault and that the man was a fool.

'Cathy had said she wanted to see the body,' he told her. 'Apparently she had some bee in her bonnet that she might know him.'

'If she isn't a relative, would they let her do that?' Alex asked.

'It happens if they think it might help them. But she changed her mind, said the idea of the murder had shocked her so much she'd started reliving bad things in her own life. Then she collapsed, poor woman.'

Alex didn't look convinced but neither did she pursue the point. 'Why did you think I might be staying at my mother's tonight?'

The look in her eyes said she already knew the answer. He tried to shrug nonchalantly. 'You had a shock. I thought you might want comfort from her.'

'You think there's a murderer wandering around up here in the hills and I should want to run for safety.'

He shrugged again. Her directness could make him uncomfortable.

'I'm not a frightened teenager, Tony. I understand the concerns – and I appreciate yours – but I'll be fine.'

'Is there an alarm system in this house?'

Her neck jerked as she swallowed. 'No. I don't like them. They go off when they shouldn't and they're a nuisance.'

'They aren't a nuisance if someone wielding a hatchet is breaking in to . . .' *Holy hell. And his father wondered why his son had said his bedside manner wasn't suitable for humans.*

'To kill me?' Alex said. 'I tend to think that all the way up here, even with an alarm, I'd be dead before anyone got here.'

Now he really felt like a heel – and the tightness in his belly was anxiety, for her.

'You never told me what the police are still looking for.'

This was not a lady who gave up easily. 'They didn't tell me, but I think I know. Did you notice one of his hands – the ring finger on his right hand?'

Her fingertips went to her lips and she glanced away. 'It looked as if it was broken. Do they think someone tore off a ring? They do, don't they? There must have been a mark from where it was. I didn't notice. I was too busy being horrified. The more I think about it, the more I'm convinced that's it.'

'You and I are thinking the same thing. But you can bet the killer took the ring with him.'

At last, Alex seemed uneasy. 'That's beastly. At the time I didn't make any connection with a ring, but stealing it from a dead man? How horrid. What could a monk's ring be worth? I suppose it's what you said, some sort of trophy. It makes me sick.'

'You could stay at the Black Dog, too, if you wanted to.' He disliked the idea of her being here alone and the feeling intensified as each new tidbit crawled out.

'I'll be fine,' she said, smiling. She hugged Bogie. 'My new watchdog will take care of me. Dogs are better than alarms. They're faster.'

He wasn't completely surprised by the announcement. Mulling it over, he finally said, 'The police just seemed to expect me to keep him. But Katie would probably appreciate not having him around tonight. Don't be disappointed if he's wary of you, at least at first.'

'I'll cook him some vegetables and chicken,' Alex said.

'Spoiled thing.'

'He deserves it – he's going to keep me safe.'

For an instant he felt physically sick but he stopped the next words that tried to leave his mouth. Instead he retrieved his coat from behind the couch.

'Oh, dear.' Alex pulled her shoulders up to her ears and put her cheek against Bogie's head. 'We know what Tony's thinking. But you would have kept your boss safe if you could.'

46

Six

Alex usually turned the central heating down at night. She didn't really need to be parsimonious but old habits stuck around.

Tonight she decided a really warm house would be comforting. Anyway, Bogie needed to be coddled a bit . . .

She was nervous and that frosted her. No, it wouldn't be stupid for anyone to be edgy given what had happened so close to this house, but being nervous could warp your judgement. That wouldn't help a thing.

A monk with a ring – possibly a valuable ring.

Weren't they into poverty, simplicity, all those Spartan habits that divested them of worldly things, the luxuries that could distract from their concentration on God?

He probably hadn't been wearing a ring at all. It was just a guess. She didn't want to, but she thought about the finger that had jutted, obviously either broken or dislocated.

The hand was covered with dried blood. There could have been less blood on the finger but she wasn't sure. Taking of a ring would automatically wipe away some blood.

When the phone rang it jolted Alex to her toes.

She saw it was Will Cummings. 'Alex,' she said into the mouthpiece.

'Will here. Just want you not to worry about

Cathy. She'll be all right. Don't forget the dart match tomorrow evenin'. They like you to give 'em a bit of a cheer on even if you don't stay for the whole thing. What they'd really go for is having you play. They froth at the mouth having the best dart player in the county in residence when she won't play.'

'Come on, Will. I don't play often enough to be in practice.' She'd started throwing darts as a kid while she waited for Lily to close up in the afternoon, and she had been very good.

'Maybe you should start practicing again,' Will said. 'You don't have enough hobbies.'

'Right.' She sensed there were things about Cathy that he was skirting. 'What made Cathy think she could identify that man?'

Will didn't answer immediately. He coughed and said, 'It's sketchy. She thinks some man came by late wanting a drink. Last night, that was. We were closed and she was cleaning up in the bar. She likes to take a last look when everyone's gone.'

'We don't serve after closing,' Alex said, puzzled.

'Oh, don't you fret. She didn't serve him but he was a stranger and when she heard about the murder her imagination got carried away.'

'You mean Cathy thought the person who came to the pub might have been the dead man?'

'That's about right.'

'So she got a good look at him?'

Will gave a little laugh that sounded forced. 'You're startin' to sound like the police, Alex. She was busy trying to finish up. I don't see her taking that much notice of him.'

It was her turn to laugh, awkwardly. 'I'm too tied up in all this. Can't quite get over it.'

'That O'Reilly chap made her describe the fella that came. She said he and the other one shook their heads like it didn't sound like the corpse. But she's that upset I don't know if she just imagined it.'

'You said she was fine,' Alex said, and wished she hadn't.

'She is. I meant she *was* that upset. Anyway, I'd best be getting back to 'er. It's snowing again. No need to get here early as usual. Wait for help putting on the chains.'

She wished him goodnight and went to look out of the window. The outside lights were off but there was no missing the fat flakes of snow that splattered the windows. At least they were fairly wet. If it didn't get much colder it wouldn't accumulate much.

Tired, but not sleepy, she put the dog down and went to the kitchen. So far she hadn't settled on what, if anything, to do with it. Glass-fronted cabinets, off-white, and solid black and white tiled counters had an old-fashioned family feel. Alex liked that. She had replaced the cracked floor tiles with stone flags.

Pretending not to watch Bogie, she boiled chicken breasts, cooked rice and added some leftover vegetables. When she'd chopped the chicken and stirred everything together, she let it cool while she found a bowl and put water down.

The dog didn't move from his spot by the kitchen door. Starting with a small amount of the food, Alex took the dish to Bogie and wafted it under his nose. With only the slightest hesitation, his bottom came off the floor and he trotted after her to eat everything down in a few bites. He ate another small bowl but she didn't give him more in case it was too much, too soon.

She had eaten little of Tony's sandwich but she wasn't hungry.

Her mother wouldn't call because she made it a rule not to intrude, so Alex made a phone call to Corner Cottage and reassured Lily, who didn't do a perfect job of pretending to be relaxed.

By ten Alex gave up on the evening. She couldn't concentrate on reading. Going to the room upstairs and at the back of the house which she still regarded as her temporary studio didn't appeal. If she couldn't lose herself in her painting she knew she was seriously rattled.

She turned off all the downstairs lights except for the lamp on a table in the hall, and started upstairs, still trying not to watch Bogie too closely. He had gone to the door when he wanted to go out and she'd allowed him, standing outside, arms tightly crossed in the wet snow, and hoped he wouldn't run away. When he came back and ran inside she felt ridiculously satisfied.

He'd lost his owner. A religious man walking through the woods with no way to defend himself and apparently having made no attempt to do so. She could scarcely swallow thinking about the stark sadness of it. Who would do such a thing – who around here? Or had it been someone passing through who'd been shocked by the man and lashed out?

Or had the victim made the gash in his own throat? Was it possible to do that?

A nagging thought echoed back that if a person was desolate enough, and beyond hope of any human comfort – or even his God's comfort – he could do it.

When they had started up the stairs, cold hit Alex's spine in what she thought of as the start of a premonition. The prickling of a thousand pins started climbing until they covered her back and sprayed over her scalp.

She turned around slowly, slowly.

Glass panels flanked the heavy front door with a fanlight above. All the panes in the fanlight were green – not what she would have chosen – and she intended to replace some of them with other colors to warm the light when it came through.

Her scalp contracted even more. Her face felt tight.

The dog had stopped beside her and he, too, stared toward the front of the house. His hackles had risen and his lips were pulled back from his teeth, but he didn't make a sound.

The motion sensors came on and a green glow washed over the hall floor.

She couldn't move, or breathe.

Call the police.

They won't get here in time.

In time for what?

The lights went out. Air rushed from her lungs. There was a wind with the snow. It could easily have blown a fallen limb across a beam and triggered the lights.

'C'mon,' she said, bobbing down to pat the dog. 'We're a jumpy pair.'

The sensors came on again. And off again. And on again, and off.

Alex felt sick.

Bogie growled but when she continued up the stairs, running now, he followed her and went with her into her bedroom where she locked the door and struggled to push a chest of drawers in front of it.

Call someone.

If you do there'll be nothing to find and you'll end up looking like a jumpy fool. It'll be all right.

With the phone pulled close and a flashlight beside it, she eventually got into bed. The sound of wind whipping around the corners of the old walls was something she'd come to love. Tonight she hated it.

But the lights stayed off.

Bogie jumped on to the bed and made himself comfortable.

In time Alex drifted, bedeviled by the half-sleeping jolts that sometimes put her into an imaginary free fall that woke her up.

The dog barking, standing on the bed and howling toward the windows, woke her completely. The clock showed it was three in the morning. She had slept after all.

After a few seconds of trying to calm Bogie, she stared at the closed drapes. Closed and illuminated.

This time the motion sensor lights stayed on.

Seven

The emergency operator kept her on the phone, kept talking. Stopped making sense.

52

She should stay where she was. Not go outside under any circumstances. A unit was on the way. Was she sure this wasn't a medical emergency? What was she hearing now? Had the lights gone off yet?

The questions went around and around in her head.

'Have the lights gone off, ma'am?'

'You ask the same things over and over,' Alex said, hearing her words slur together. 'The police always ask questions like that – the same questions. The lights are still on. They must be right outside.'

'Are there sensors at the back of the house?' the operator asked.

'Why? I mean, yes.'

'Are those on, too? Are they on the same circuit?'

Alex rubbed at her stinging eyes. The dog jumped up and down and barked. He flew up at the windowsill, then threw himself against the wall, howling.

'I'm sorry,' Alex said. 'I'm making a mess of this—'

'It's OK. It won't be long.'

'I can't see the back of the house from here but those lights are on the same circuit, yes.'

Barely at first, then steadily louder came the urgent warning from police sirens.

'They're coming!' Alex tried to straighten her knees, to stand without shaking.

The lights went out.

Alex closed her eyes. 'Bogie,' she whispered. 'Come here, boy.'

In an instant the dog's front paws landed on her thighs and Alex dropped to her knees to hold on tight to the warm, wiry body.

When more lights flashed across her closed eyelids she knew the police car had turned down the driveway. And another vehicle came. Doors slammed and pounding came from the front door.

'They're here,' she said into the phone and dropped it to shove the chest of drawers blocking her bedroom door. She'd only moved it a foot before she unlocked and opened the door enough to squeeze through on to the landing.

Clinging to the banisters, she ran downstairs but stopped by the front door. 'Who is it?' she cried, and her voice broke.

'Police, Ms Bailey-Jones. It's Dan O'Reilly.'

The detective inspector? She let him in, stood there on bare feet wearing her flannel pajamas.

What felt like hours later, Dan O'Reilly came through the back door, passed through the little mud room and met Alex where she paced in the kitchen.

At least the inspector didn't look either annoyed or disbelieving, but she knew before a word was said that the men who had been searching her gardens hadn't found anything to put her mind at rest.

'Coffee smells good,' O'Reilly said. He picked up a mug, raised it and waited for her invitation before filling it from the percolator. He drank, looking from her to the kitchen over the rim of the mug.

'So, nothing?' she said. 'It's weird to hope there's a maniac found in your garden while you

54

also hope there's no one at all out there. I feel like a fool.'

He shook his head slightly. There were strands of gray in his wind-ruffled dark hair.

Alex looked away. She'd already drunk too much coffee. At least she'd been able to pull on clothes, jeans and a sweater that felt comfortable.

'I don't understand how you were the first to get here,' she said.

'I was at Constable and Mrs Frye's. They were good enough to insist I stay when I said I wasn't comfortable getting too far away at this point.'

Alex's mix of relief and self-consciousness evaporated. His simple statement creeped her out.

Snow had turned the shoulders of his tan raincoat dark and wet. 'It's not unusual to block reality when you're faced with death. Particularly sudden and violent death.'

Without looking, Alex found the back of a chair and scraped the legs away from the table. She sat down and propped her elbows.

'We're glad you called,' the officer said. 'I wouldn't have wanted you to do anything else.'

'But there wasn't really a reason to be scared,' she told him. 'Now I almost wish you'd found him out there. This would all be over then.'

'Are you sure you saw the lights go on?'

Anger flashed at her, stiffening her body and making blood rush to her face. 'You think I imagined it? I didn't imagine it. It was like being played with, like someone trying to frighten me. And the dog barked, too.'

O'Reilly had already expressed his surprise at

finding Bogie there. 'Dogs are sensitive to human moods, or some of them are. He could have felt your anxiety.'

Staying in her seat was an effort. 'OK, I made it all up because I wanted to feel like a fool. Sorry I bothered everyone.' She sounded childish in her own ears.

'No,' he said quietly, and his dark eyes held hers steadily. 'You're in the middle of an unsolved murder case. I don't say that to worry you even more but you have to be careful, very careful.'

'The next thing you'll say is that I should move out of my house. I'm not going to. If someone wants to find me badly enough, they will. Wherever I go, I'll be vigilant. OK?'

He smiled and sat opposite her at the table. 'We'll all be more comfortable if you're down in the village. You included.'

Bogie sidled up beside her and rested his head on her thigh. If she didn't believe dogs got sad, she'd tell herself she was making it up. He was sad and lost and she was the only thin thread he had to safety. She considered what O'Reilly was suggesting. It was time to stop proving how independent she was. Staying here tonight would be stupid.

Alex scratched the dog's head. 'OK, I can go to the Black Dog.' She *would* feel better with people around.

'Looks as if you've found a friend,' O'Reilly said.

'He's my kind of fellow,' Alex responded. 'What are you trying to find from the crime scene?'

The blank look she got was completely convincing but she wasn't one to give up so easily.

56

'You were looking for something in the woods where the man died. I watched your men. And you asked me if I'd found anything.'

Mentioning the ring theory didn't feel right. Let him tell her.

He smiled at her and drank more coffee.

There were digestive biscuits in a tin on the counter. Alex got up, thought about putting some on a plate but opened the lid and set the tin in front of him instead. O'Reilly promptly took out two biscuits and demolished the first in three bites.

'You're stalling,' she said while his mouth was full. 'I bet you've had people searching for something all through daylight hours. What?'

He finished the second biscuit with more coffee.

'Had enough time to think of an excuse not to answer?' Alex said.

O'Reilly laughed. 'You almost think like a detective. We may make one of you yet.' He held up a hand. 'Forget I said that. The question was routine.'

'You didn't have anything specific in mind?' She wouldn't mention she knew Tony had been asked the same question.

'We would be interested in anything that caught your attention.'

How to deny the truth without telling a lie?

She'd leave it for now. 'Do you know who the man is yet?'

'No.'

'No wallet or anything?' Tony had said there wasn't, but . . .

O'Reilly let out a long breath. 'Not a thing.'

57

'Can anyone tell what order he was from?'

'Not so far.'

'Couldn't you have someone go through descriptions of the habits different orders wear?' She leaned toward him.

'Thanks for the tip.'

There was laughter in O'Reilly's voice. He thought she was playing amateur detective, but she didn't regret the question. She would see if there was a way to find out the details of that habit. If she could find out something useful, where was the harm?

A rap at the back door preceded the entrance of a uniformed policeman. 'Sir,' he said. 'Could you come and have a look at this, please?'

On his feet immediately, O'Reilly said, 'Stay here.'

Ignoring the order, Alex followed as closely as she could without running into his back.

Several officers stood at the back of her Land Rover, parked beside a dry stone wall that ran from the front of the property to disappear behind the garage.

'I asked you to stay put,' O'Reilly said, still striding purposefully toward the vehicle.

Alex didn't answer, just kept on following.

Flashlights illuminated the Land Rover and she saw one policeman kneeling to train his light on a wheel. 'There,' he said, pointing.

Then she saw the way the whole vehicle canted to one side. The right, rear tire was flat.

'He was out here,' Alex exclaimed. A deep slash from some sort of sharp knife or tool must have done the job, but another dart with a yellow flight had been embedded in the tire.

'Shit,' said O'Reilly. 'Window dressing. He's into games.'

Eight

The Burke sisters' tea room and book shop, called Leaves of Comfort (to the overt disgust of Harriet Burke), took up two terraced cottages on Pond Street, just around the corner from the Black Dog and butted up against the churchyard of St Aldwyn's plain little Victorian church.

Shortly after eleven in the morning, Alex knocked tentatively on the dark blue front door at the rightmost cottage. Although the entire lower floors of both cottages were used for the business, when the shop was closed this side was where the sisters came and went to their upstairs living quarters. Customers used the left door, although both accessed the same space.

From a window over Alex's head, a voice called, 'Come on in, Alex. Unless you'd prefer not to catch whatever Mary says is wrong with her.' Harriet smiled down at her. 'It's not locked.'

Alex went in, immediately relieved to feel both warm, since she'd hurried over without a coat, and closed away from the world outside. When the Burkes said afternoon tea, that's what they meant, and nothing was served before three. Until then, this would be a peaceful place. At the Black Dog, continual chatter about the murder had been too much strain to bear. That and following O'Reilly's instructions not to spread around what had happened last night.

'Someone may be watching you,' he'd said. 'They want to frighten you and we need to know where you fit in. If you don't say anything he may get rattled and do something to give himself away.'

Alex swallowed several times. *Do something . . .*

'Take your time.' Harriet's voice floated down the stairs this time. 'We took in a few Enid Blytons yesterday. You might like to look at them.'

'I'll do that,' Alex said.

'And there's a sweet old copy of *Heidi*.'

'Ooh, lovely.'

She collected children's books. On her library shelves were some beautiful, classical books, but she also gathered in childhood favorites recommended by older or even current generations, even if the condition was far less than fine. She loved the charming illustrations, especially the line drawings in so many of them.

As expected, a pile of books was stacked against the wall at one end of a dark wooden counter. Alex skirted the tea room tables, no two alike, sniffing appreciatively at the warm smells of fresh cakes and pastries in large white boxes from George's Bakery. Leaves of Comfort used the village bakery shop rather than have their goodies made on the premises. Not needing a large kitchen made space for at least two or three more tables in the tiny establishment.

She saw how torn the top book's cover was. Torn and taped together. But she also saw it was an original cover on a copy of *The Circus of Adventure* and swept it up. This was the only one missing from the books she already had in that series.

Johanna Spyri's *Heidi* had a slightly faded blue leather binding and Alex shivered a little with anticipation.

She would examine the stack more closely later.

Books crowded every available space in the shop, including a shelf that ran around both of the downstairs rooms just above eye level. Here and there hand-made tea cozies and teapots were on display and for sale like the jars of homemade jams and chutneys, tins of biscuits, packages of loose tea and bottles of sweets; all of these worked well as bookends. A pelmet of heavy, homemade lace hung in points from a rod along the edges of the shelves and lavender vied sweetly with the scents of delectable food.

Each table was covered with a white lace or embroidered cloth and among the china settings of various patterns were one or two strategically placed books. Village women, in both Folly and Underhill, made the cloths and similar ones were for sale.

Harriet and Mary couldn't have chosen a better outlet for their so-called retired energies.

'Doc James says Mary's under the weather,' Alex said loudly as she started up the stairs. 'Thought I'd better get over here to offer comfort and solace.' And snatch the first chance of the morning to get away from Major Stroud's prodding for ghoulish information on the murder victim.

Being exhausted and scared had nothing to do with anything, she told herself, trying to lift her spirits with sarcasm aimed at herself.

'There you are,' Harriet said when she saw Alex. 'Where's that Bogie? We heard you've taken him in.'

There were no secrets about inconsequential details in Folly-on-Weir and the local mouth-to-mouth was fast and efficient.

'I left him with Cathy. She already loves him.'

'How is Cathy?' Harriet said. 'Someone said she was very upset yesterday.'

'Still not good.' Alex suppressed a smile.

The kettle whistled in the kitchen and Harriet got up from a hugely overstuffed chintz chair. With the window behind her, open to frigid air, light turned her almost white hair into a silvery aura. 'We already have our delivery of pastries. I brought up some pieces of Battenberg cake, just in case you came by.' She rolled her eyes as she passed Mary, indicating, Alex assumed, that she was irritated with her sister. They spent a considerable amount of time being tetchy with one another.

'Sounds heavenly,' Alex said. 'I didn't finish going through the books because I wanted to come up, but I'll take the Blyton that was on top and the scrumptious *Heidi* for sure.' And probably the rest. She usually did.

Mary, wrapped in a shawl apparently crocheted from odds and ends of mismatched wool, didn't turn around, so Alex went to the other side of the woman's spindled rocking chair and looked quizzically at her.

Once the kitchen door closed behind Harriet, the elder of the sisters said, 'You know cats don't agree with me.' Mary's hair was pure white, thick, and pulled up into a bun at the back of her head. She favored various decorative combs and wore a tortoiseshell one inlaid with ivory today. It stuck up in the manner of a Spanish dancer's, minus the *mantilla*, which might disconcert some.

'Well,' Mary said, 'you do know that, don't you?'

'Um – no,' she answered succinctly.

'Of course you do. I've told you before.'

The kitchen door opened a few inches and Harriet called through: 'Are you hearing about Mary's newly acquired allergy to cats? Don't believe a word of it.'

Alex narrowed her eyes and lowered her voice. 'Honestly, Mary, I don't recall anything about a cat allergy, but so what? Stay away from them.' There wasn't a person in the village who would forget how upset Mary had been over the loss of a beloved old cat but Alex wasn't going there.

Mary shook her head and pointed.

A skinny, scraggly tabby sat tucked into a corner by the fireplace, watching them with disconcerting suspicion. An electric fire burned in the grate and the animal clearly sought out the warmth.

'Oh, dear,' Alex said. 'It doesn't look very well. It's so thin.'

'Then it should go to someone who'll get pleasure from fattening it up. Could you take it to that nice Tony Harrison for us?'

'Oliver isn't going anywhere,' Harriet said, marching across the room with a laden tray in her hands. She put it on a drop-leaf table polished to a glassy shine. 'He's doing beautifully. He particularly likes whitebait. I got some at the fishmonger's and popped it under the grill – made it all crispy, curly, and he ate every bite.'

'Fish isn't good for cats,' Mary said, her eyes closed. Her softly lined, deceptively sweet-old-lady face had a touch of rouge and powder, and she looked the perfect grandmotherly type. What a laugh.

'Of course it's good for them,' Harriet said.

'No, it isn't. They get eczema from it and their fur falls out.'

Alex's glance settled on the pink and yellow squares in some tender-looking slices of Battenberg cake, a sponge checkerboard held together with raspberry jam and all wrapped in a thin skin of marzipan. It was her favorite and she realized she was hungry. 'This looks good,' she said. 'I'll pour the tea.'

'*You* don't look good,' Harriet said, deliberately not giving Mary any attention. 'This nasty death is too much for you. It would be too much for anyone. What's going on about that? Is that policeman still being hard on you?'

Alex had a reason for coming, other than seeking out a haven, but before she launched into her own questions she supposed she'd have to give the Burkes some of the information she'd rather they got from her than the village gossips who were bound to find out eventually.

'She's forgotten I had Rupert for eighteen years,' Mary said, still eyeing the tabby. 'I'm an expert.' Rupert had been Mary's cat.

'And you haven't got over not having him any more,' Harriet said sharply. 'Five years and you're still grieving. Well, Oliver showed up in our garden and now you're going to live with him. Like it or lump it. He's mine. I found him shivering in the snow. And you weren't allergic to Rupert so stop being so selfish. Getting Doc James over here like that with some silly tale about cat allergies. Shame on you.'

'The doctor said I had a cold,' Mary pointed out, managing a couple of dry sniffs.

Alex cleared her throat and sat in a red velvet slipper chair in need of reupholstering. 'The police were at Lime Tree Lodge half the night,' she said. 'But you mustn't tell a soul until I give you the word. You'd get me into trouble with the police if you did.'

She had the full attention of two bright-eyed women instantly. Mary enjoyed a good gossip but she was devoted to Alex, who knew she could trust her.

'Somebody's playing games. Trying to frighten me. It worked. I spent what was left of the night in my room at the pub.'

Harriet gave her a skeptical look. 'What happened?'

Another thought grabbed Alex's attention. 'Mary, you won't be able to play in the darts match tonight. I'd better make a quick call and have a replacement found.'

'I will be playing,' Mary said imperiously. 'It will do me good to get away from the source of my misery.'

As if called, Oliver got up, stretched his long, thin body, and strolled to rub himself back and forth on Mary's legs. She put a handkerchief over her nose and mouth and shook her head.

Exceedingly short-sighted, for dart matches she donned heavy glasses with lenses the thickness of the bottoms of Coke bottles but tended to wipe out all competition. Since she was arthritic and walked with a cane, she had given in a couple of years earlier and agreed to stand within the safety shield of a walker for matches. She couldn't play with a cane in one hand, but with the promise of grabbing the walker in an emergency, she was fine – more than fine. Mary was an ace darts player.

Alex noted that the woman didn't try to stop the rangy tabby from leaning on her and rubbing his face against her shins.

'What happened last night?' Harriet's thin patience was well known. '*If* we've finished pandering to Mary's eccentricities.'

Pouring more tea, Alex said, 'It sounds silly when you put it into words. Someone fooled with the motion sensor lights. Whoever it was turned them on and off till I thought I was going mad. Must have been moving in and out of their range, which wouldn't be easy unless you figured it out first.'

'Horrible,' Harriet said, aghast. 'That's mean, if not evil.'

'And they let the air out of one of my tires,' Alex said, leaving out the bit about a dart.

'You shouldn't be up there on your own at all until this mad person is caught,' Mary said at once. She hadn't touched her tea and it must be cold. 'If I were your mother, I wouldn't allow it.'

'Alex has been married and divorced,' Harriet said, exasperated. 'She owns a pub and she won't see thirty again. She makes her own decisions. What are you talking about, Mary?'

'If you get tired of staying at the pub, and if your mother doesn't want you, we do. We can make room here.'

'Stop, stop.' Alex laughed and scooped up another piece of cake. 'I'm fine where I am and I can get what I want from the lodge in the daytime. No way will I let a bully completely get the better of me.'

Mary gave her an arch, nursing sister look, 'Not even a murderous bully?'

A lull in the conversation didn't last. Harriet said, 'We all know something's wrong with Cathy Cummings. What is it? Is she looking for attention? Why would she get hysterical about a stranger's death?'

'The past,' Mary said under her breath.

Alex waited for more and when it wasn't forthcoming, said, 'What about the past?'

'I think everyone's just about forgotten what that woman went through. People hardly knew her then. But you don't get over things like that.'

Harriet frowned and then looked chagrined. 'The son,' she said. 'You're right. It's so long ago I tend to forget the Cummings lost a child.'

It didn't seem the right moment to probe, so Alex waited.

'He drowned,' Mary said. 'In the Windrush down that back way in Bourton-on-the-Water. I think he was about four.'

Alex set down her cup and saucer with a clatter. She got up and went to the windows. Moss-covered gravestones in the churchyard, mostly very old and leaning this way and that, accentuated the silence everywhere. In early spring there would be snowdrops, bluebells, then daffodils beneath ancient trees to soften the scene. But in winter it was stark, like that place in her heart that waited to ache at inconvenient times.

Black mould stained the church walls but some of the original stained-glass windows remained to brighten the chilly building.

'Alex?' Harriet said quietly after a while. 'What is it? I've seen you go off into yourself like this before. You never did it before you went away.'

Alex put on a smile and turned around. 'I feel bad for the Cummings,' she said. 'What a horrible thing. I don't remember anyone drowning in the Windrush. It's so shallow.'

'The boy hit his head,' Harriet said. 'That's what they said at the time. Slipped and nobody saw him until it was too late.'

'Poor Cathy and Will.'

'Cathy hasn't had it easy,' Mary said, 'what with—'

'No point in gossiping about old things,' Harriet interrupted.

Mary set her creased mouth. 'I think Will still has his moments. Likes the horses too much. That's how they ended up selling the Black Dog, or so it's said. And it makes sense.'

The gambling problem was something Alex already knew about but Will seemed to have himself under control these days. 'Let's hope he's put all that behind him,' she said. 'Doc James said something about Cathy overreacting to someone else's tragedy. I can imagine how all the recent police activity and the horror of what happened in the woods up there could upset her badly.'

68

Harriet gathered the three cups and went to the kitchen to empty the cold dregs. She returned and poured boiling water to top up the pot.

Someone rapped on the front door.

Harriet beat Alex to the window, leaned out and said, 'Must be our day for visitors. In you come.'

She poured tea, making no attempt to say whose feet they heard on the stairs. When Tony Harrison came into view she scurried off, muttering about getting another cup.

'Hello, Tony,' Alex said.

He didn't smile, but spread his feet and put his hands behind his back in a stance that was becoming familiar. Then he saw Oliver. 'New family member?' he said, and his features softened a little. 'Looks like he needs some meat on his bones.'

'I'm making sure he gets it,' Harriet said, returning with a cup and saucer. She buttoned the cardigan to her beige twinset but Alex thought it was more to have something to do with her hands than because she was cold.

'I'll take a look at him,' Tony said and gently lifted the cat from his warm spot. Kneeling, he put Oliver on the soft if worn silk rug in front of the fire. 'Welcome, fellow,' he said, palpating his body while the cat looked up at him, unblinking, and made no attempt to escape the intrusion.

'I came looking for you, Alex,' he said, continuing to examine the animal. 'I heard about last night.'

Wishing she could warn him off talking in front of the Burkes, Alex didn't answer. They already knew too much. Who had told him, anyway?

'If I'd had any idea, I wouldn't have left you. It's not safe up there on your own.'

69

'Bogie came up trumps. He alerted me.' Being cared about might be nice, but all this interference grew tiresome.

'Did he catch and kill the murderer?'

Alex groaned. Both sisters had sucked in noisy breaths and slapped hands over their mouths.

With Oliver happily purring on his shoulder, Tony got up. 'This boy is in great shape, or he will be once he's had some TLC and his shots. He'll also have to be neutered.'

Harriet and Mary weren't listening. They looked at Alex with wide eyes.

'It was a silly prank last night, that's all,' Alex said. She pulled down the hem of the baggy gray T-shirt she wore over a thin sweater and realized she was doing exactly what she did as a girl when she was uncomfortable. She stopped tapping her feet on the floor and let go of the shirt. 'That's *all* it was. But I did come down and stay at the Black Dog for the rest of the night.'

'I think it's time everyone in this village was warned to take security precautions.' Tony repeatedly ran his hands over the cat. 'I'd like you to come with me to talk to O'Reilly, or his boss if that's what it takes. We need more patrol cars, particularly at night. There are too many people around here who aren't capable of defending themselves.'

'Tony—'

He cut her off. 'Just listen. I was up at Derwinters earlier, looking at a filly. It was Leonard who told me what went on last night.

'While I was there, Heather wandered in on foot, without her helmet, covered in mud – and blood. All scratched up and she was probably lucky it wasn't a lot worse. She'd been riding and her horse got spooked and threw her when she was about to jump a hedge.'

Now Alex really wished he'd waited until the two old ladies weren't around to hear. They were both pale but, oddly, appeared more quizzical than frightened. They wanted to hear the rest of the story.

'She must have been thrown,' Alex said quietly. 'I'm very sorry to hear that.'

'Her horse came in fifteen or so minutes later. He'd been riding hard and was screaming and bucking. Good job I was there. Also a good job the dart had landed in a fleshy part of his rump.'

Nine

Heather Derwinter beat Tony in stirring up the police and local attention. He and Alex had just got into his car when she got a call from O'Reilly with the news that, at Heather's insistence and with the backing of the mayor, there was about to be a police briefing in Folly-on-Weir.

'I don't want to go,' Alex said after repeating O'Reilly's message. She pushed the phone back into her pocket. 'Do you?'

He had expected something like this. 'Yes, I do. We need to know what's being done and said publically.'

'We already know.'

'Nothing's been said to the public until now. I haven't heard or read a word about it.' He drove to the church parking lot off Mallard Lane and got out.

Alex joined him. She wore no coat and looked shivery. 'Look around. There are hardly any cars here. They didn't get the word out so there's no point in going.'

He wasn't sure why she didn't want to go to the meeting but would put money on her not wanting to admit how serious a threat she had to face. 'Most people will come on foot. We already passed some. Just a minute.' From his Land Rover he took a quilted vest and draped it around her shoulders. He knew she wouldn't accept the coat he wore. 'Wear it,' he said when she opened her mouth to protest.

Quietly, but with a faint flush in her face, she put the vest all the way on and fastened the zip. Someone else could have worn it with her. 'Thanks,' she said, setting off to leave the parking lot without saying if she would go to the meeting or not.

Alex turned right. The meeting it would be.

As he'd predicted, more villagers were straggling along the little road and there were also vehicles, including a police car, parked on a verge.

Walking at her shoulder, Tony ducked his head going through the low entrance to the seventeenth-century parish hall on the far side of St Aldwyn's. It was when he looked up again that he saw members of the press for the first time.

Alex backed up, trod on his foot and pressed against him. She'd seen the cameras and recorders, too. 'I'm getting out of here,' she whispered. 'If my name is mentioned and they figure out which one I am, I'll be asked stuff. I don't want that. Most of all I don't want my picture in the paper.'

'We'll cut up the gallery stairs,' he said quietly in her ear and took hold of her elbow. 'But they won't say your name. And it's probably only fairly local stuff.'

Her low boots scuffed on the stone stairs to the gallery. 'The whole village knows I found the body. Anyone might talk about it if they were asked.'

She had a point.

'Good thing we aren't the only ones up here,' he whispered. 'We'd really be obvious if we were alone. I should have thought of that before we came up.'

As it was they sat immediately behind George from the bakery and his wife. The couple seemed half asleep and didn't turn around. Bakers probably got up long before dawn, Tony thought. They had a right to nod off in the middle of the day.

'We should have made sure Harriet and Mary knew,' Tony said. 'Doesn't look as if anyone else did.'

Alex smiled at him. 'They probably wouldn't come anyway. They avoid meetings. Mary knows they'll learn anything they want to know soon enough.'

'And we wouldn't change them, would we?' He liked being with Alex, liked it a lot. Why hadn't he taken notice of her before she met Michael Bailey-Jones? *Because she'd made such a good friend and then you thought you'd already met the love of your life.*

73

'More people keep coming,' Alex said. 'Funny to see the mayor chin-wagging with the police.'

Joan Gimblet, Mayor of Folly-on-Weir, stood at the far end of the lower room with O'Reilly, Lamb and Constable Frye. Her mayoral chain glistened on her considerable bosom and her blonde hair looked freshly gussied up.

'They'd have sent some honcho or other if this was really newsy stuff,' he whispered to Alex. 'O'Reilly's boss, or his boss.'

She made a grumpy sound and said, 'It's a sad testimony to the state of things when murder isn't newsy.'

Of course, she was right, but that discussion could wait for another time.

Dan O'Reilly walked to stand in front of the rows of chairs carrying the ancient microphone. 'Good afternoon. I'm Detective Inspector O'Reilly and this is Detective Sergeant Lamb. Your own Constable Frye is here and you all know Madam Mayor.'

While a murmur of agreement went through the small throng, Tony saw Heather Derwinter take a seat near the front. Either Leonard was parking the car or she'd come alone. Tony would have expected her to take it easy for the rest of the day, but evidently she felt she couldn't stay away when it had been she who'd raised the alarm with the police.

'You all know a man met his death in the woods on the hill.' With a nod, O'Reilly indicated the direction of the hill. 'We felt there were a few things you should know and some safety issues to address.'

'Did someone else get murdered?' a male voice

shouted. Tony couldn't see who had spoken but assumed it was a reporter at work.

'I'll have a few minutes for questions when I'm finished,' O'Reilly said neutrally. Apparently he wasn't a novice at this sort of thing. 'I'd like to ask anyone who thinks or knows they've seen someone who seemed out of place to contact Constable Frye or come directly to us. Please don't hesitate to let us know even the smallest thing. If it isn't relevant, you will still have done a service.'

'He sounds so . . . I don't know. In charge, I suppose.'

Tony noticed how intently she watched the detective, as if he really interested her. He shouldn't find that remarkable, or get an uncomfortably sinking feeling.

'I don't want to alarm you, but basic safety precautions are important. You know what they are but village life is friendly and quiet and sometimes people forget that it's wise to make sure all windows and doors are locked. Don't go alone into isolated areas or be out after dark if you don't have to be. We're fully engaged in this investigation and we'll make sure you're kept informed. Don't forget, if something concerns you, pick up the phone.'

'He isn't going to give any details,' Alex said, and sounded relieved.

Another stranger's voice rang out: 'You said you'd tell us about someone else being murdered.'

His face calm, O'Reilly said, 'There hasn't been another death.'

'Why are you avoiding talking about murder?'

'I answered your question,' O'Reilly said.

'Is it true the dead man was a priest?' A woman this time.

'No.' O'Reilly didn't elaborate.

'He's being cagey,' Tony said. 'Not that I blame him.'

Alex kept watching the detective. 'I hope he stays cagey,' she mumbled.

'Was he shot?'

'I can't discuss those details,' O'Reilly said.

'That isn't something you normally keep mum about.'

'This time it is.' Now O'Reilly shifted as if he was getting ready to cut off questions.

But the woman wasn't to be silenced. 'So what's the identity of the victim?'

'The next of kin will be the first to hear that.'

Ten

Alex had insisted on walking back alone from the meeting at the parish hall. It would be too easy to become reliant on Tony and she didn't think he wanted that. Maybe she needed – and wanted – his friendship but there were always potential hang-ups when a man and woman tried to have a platonic relationship.

She and Tony had parted with a wave. He insisted she keep his gilet until she had something else. He'd pick it up from the pub later, which reminded her that she needed to get more clothes and other supplies from Lime Tree Lodge for her stay in the village. *Bloody nuisance.*

When she left Tony, they'd both started walking away, only to turn back and frown at one another. Alex was the first to shrug and leave again. They didn't know what to make of O'Reilly's parting comment at the hall.

'The next of kin will be the first to hear that.'

The afternoon dragged on, but only until both regulars and villagers who rarely stopped by began trickling into the bar.

Within an hour the place was filling up. 'You've brought this place up to what it was at its best,' Reverend Restrick said, surprising Alex, who hadn't seen him come in. 'It's warm and inviting. A comfortable place to be. It's important for a community to have safe gathering places.'

'Thanks,' Alex said, smiling at the big, florid man who asked for his usual, a whiskey neat.

The vicar moved along the bar to join Doctor James Harrison and Lily. Alex's mum rarely spent her own time in the pub but she and Doc James occasionally had a drink together.

So the vicar thought her place was warm, inviting and safe. Until a few days ago it had felt that way to Alex, too. Not any more. She felt as if a layer of glass sat between her and everyone else, cutting her off from interaction but not from watching and waiting for something horrible to happen again, perhaps to one of them.

Or to herself.

Tony came in with Katie sticking close to his legs. He beckoned to Alex and moved to the end of the bar closest to the door.

'What?' she said, hurrying to lean toward him. She closed her eyes for an instant and took a deep breath. 'Sorry. I'm snapping before I can stop myself.'

'Forget it. You're strung out. Why wouldn't you be? I've never played darts.'

'What?' She heard her voice biting out again and shook her head. 'I've got to get my cool, collected face back on.'

'Not your fault. I didn't make any sense. I had a thought and wanted to ask you about it. Are there three darts in one of those boxes they have?'

'Tony . . . don't tell me you don't know a player throws three darts.'

'I never noticed. I wasn't interested. Anyway, that wouldn't have to mean there weren't more than three in a box. Maybe there's a spare. Or two sets in one box.'

For the first time all day she felt like laughing. All she allowed herself was a grin. 'No spares. One set.'

Leaning even closer to her, he said, 'So all three darts are accounted for – for now.' He made a wry face. 'At least from one box. I say we hope only one set went missing.'

'I'd like to believe we don't have anything else to worry about,' Alex said. 'Maybe we don't. But there are plenty more darts around.' Unwillingly, she wondered how she would feel if the dart artist suddenly stopped. If that happened, he or she could be trying to lull them all into thinking the danger was over.

'Listen, I think you should be more positive about this. Whoever our maniac is, he wanted to tie the crime to this pub. Otherwise why use darts easily traceable . . .' He whistled softly. 'Maybe there's a good reason I'm not a detective. Doesn't mean anything, does it? Not without more information. That'll teach me to get carried away by the first cheerful thought I've had in days.'

'It could be significant,' Alex told him. 'I just wish we had a record of how many we had to begin with. But something will break soon.'

They looked solemnly at each other.

'Do you think O'Reilly slipped up this morning?' Tony asked. 'I've thought about it all afternoon.'

'In other words, have they identified the dead man? We couldn't decide then and I don't have any more insights now. But if he didn't slip up I think he may have been throwing out an ambiguous comment to see if it stirs something up.'

Tony lowered his voice even further. 'Do we still think the man was wearing a ring at some point?'

'I don't know, but I intend to find out.' She hadn't meant to admit that. 'And I don't see anything positive in telling O'Reilly we noticed the damaged finger. Not when we don't know if there really was a ring.'

'Right,' Tony said, giving her a long look. 'Call if you need me. I've got to check a couple of patients at the clinic. See you later.' He headed for the exit from the inn and restaurant on the far end of the bar, giving his dad a slap on the back and a salute as he passed.

Alex felt watched as she moved about the bar, and wished she could leave. She had to stay at least until the dart match was underway. Perhaps she needed to be down here for the whole evening, just to put on a good face and help make customers feel all was well. She had tried to make a call to O'Reilly, left a message to ask for a brief talk in the morning. Alex hoped she wouldn't regret the move. If he would take her seriously, maybe she had some ideas worth thinking about – and maybe she could get something useful out of him, like whether or not they knew the dead man's identity.

Kev Winslet from the Derwinter estate held court, his voice booming loudly enough for snatches of what he said to make it past the din.

Cathy Cummings was back at work and looked settled again. She had a definite soft spot for Bogie, who already had his own blue tartan blanket folded up on the hearth. Cathy took treats to the dog and he gave her doggy smiles, but it was to Alex he went regularly to make sure she hadn't forgotten him.

'Al reckons what happened up there was an accident,' Cathy said, standing behind the bar with her hands on her hips. At least the color was back in her cheeks. 'He could be right. Who would want to kill a man like that?'

Alex pulled some pints of Guinness and slid them across the bar. She didn't feel talkative but she didn't have much option. 'I wish we were sure it either was or wasn't one of our darts that killed him.'

'Did they ask you how many boxes we keep in the cupboard?'

Alex nodded. 'Yes. But I couldn't tell them anyway. Never counted them. Did you?'

'Never had a need,' Cathy said.

Kev Winslet had a rapt audience in front of the fire where he stood with the back of his jacket flapped up, warming his corduroy-clad rear. There had to be twenty people gathered around him. 'You know what coppers are like,' he said. 'Like to make themselves important. I reckon this lot's stringing the whole thing along, making more of it than needs be.'

'I doubt they've time to do that, Kev,' Reverend Restrick said. 'It must take patience to pick up all the little puzzle pieces and turn them into a picture.'

'What about those boys Frye had to deal with for knocking down gates and putting soap powder in the pond? They may have behaved themselves for months – at least, I haven't heard they've been up to anything else – but that doesn't mean the little buggers didn't get bored again.'

'And start killing strangers?' Lily said. 'Oh, Kev, no.'

A dark frown pulled down Kev's bushy brows. 'Ah, well now, sometimes things go wrong. Or they could have decided to tag on behind the death thinking no one would think other things could be them – like Mrs Derwinter's—'

'Kev,' Alex said quickly. 'Let me buy you a drink.'

Tony's dad, Doc James, turned and hooked his elbows on the bar behind him. He resembled Tony but his hair was almost entirely white. 'Listen to the vicar, Kev,' he said. 'The victim wouldn't think the police are making too much out of what happened – and there's nothing to suggest a prank gone wrong as far as I know.'

81

Normally good-natured, Kev did have a temper and he scowled, his face turning a deeper shade of red. He didn't like to be contradicted.

'Best let the police do their job, Kev,' the reverend said quietly. He was a man who considered what he said and Alex could tell he was concerned about so much speculation. She slid a fresh pint of Trooper ale in front of Kev.

Will pulled Alex aside. 'Just got a call from Fred at the Horse and Hounds. They're forfeiting tonight's match. He said they've got a bug going around and they can't get a team together.'

'You think they're not coming because . . . well, because of what's happened?' Alex turned her back to the room. 'Can't be. Fred came in himself yesterday.'

'Too true, he did,' Will said. 'Maybe he thinks he can help turn everyone off us and he was sizing up how many extra customers he might get.'

'It's not like you to be into conspiracies,' Alex said. 'We'd better ring round and let our people know there isn't a match.'

'I'll do it,' Will said. 'I'll tell 'em there's a drink on the house if they still want to drop in.'

Alex nodded agreement. Will was good with customers and with bringing in new business – and soothing feathers.

Lily caught Alex's eye and beckoned. 'Did you get your wheels mended?' she said. It was good to see her relaxing for once.

'Yes,' Alex told her. 'The garage sent someone up earlier. The Land Rover's out at the back now. They drove it down for me.'

'Um . . .' Lily rarely seemed awkward but she

did now, and Alex knew what was coming. 'It'd be lovely to have you stay with me if you'd like to. Unless you're more comfortable using your room here.'

Resisting the urge to be a bit sharp over motherly concern wasn't always easy but Alex said, 'Thanks, Mum. If I'm coming over, I'll let you know.' She had planned to continue staying at the Black Dog.

'Bogie's welcome, too.' Lily nodded and turned back to Doc James.

He smiled at Alex. She had always liked him and they got along easily, but this time she thought he gave her a more searching look.

One of the kitchen staff came through and left a steaming plate on the bar. He said something to Cathy and left again. She took the meal of bangers, mash and mushy peas doused with thick onion gravy to one of the tables dubbed 'step-up' because they were on a raised area behind a half wall of blackened wood paneling. A single step separated them from the main pub floor.

Cathy slid the plate in front of a thin man in dark clothing with iron-gray hair cut very short.

He glanced toward Alex, met her eyes very directly and moved to sit on the opposite side of the table with his back to the room.

Alex's heart flipped. He wore a long habit. The sound of a pinball machine in a side room became grating. Voices around her rose and fell and collided together in a meaningless babble.

Without turning around, the man raised a hand in a wave as if he knew she was watching him. Slowly at first, then with firmer steps, Alex came from behind the bar and approached the customer. She saw he had a glass of red wine beside his plate.

'Can I help you?' she asked pleasantly, although her voice sounded breathy in her own ears.

Bright, light blue eyes settled on hers, at close quarters this time. 'Are you Alex?' he said. His cheeks were sunken and weathered but she didn't think he was an ill man, just a naturally thin one.

'Yes, I am,' she said.

'Can you spare a little time?' His voice had a rusty edge.

'Yes, of course.'

'Good. I hope we can help each other.'

She sat on the worn and slippery banquette facing him and he added: 'I'm Brother Percy. I would be happy for you to call me Percy.'

Eleven

The man took a healthy swallow of wine, propped his elbow on the table and continued to hold the glass in long, almost transparent fingers. 'I understand you own this place.'

'I do. How can I help you?' His age was difficult to guess. He could be fifty or seventy – he had an unworldly air.

'Please tell me about Dominic, about what happened to him. I spoke to a policeman. At first he was interested. Had all sorts of questions. But I couldn't tell him anything he wanted to know. I wanted to say what I knew about the brother, and that I'd like to see him. I learned you found Dominic so I came to find you.'

Slowly, Alex slid to the edge of the bench and rested her forearms on the table. She couldn't feel her hands any more. Cold anticipation made it hard to talk. *Dominic.*

Her breath shortened and her skin began to prickle. The start of a panic attack? She hadn't had one in months, not even when she'd come upon the dead man. Panic could describe what she'd felt when someone fooled with the motion sensors at her house, but that was different from the real thing. Alex knew all about that.

'Dominic was the man who died in the woods up there?' She nodded toward the hills opposite the pub.

'I believe so.' Percy nodded and demolished a sausage while he waited, with apparent patience, for her to say something else.

'You're hungry,' she said, startled by her own comment. 'I mean . . . Yes, you are hungry.' With an awkward little laugh, she rubbed her hands over her eyes, taking deep, calming breaths. 'His hair was cut like yours. For a moment . . . I knew you must be something to do with him.'

He smiled and papery wrinkles drove webs of fine lines around his eyes and mouth. Transformed by the kindness of that smile, Brother Percy warmed Alex a little. Her muscles started to ease out of the grip of tension.

'Who was the policeman you talked to?'

'A detective,' Percy said. 'Lamb, his name is. Nice fellow I imagine, but busy.'

'Wasn't interested in what you had to say?' The

idea amazed her. Surreptitiously, she placed the flat of her right hand just above her waistband and felt the next inhalation. She kept it slow.

'He was interested but since I couldn't give him the name he was looking for, he took what information I had and said he would have to verify who I say I am before letting me see Brother Dominic.'

Ethereal – that described this person. Almost as if he might disappear if she closed her eyes for too long, although the speed with which he dispatched his meal suggested he was quite human. His hooded cowl stood away from a corded neck. Beneath a threadbare raincoat far too flimsy for the weather, his tunic was a very dark brown and tied high at the waist with a rolled and knotted raw linen cincture.

'You have a name for the man who died. Dominic. And you're Percy. I'm sure they can check the rest.'

'I should explain, although it won't interest you particularly.' He smiled again. 'Once we were called Gyrovagi – monks without a cloister. Wanderers on a quest others didn't understand or felt threatened by. We were considered undesirable. Charlatans, even. I won't bore you with more of that. I don't know Brother Dominic by any other name, not the name he was given as a child – if he even knew it. But he was a man in search of simplicity and truth, not the name he was once given. And I long ago shed my own. It's irrelevant. I cannot give the police the pieces of paper they want. They would have to accept my word that my path crossed that of Brother Dominic.'

'You must see him.' Desperation didn't make for a clear head. Brother Percy admitted he didn't have a home. That meant he could disappear.

Sadness dragged the lines of his face downward. 'I would have liked that. And to spend a few minutes with him. I have something of his by mistake. He would have missed it by now. Not important, I suppose, but I'd have liked to . . . leave it with him. Some would have called him inestimably sweet – perhaps he was – but I was only caught by his goodness, and I supposed what I felt was a troubled spirit still searching.'

Wanting nothing more than for him to keep talking, Alex sat still and held his gaze. She wanted to ask him if Brother Dominic wore a ring. Not yet, though.

Cathy wiped the table and asked if Brother Percy was ready for more wine. He only smiled at her.

'Dominic was dissatisfied with himself. I felt that. Once he talked of things he had yet to put right, if he could ever discover how to do that. He missed someone called Lennie but I wasn't sure who he meant. It isn't our way to ask questions, simply to listen. We are essentially silent.' His sudden laugh jolted Alex. 'He had a dog. It caused him more problems than he already had but he would never have given it up once it came to him. It's hard enough to feed oneself as we live. I think Dominic sometimes chose not to eat in favor of that little fellow.'

Cathy picked up Percy's empty plate and glass. 'Will you have pudding?' she asked Brother Percy.

'No, but thank you,' he said, and took the bill from her.

This man would go away, Alex knew it, and then she might never find out more than the few insights he was giving. She glanced toward the fireplace where Bogie lay curled up on his blanket. 'You know . . .' No, Percy was unlikely to want Bogie but she couldn't risk it. Silly when she'd only had the little dog since yesterday.

'It's all right,' Percy said, his clear eyes shining with a touch of humor. 'I saw him by the fire when I came in, but I couldn't look after him anyway. And I'm glad he's here. Dominic will be glad.'

Alex shivered. A calmness hovered about Percy and when he spoke of Dominic as if he were somewhere around she thought she felt the other man's presence, too.

Cathy approached with two glasses of red wine. She put one in front of Alex. 'The gentleman was drinking your favorite Burgundy,' she said. 'I thought it might be nice for you to have some together. These are nasty days and the nights are enough to freeze your bones. It'll warm you up.' She set down the other glass near Percy and left.

With a slight frown, Percy regarded the second pour of wine.

He can't afford it. 'You didn't ask for that one,' she said with a smile. 'It's on the house.'

'I should be going,' Percy said. 'But thank you.'

Alex furiously thought of ways to keep him. In the morning she'd see Dan O'Reilly and she'd like to take Percy with her. 'Stay and chat,' she said, knowing she sounded forced. 'Where will you spend the night?'

The Burke sisters had come into the pub, Mary leaning heavily on her cane and forcing a few coughs. Alex waved at them.

'I'll know when I get there,' Percy said and picked up the new glass of wine. 'I'll be warm enough,' he added and smiled.

Laughter followed Harriet and Mary toward their table by the fire. Alex could only imagine what outrageous complaining Mary was tossing out. She was a one-woman put-down artist when it came to the darts team from the Horse and Hounds – or just about any other team that competed with the Black Dog. She'd be full of derisive comments tonight. The laughter grew and, from the gesturing of the woman's free hand, Alex could tell she was enjoying herself.

Will kept a 'reserved' sign on the sisters' table to avoid any scenes should someone else try to sit there, and the two were soon ensconced amid a chuckling group of neighbors.

'You like what you do here,' Percy said. 'You would have enjoyed Brother Dominic if he ever managed to put his worries to rest. It seemed important for him to get to this place.'

How she wanted to ask about those worries and the tiny bits of information the monk had told her. But if she started asking too many questions it could be a big mistake.

'I never expected to do anything like own a pub,' she told him. 'I came back to the village when my life changed a lot. I worked in London as a graphic artist, but I don't miss it.' Not completely true, but the rest was too complicated.

He raised one eyebrow quizzically but didn't press for more information.

'Did you read about Dominic in a local paper?' she asked. 'What happened, I mean?'

He looked vague. 'I heard,' he said and reached into the pocket of the raincoat he wore, pulling out a small leather purse. 'I knew it had to be him. Someone he knew should say what needs to be said.'

'Please stay here at the inn tonight,' she said. 'We have plenty of room and that way you'll have a comfortable bed to sleep in and a healthy breakfast before you set off again.' All she could visualize was the elderly man trudging along, who knew where, in the darkness.

Then there was the spectre of a malevolent presence lurking out there.

'That's not my way,' he said. 'But I do thank you for your kindness.' He opened the purse and began to assemble coins on the table.

She had to keep him here. 'Reverend!' She called to the vicar, who immediately saw her signalling him and came toward them. 'This is someone I want you to meet. Brother Percy, this is Reverend Restrick, the vicar of St Aldwyn's here in Folly-on-Weir.' Sending a distress signal without Percy noticing stretched Alex's inventive abilities. 'I'm trying to get Brother Percy to stay the night in the village. Tell him it's too cold and getting too late to go on.'

The vicar waited for the other man to shift along the bench and sat beside him. He shot Alex an understanding glance.

She excused herself and fetched the vicar's

drink from the bar. In the short time it took for her to get back the two men had fallen into easy conversation and she wished she could just creep away and leave them to talk.

'Drink your wine,' the vicar told her. 'It's good to see you relax.'

If only he knew how she really felt.

'Brother Percy knew the dead man,' she blurted out.

Before she could apologize for her clumsiness, the vicar said, 'Yes, so he's said. Brother Percy . . . perhaps we shouldn't talk too much more about it all until he's had time to rest and think. He isn't a man accustomed to being with so many other people.'

Percy raised a hand in protest. 'I don't expect my peculiarities to be accommodated, Reverend, but thank you for your consideration. It doesn't seem I can be of any more help anyway and the longer I stay – comfortable as I am here – the later it gets.' He smiled a little and emptied the second glass of wine. 'Not that the night has ever held any fear for me.'

'I'm not as comfortable with my own company as you, Percy,' the vicar said. He had already drained his whiskey. 'Charlotte, my wife, is visiting her sister so I'm fending for myself. It would be a pleasure to have you use the spare room at the vicarage. It's always made up. Then I'd have a companion for breakfast in the morning before you go on your way – if you'd like that. I make good coffee, I'm told, and fry an edible egg. I've some Cumberland sausages, too. Best there are.'

Brother Percy fiddled with the coins on the table.

'I don't want you to feel pressured, of course,' Reverend Restrick said.

'Thank you, Reverend, thank you. Yes, I'll be grateful to stay with you, but I'll be away before breakfast.' He started to move and the vicar immediately got to his feet to let the monk out from behind the table.

'We'll see,' Reverend Restrick said, smiling at Alex as the other man walked ahead of them.

Twelve

Whatever Tony felt, it wasn't good. There had been something off in his father's voice. Come to that, it was off for him to call late in the evening at all. If there had been something worth saying, something that couldn't wait for a more reasonable hour, they could have spoken at the Black Dog, or so he'd have thought. This summons, and that's what it had sounded like, pressed all of Tony's warning buttons.

Katie ran ahead along the pathway toward the doctor's home and surgery. Multiple rose arches punctuated the way where, if it were light enough, the dormant vines would show, thick and brown. At 39 Bishop's Way – the house wasn't named – a fifteen-foot-high stone wall with impressive ball-topped gateposts edged the narrow verge that butted the roadway. A brass plate with the number and Dr Harrison's surgery information was set into one gatepost. The property stretched back a deceptively long way and James Harrison's all but lifelong gardening hobby had produced a lush, mature half acre that became a destination view in summer when great splashes of color vied for attention among mature trees, and the lawn behind the house rolled, emerald, down to a bubbly feeder stream.

Curtains were drawn over the study window but the conservatory lights glowed and Tony ran to catch up with Katie before she could scratch the door.

He pushed between counters crowded with pots where the air smelled of mulch and loamy soil.

Another half an hour and he would have left for home. If his paperwork weren't in such need of a major attack, he would already be on his way. His assistant in the office and surgery was on holiday.

'Dad,' he called, crossing the old stone tiled back hall and putting his head around his father's study door. 'You called – I came.'

Looking at him over the top of his half glasses, his dad didn't return Tony's smile. A book lay open on his knees but it had slid sideways, as if unread.

'Good, good. Get us a drink, would you? I'll have a splash of soda in mine.'

The Scotch wasn't decanted. An almost full bottle of Macallan and a soda siphon stood on a shelf among a cluster of mismatched crystal glasses. James Harrison liked good crystal and picked up any piece he fancied, regardless of size or pedigree.

'Damn frigid out there,' he said, holding his hands to the wood fire that curled up the soot blackened breast of a fireplace surrounded by royal blue and dark green tiles. 'Cold enough to knock the bottom off a brass monkey,' he added in what was about as lusty as his language ever got and clearly an attempt to take the edge off an already strained atmosphere.

Tony poured the drinks. He didn't believe in diluting good scotch with anything and took his own neat. 'This'll warm me up for the drive home,' he said. 'Probably shouldn't be too much longer – got an early call in the morning.'

'Mm.'

His dad's mind was elsewhere, apparently buried in whatever topic had also distracted him from the book now sliding, unheeded, toward the floor.

Although the room was small, when Tony's mother had been alive she had sat in the chair he used now to read or sew while she kept her husband company in the evenings. He could imagine the two of them there now and, although he was grateful for the closeness they had shared, thinking about how his father had missed his wife saddened Tony. At least his dad got out more these days.

'Never thought I'd see the day when this village got turned into a horror story,' his dad said. 'A lot of people are frightened. You can feel it but there's only so much you can say when you try to soften things a bit.'

'I know. And I can't get my head around the idea of it being a religious man who's been victimized. You can't get away from that being true, can you?'

'No, son.' The doctor sank more deeply into

his cracked, green leather chair and didn't react when the book hit the carpet.

The room still looked as it had when Tony's mother had been alive. The greens and blues in the old fireplace tiles were repeated in draperies, carpets and cushions. In summer, with the windows open, it felt as if the inside and outside were one.

He waited but his father didn't say anything more.

'You said it was important for me to come by tonight, Dad.'

The doctor took a thoughtful swallow from his glass. 'I was sorry you and Penny didn't have a smooth path with your marriage but not completely surprised. You were very young when you met and I think she expected to carry on in a sort of fairyland where she was the princess forever.'

Penny had not been the topic Tony expected.

'I don't blame Penny for anything,' he said, although the words didn't ring completely true even in his ears.

'We'll have to put you up for sainthood then. But I need to organize what's on my mind. You like Alex Bailey-Jones, don't you?'

So that was it. 'We've known each other since we were kids and it's easy for us to be together.'

His father still looked expectant.

'In the past couple of days we've had reasons to talk a lot, but we don't know a whole lot about one another's lives between leaving Folly and coming back again – permanently, I mean. But, OK, yes, I like Alex. She's kind and smart and she isn't a quitter.'

95

'She's also a pretty woman who knows how to stand on her own feet,' his father said. 'And I think she's been through a lot, although she keeps it to herself.'

'Has Lily ever talked about what happened with Michael?' Tony asked without thinking. His dad wasn't the kind to discuss other people's confidences.

'Only that there's been real sadness and Alex likes to keep her own counsel. Does she know about you and Penny?'

Tony breathed deeply through his nose. 'She knew Penny a long time ago – only through me, of course. I was already at university. You remember how I used to bring Penny home. That's how Alex met her.'

'Don't beat around the bushes with me, son.'

'No, then. She hasn't asked about Penny or anything else in my past and there's been no reason to bring it up.'

His dad gave a short, humorless laugh and bent to give Katie an absent-minded scratch between the ears. The dog liked to lie with her head on his checked woolen carpet slippers.

'Why don't you just spit out what's really on your mind?' Tony said. He drained his glass and got up for a refill.

'I've seen you and Alex together several times in recent days. You're protective of her. I may be old but I'm not dead yet. I can still read these things. I've seen the way you look at her – and you aren't and never were obvious about those things. But you want to be around her.'

It was his turn to laugh, or more, to snort. 'I

don't know how you get all the way there. Just because I get along well with an old friend doesn't mean there's a great romance in the wings.' He shouldn't drink any more Scotch, it was making him tired. When he was tired he could get short-tempered and that would be a mistake here.

'At the pub earlier, you stopped by just to talk to her. You aren't much for being in the pub, never have been. That's changed, hasn't it? Now that Alex owns the place and she's there so much of the time. The murder just turned out to be something that gave you a chance to get to know her again. What exactly does she know about you? Since you went your separate ways, that is?'

Everything Tony looked at took on sharper focus; colors became more intense. He felt his skin tighten. 'I'm sure she's figured out I'm not married any more.'

'Would she know, by some sort of instinct, that you're a widower?'

'I told you, it hasn't come up.' He rubbed a hand over his face, ashamed of his tone. 'No, Dad, she doesn't know. Sorry to snap. It's still raw.'

'It's been more than five years and before she died you two weren't having an easy time of it.'

'Thanks for reminding me.'

His father took off his glasses and set them on the hearth. 'Every parent says this, but I only want what's best for you. Alex might be that but you could blow it with the secrecy.'

'Damn it, Dad. I don't even think Alex knows I was in Australia or that I had a practice there for a year.'

'She would if you hadn't made a neat job of

97

getting back here without talking about what happened. I still can't believe nothing was picked up by the media in this country. But don't think there aren't records in Australia, and if our local plods decide they want to dig around in your past, they'll find them.'

'I wasn't charged with anything.' Tony sat down again, hard. 'You never said any of this before. You kept telling me you believed the way I explained things and we didn't need to dwell on any of it. Those were your words, or damn close.'

'And I meant them,' his father said, leaning forward, urgent. 'But I'm your father, not a woman you want in your life.'

Tony opened his mouth to say he didn't know what he wanted in his life, but he thought he might want Alex. What he didn't have a strong idea about was how she felt about him.

'You know she's divorced, son, and you know there's been some bad stuff in her life even if she doesn't say a lot. And you'd know if that ex-husband of hers had died in . . . if he was dead.'

'In unusual circumstances? Isn't that what you were going to say? Might as well be completely open with me, Dad. You and I already know the whole story. What I don't get is why you think I would bring up the mess with Penny. I had no part in it.'

His dad got up and walked behind his chair. He braced his arms on the back. 'Even you know how anyone else would take what you just said. They would think you were playing games. Of course you had a part in it. She was out there with you – because of you.'

'But I didn't have anything to do with her death.' He refused to allow himself to crawl back into the dark hole it had taken him too long to escape. In that hole, he had even questioned himself.

'Penny drowned,' Dad said. 'They never found the body, just some of her diving equipment. But *she was gone a week* before you reported her missing. That's what could have changed your life forever, too.'

'I hate this.' Tony put his glass aside. 'There was someone else. I thought she was with him the way she had been on other occasions. I don't want to go through it all again.'

James Harrison's sharp eyes softened. 'And I don't want you to either. Or to lose a chance at happiness because you lied.'

'I haven't lied, dammit.' He was on his feet.

'By omission. Same thing. If you don't bring it out in the open, and soon, she may never trust you.'

Tony picked up his coat and wound it over an arm. 'Dad?' He had hoped never to ask this question but it was inevitable after tonight. 'You're not sure you believe I didn't murder my own wife, are you?'

Thirteen

By four thirty in the morning, Alex gave up trying to sleep. As long as she kept counting the minutes until she could turn up at St Aldwyn's, and try to persuade Brother Percy to go with her to see Detective Inspector O'Reilly, she would not manage to keep her eyes shut.

A full moon lighting the room through thin curtains didn't help.

It was almost time to think about going to St Aldwyn's.

Already dressed and lying on top of the bed at Corner Cottage, she tried to gage how long she should wait before going to keep watch on the vicarage. She feared Percy might leave very early and she'd miss him.

Bogie shifted restlessly and whined. He jumped to the floor and she could see the shine of his eyes staring up at her. She had no way of really knowing his schedule yet but she'd better get him out for a run.

Staying like this was hopeless anyway and only made her more edgy and tired. She got up quietly and lifted Bogie into her arms. It was easy to shove her feet into her boots.

Her mother had been so pleased when she arrived – almost giddy but trying to be cool. Alex vowed to come and stay again soon, and spend more time with Lily, but after tonight and until she could go back to the lodge for good she knew the freedom of her own quarters at the Black Dog would be best.

The spare parka her mother kept for her was hung over the newel post at the bottom of the stairs, where Alex had been in the habit of tossing her coat when she was still living at home in Underhill.

With moonlight acting almost like sunrise, she

wasn't afraid to go out. They would still stay in the garden, from where she could get back inside quickly. At least she didn't have to go into those isolated woods that had become so ominous. Alex gave an involuntary shudder and closed the back door of the cottage behind her.

Pulling on a woolen hat and gloves, she followed Bogie only to see him whip to the stone wall at the bottom of the vegetable garden and slip through the gate that had been left open. She muttered under her breath. That gate was supposed to be closed and bolted.

The garden backed on to the village green and she ran after Bogie, knowing where he was heading. Calling him in a low voice to avoid rousing anyone in the cottages, she caught glimpses of flying dog heels and followed them until she made her way through scrubby grass on a narrow path trodden by many feet over a lot of years. Dirty snow still clung to ruts and hillocks on the ground. Each step she took crunched. As Cathy had suggested, the cold was bone freezing.

Bogie leaped about, gleeful at an unexpected chance to be outside. 'Come here, *now*!' Alex hissed. 'We're going back.'

He wasn't giving up this treat so fast and made for the trail all dogs and their owners used to go around the pond.

When he stopped, suddenly, one foot raised, Alex's stomach and heart raced for first place in her throat. The dog growled. She spun around and her knees wobbled at the sight of a man bearing down on her in the silvery light.

'It's O'Reilly,' he said.

101

She recognized his voice and squeezed her eyes shut, caught between relief and awkwardness.

'Are you out of your mind?' He sounded more angry than incredulous.

No surprises there. 'Good morning, Inspector,' she said – calmly, she hoped. 'Bogie needed a walk but I'm glad to see you.'

'You can hardly see me. Wasn't that you I saw at the parish hall when I advised people not to wander around alone at the moment?'

'It's like broad daylight,' she pointed out. 'And life has to go on. Bogie needed to come out and I was suffocating inside.' He didn't have to know just how descriptive that was of the way she was starting to feel most of the time. 'A little fresh air was all we needed. The gate wasn't supposed to be open but he slipped out.'

'We'd all feel better if you slipped back in with him. You came from that cottage, didn't you? Your mum's? I'll walk you back now.'

Now that Bogie knew there was no threat he ran ahead and back again, only to turn and repeat the process.

'Don't let me keep you from what you were doing, Inspector – we'll go back soon.' She paused and looked him in the eye. 'What were you doing wandering around out here at this time of the morning?'

He took in an exasperated breath and let it out. 'Police work often requires long hours.'

She waited. He'd have to say something more illuminating eventually.

'We're thinking of setting up an incident room in the parish hall,' he said.

102

He was good at diversionary tactics. 'Really?'

'Unless we get a sudden break in this case it looks as if we'll be around for . . . well, for as long as it takes.'

'I'm coming to see you in the morning. Should I come to the station still, or the parish hall?'

'You're seeing me now. What's on your mind?'

He sounded tired but he was trying not to be too short with her. Talking to him now might have been fine, if Brother Percy hadn't shown up at the Black Dog earlier. Now there seemed so much more focus to what she wanted to talk about.

'Bogie,' she called, hurrying after the dog. 'Don't get too far away.' This was an opportunity to see if O'Reilly would reveal something she didn't already know.

Unfortunately, Bogie ran obediently back, and at once, taking away her excuse for staying out here. Alex shot off with the dog beside her, forcing a laugh and pretending to play with the animal, who leaped on a bench. He gave her a huge, doggy grin. Alex went to clear snow from the bench and sit beside him. He promptly climbed on her lap and she clipped on his lead.

O'Reilly followed and sat down without being invited.

Neither of them spoke for what felt like ages. Wood smoke drifted, pungent, on the air; some the remnants of fires now little more than embers in the grates of still-sleeping households, some the fresh work of the earliest risers.

Alex looked over her shoulder toward the Black Dog. They kept the colored lanterns on all night. They looked washed out now but she still liked the idea of being a welcome sign to anyone passing by.

'Is Alex short for Alexandra?' O'Reilly asked.

'Yes.'

'Nice.'

'Prissy,' she said, and laughed. She hadn't expected a personal question. 'Why are you walking around out here – really? Following up a clue?'

'You could say that. In a broad sense.'

She laced her gloved fingers together and hunched down into the neck of her parka.

'It's getting on for five,' he said. 'Won't your mother be worried if she gets up and you're gone?'

'Mum doesn't get up at five. Anyway, she'll only think I'm out with Bogie, which I am. What kind of clue are you following?'

'You don't need to worry about that. I wanted to ask again if you saw anything unusual on the morning you found the body. Anything that's come back to you? Doesn't matter how small and insignificant you think it is.'

So she wouldn't get any information from him, but he expected her to keep answering questions. 'Other than finding the body, you mean?' Facetious remarks weren't one of her habits but he frustrated her.

O'Reilly didn't answer.

'I didn't,' she said finally. 'What I'd like to know is what you and your people found that *I* didn't notice. I was too shocked to be looking around the way I should have.'

'Don't worry about anything you didn't see,' he said. 'That's up to us.'

In other words, mind your own business while the grownups do their work. 'You've probably done me a favor by showing up,' she said in a rush, unsure why she chose that moment to come clean. 'I should tell you something. You'll save me a trip.'

'Go on.' He meant to sound casual, but the timbre of his voice edged down.

'Something happened last night. I met an interesting man and I want you to meet him, too. Evidently he did come to see your people but he didn't think they were interested in what he had to say so he didn't push it.'

'What are you talking about?'

O'Reilly stood up and Alex joined him, clutching Bogie to her. She didn't want the man looming over her while she remained seated.

'What man?'

Brother Percy's permission should have been asked before she threw him to the police again. He obviously wasn't keen on them. 'He'll leave Folly sometime this morning. I don't know how early but I want to catch him first. I think you ought to talk to him yourself. He's a monk, like the dead man.'

O'Reilly sighed. 'It might have been useful to keep that connection out of the public eye. Between you and your friend the vet, it was impossible.'

Alex ignored the remark. 'He wanted to see the dead man but they wouldn't let him because he doesn't have proper ID.'

'What's this monk's name?'

'Percy. Brother Percy.'

O'Reilly looked skyward. 'Anything other than that, like a last name, I can hope?'

'His order leaves all that behind – they travel light and that includes taking simple names that have nothing to do with given ones.'

'Who did he talk to among my people?' He was growing more intense.

'You can ask him all that.' She didn't want to grass Lamb up. 'He's staying at the vicarage with Reverend Restrick. I wanted to get there early so I didn't miss him.'

'Why didn't you call me as soon as you thought this was important?'

Now he was unsettling her. 'I don't know. I was going to see you this morning and I decided I'd bring Brother Percy with me, if he wanted to come. He knew Brother Dominic.'

Heavy silence lasted only seconds. 'Is that what you think the dead man's name was?'

'Probably. Brother Percy is sure it's him. He knew about Bogie.' She rubbed her chin on Bogie's head. 'He did say he's got something he wanted to return to Brother Dominic.'

'And you didn't think you should come to me with that information at once?' O'Reilly took her by the arm, gently enough, and set off purposefully for the street and the village itself. A thunderous atmosphere descended on them and it was generated entirely by the policeman.

He strode along until Alex was running to keep up with him.

'Hey, stop!' She planted her feet. O'Reilly released her arm immediately. 'Are you planning to barge into the vicarage at . . . at whatever time it is now?'

'Past five,' he told her, illuminating his watch.

106

'And that's what I'm going to do. Or rather I'm going to ring the bell and ask to see this Brother Percy.'

'Why can't you let me give him some warning first?' Now she really felt guilty.

'You've done your part. Better late than never. You've told the police what you should have told them the minute you spoke to this man. Why don't you go home? I'll make sure you get inside.'

Bogie squeaked and she realized she was holding him too tightly. 'I'm not a member of the police force.'

'No, you're not, and—'

'And I don't follow your orders, Inspector.' She cut him off. 'Nor have I done anything wrong. I didn't ask to be involved in this case but I am, and I'm not going to get much peace until it's solved. So forgive me if I'm interested, and for feeling responsible for the person I just alerted you to. If I hadn't persuaded him to stay with the vicar, he'd already be gone.'

'Don't interfere in police business,' O'Reilly said shortly. 'Your actions suggest you want to be in the middle here. It isn't your place to decide when and where we do our job.'

Not trusting herself to say another word, Alex took off toward St Aldwyn's and the vicarage. Her face burned and she was glad he couldn't see how he had embarrassed and angered her.

'OK, OK.' O'Reilly fell into step beside her again. 'I was harsh, but you asked for it.'

Her teeth ground together with the effort of not saying something she could regret later.

The walk to Mallard Lane and St Aldwyn's

took only minutes. In the unnatural early light, the church with its leaning gravestones and the hulking silhouettes of whispering old trees took on an ominous cast.

In seconds the moon disappeared, leaving only matte gray skies in its wake.

'What's the quickest way to the vicarage?' O'Reilly asked.

'Through the churchyard. I still think it's too early to do this.'

'You may be right.' He sounded less belligerent. 'But I can't afford to take any added risk of losing him. If I haven't already.'

Light rain began to fall and Alex yanked up the hood of her parka. Still her face quickly became damp. It felt good.

They walked along beside the church. Faint glowing shone through stained glass windows. Moss-slick gates opened with a creaky whine beneath the roof of a lych-gate into the modest grounds around the vicarage. Bogie was getting heavy in Alex's arms but she didn't want to put him down here.

The Victorian house was handsome, if dark and forbidding. There was no sign of life.

O'Reilly went directly to the front door beneath its heavy arch of bare vine.

He halted abruptly and held up a hand for Alex to do the same. The thick door wasn't quite closed.

The sharp ring of the bell startled Alex. She'd been rattled more than enough for one night.

That ring didn't echo through the house, but sounded as if it hit a sodden blanket just out of sight.

O'Reilly waited a few seconds before hitting the bell again, and lights came up on an upper floor, filtered, dull yellow, downstairs and across the narrow visible wedge of black and white stone tiles on the floor inside the door.

Reverend Restrick arrived, minus his clerical collar and scuffing in check wool slippers. His white hair stood up and he looked harassed. 'Look at this,' he said of the door. 'It's a good job Charlotte's away. She's always after me for not shutting it properly. Is something wrong?' he added, which should be expected since calls like this were only likely to be a sign of trouble in the village.

'I hope not, Reverend,' O'Reilly said.

Alex pressed herself forward. 'Sorry, Reverend. Brother Percy came back to spend the night with you. Could we speak to him?'

O'Reilly's stare bored into her face.

'So early?' Reverend Restrick asked. 'I think the poor man was exhausted . . . I don't suppose you opened the door?' He looked hopeful.

'It was already open,' O'Reilly said, all business. 'I want to make sure I see the brother before he leaves the village. Ms Bailey-Jones has told me what the man said last night.'

So formal now.

'Yes,' the vicar nodded and stood back to wave them inside. 'I understand, but he really was worn out. I was hoping he'd get a good long sleep. He thought he'd be away really early but I doubt it.'

'He could have left,' O'Reilly said, ever the logical one.

'I'll wake him.' The glance Reverend Restrick

gave O'Reilly was disapproving. 'Wait in there.'

He left, using the passage that led deeper into the lower floor of the house, and they stepped into a library that had always been a favorite place for Alex from when Harriet Burke used to bring her there for extra study cramming after school hours. They'd had the run of the extensive collection. She put Bogie down and he immediately curled up as if exhausted.

Before a couple of minutes had passed, O'Reilly said, 'Where the hell are they? The place isn't that big.'

Shifting light crept into the sky beyond leaded windows.

They were looking at one another when a shout came from deep in the house.

'Stay here.'

The detective strode from the library and his shoes echoed on those stone tiles. He was forever telling her where to be. Alex followed him. This was not her style, not her thing, not her business. She didn't want it to be but fate had brought it her way and O'Reilly wasn't going to be unreasonable with her and get away with it.

Bogie's claws clicked along beside her while she followed aim lights toward the far side of the house. She hadn't been there since she was a teenager but knew the vast, antiquated kitchen was this way together with several other rooms she had never entered.

At last she heard muffled voices and her heart speeded up. The closer she got the clearer she heard the detective barking out questions, and the low answers he got.

110

Alex hurried. She'd better be ready to be blasted for sticking her nose in but without her, O'Reilly wouldn't be here. Abruptly, Reverend Restrick half ran, half staggered into her. He stared, unseeing, and stumbled in the direction of the kitchen.

One more corner and another door stood open, but blocked by O'Reilly's broad back.

He didn't block the chair that lay on its side, or the rope hitched over an exposed beam. Straining upward with the man in his arms, he struggled to take the weight of Brother Percy's hanging body.

Fourteen

'Hi, Tony. I don't want to give you a shock.'

Startled, he slammed the door of his Land Rover and looked toward the back door of the clinic. Alex perched on the single narrow step with Bogie at her feet.

'Hello.' He frowned at her disheveled appearance. 'Didn't see you there. Just let me get Katie out.'

This was early surgery morning, which meant he put in a couple of hours here in the village before taking off to the surrounding farms. As often as not, no patients showed up and he used the time to catch up on paperwork. Alex had never come here before.

Keys in hand, he hurried toward her with Katie running ahead.

Trying not to stare, he unlocked the door and

111

pushed it wide. Alex didn't resist when he took her by the hand and helped her get up.

'Do I look scary?' she asked with a half smile. 'I feel scary. And maybe scared, too.'

He almost put an arm around her shoulders but waved her inside instead. 'You look worn out and rattled,' he said, choosing diplomacy and caution.

'I remembered you had your clinic here in the village today,' Alex said. She went uncertainly through what had been the kitchen in the cottage he had renamed Paws Place when he bought it. The room now doubled as a dispensary and operating room for minor procedures.

'Go on through,' he told her. 'The sitting room is on the left.'

The sitting room was also where he had a desk and dealt with records.

'Alison will be in at any time, I suppose,' Alex said of his assistant. 'She'll wonder what I'm doing here.'

He stopped himself from saying the woman would assume she was there for Bogie and told her, 'Alison's on holiday,' instead.

'This isn't going to work,' she said. 'You'll have patients shortly. I'll get out of your hair.'

He cut off her attempted retreat. 'If I have a patient, I'll deal with it. Do you have somewhere else to be now – or soon?'

She shook her head, no. Her hair was uncombed and twisted into wild curls. The blue parka she wore was too small; the rest of her clothes were rumpled. Purplish marks underscored the inner corners of her eyes.

'There isn't anyone else I can go to, Tony.'

'Flattery will get you anywhere.' His regret was instant. 'Sorry, kiddo. I didn't mean that the way it sounded.'

'I didn't mean what I said the way it sounded, either. I would have come to you anyway because I think you've got some of the same concerns I have. Or maybe I should say doubts.'

Furnished with a hodgepodge of comfortable but mismatched furniture, the sitting room still managed to look inviting. He led Alex to a deep chair covered with a rose damask even his father laughed at, and urged her to sit. Panels of gathered lace hung at bay windows on to a pathway beside a stream where ducks plied back and forth.

He lit the gas fire and both dogs promptly arranged themselves as close as they could get to the warmth.

'You need tea,' he said.

Alex laughed.

'What's funny?'

'You, playing mother. What I need is to find out if you think I'm on to something, or I've lost my marbles.'

An electric kettle and tea supplies sat on a tray atop a small refrigerator draped with a checkered cloth. 'We can have it all.' He plugged in the kettle and pulled a ladder-back chair close to her. 'Let's have it.'

'That man who died in the woods wasn't a random victim of some passing lunatic.' She struggled out of her parka and spread it over her knees.

'Probably not.'

'He was part of something bigger. Something

113

really creepy, not that murder isn't creepy enough to begin with.'

When she flopped back in the chair and closed her eyes, Tony got up and tossed tea bags into mugs. The water boiled on cue. He used a generous helping of milk for each of them from a carton kept in the refrigerator.

A paper bag of Bourbon biscuits in individual plastic wrappers was the best he could do but he pressed several into Alex's hand and said, 'Eat, you need the sugar.'

'No one needs sugar,' she muttered, fumbling with the packaging.

'You do if you're in shock. And that's how you look right now. Eat the biscuits. I've put sugar in your tea, too.'

She wrinkled her nose and said, 'I hate sugar in tea.'

Tony ignored what she said but the wrinkled nose suddenly reminded him of Alex Duggins, the girl who didn't take crap from anyone, the girl from Underhill who outstripped most of the people in her class and laughed her way out of the slights and into a career that took her places.

He handed her the tea. A boy who had shouted, 'There goes the uppity little bastard,' after her one day had felt Tony's fist. She never actually thanked him, but he'd found the plastic figure of a knight, complete with shield and broadsword, in his desk and knew who had put it there. And he still had the plastic figure somewhere. For a moment, he touched her cheek and she glanced at him with a tentative smile.

He sat opposite her again and waited until she

114

drank some tea, wrinkling her nose again. 'Give me that.' Removing a biscuit package, he took it from the wrapper and gave it back. 'Eat, then we'll talk.'

Munching a biscuit, she took a giant swallow of tea and gulped it down. 'I think I need a collaborator,' she said. 'You won't be interested but I've decided to ask anyway.'

The words were intended to be light but there was nothing slightly humorous about her worried face or her increasingly rapid breathing. A sheen of sweat popped out along her hairline.

'I'll help if I can, you know that. Just tell me what you need.'

'Another man died early this morning. Another monk. We found him at the rectory.'

He swallowed his tea with difficulty. 'We?'

'O'Reilly and I. That's another story. He showed up when I was walking Bogie. Just before five this morning. Forget that. Concentrate on Brother Percy. He came to the Black Dog last night. He was looking for me because he heard I found Brother Dominic – that was the name of the man in the woods.

'I'll spell out the details later but for starters, the police gave Brother Percy the brush off so he was going to leave last night. I wanted him to talk to O'Reilly with me today and Reverend Restrick offered him a bed for the night. That's why Percy was at the rectory. I told O'Reilly about him this morning. He didn't know he'd tried to talk to the police already. O'Reilly roared over there with me in tow and found the body.'

'Oh, for God's sake.' Tony ran a hand through

115

his hair. His next thought was that someone could make nasty connections between Alex being around at two murder sites. 'Tell me it wasn't another dart.'

'He hung himself with his belt thingie – cincture or whatever it's called.' Without warning, tears filled her eyes and she blinked rapidly.

'You've had a terrible shock,' he said.

'Stop telling me I'm in shock. I know all about shock. I'm upset and angry. If I hadn't insisted on him staying in Folly last night he wouldn't have been hanging in that room.'

She trembled visibly and Tony reached out to squeeze her hand. Alex surprised him by holding on tightly. With her other hand she felt around in her pocket. He put a box of tissues where she could reach them.

'Oh!' She withdrew the hand again as if it burned. 'Damn, I forgot I had this.' And she held out a short knife with a serrated blade from which a scrap of frayed white cloth trailed. 'I had to get a knife from the kitchen to cut through Brother Percy's belt while O'Reilly held him up. I did it all wrong.'

Blood dimpled out at the end of her forefinger. She looked at it absently, and sucked on the spot.

Tony reached for the knife. 'You did the best you could. O'Reilly shouldn't have involved you.'

Alex held on to the knife. She picked the frayed material away with a shaking hand. It had some-how become stuffed tightly into the serrated edge.

A tiny end of fine lace wriggled free.

Tony shifted forward to the edge of his chair, setting aside his mug. 'What's that?' he said. 'Doesn't look like part of a cincture – not that I've seen many up close.'

'I wasn't thinking properly,' Alex said. 'It was hard to cut through and I had to tear the knife through the last bit.'

Very gently, she pulled until a strip of fine lawn fabric, edged with lace, came free. She spread it out carefully on one thigh. 'It must have been white once,' she murmured. 'The lace is so delicate.'

He didn't know one kind of lace from another but the fabric looked old. 'Is that machine made?' Looking closer, he touched little balls formed at the edge of each point of worked thread.

'No! Handmade and someone took a lot of trouble with it. See the tiny filaments of silver wound in? Harriet and Mary know about this stuff. They sell things made by ladies for miles around. If it was made in the area they might recognize this as a style . . . not that it's likely to mean anything.' She sounded defeated.

Her increasing distress worried him. Flopping back in her chair, she lost interest in her find and her lips parted. Her skin shone as if it were clammy and her breathing became gasps interspersed with short coughs. Quickly, he grabbed the biscuit bag, emptied the contents on the floor and scrunched the open end together. 'Breathe into this. You're having a panic attack.'

She gave a nod and used the bag. Gradually she calmed down but her face was chalky.

'Is this the first panic attack you've had?'

Alex shook her head, no.

There would be another opportunity to find out if she had issues he knew nothing about, which she almost undoubtedly did.

'Alex, if someone intends to take their own life, they do it. You're blaming yourself for what happened but if it hadn't been at the rectory it would have been somewhere else. He must have been upset about the other brother. He could have been going through a crisis of faith even before that. Where's the vicar? What does he think?'

'I don't know.' Her shaking became close to violent. She drove her fist into her diaphragm and breathed through her mouth. 'He rushed away. I didn't see where. That's why there was only me to help O'Reilly cut the body down.'

Fifteen

'This is wrong. I don't want to wait here.' Evelyn Restrick wanted agreement, he wanted to be told it was time to go to the police and tell them everything.

'You came after me, Restrick, not the other way around.'

The mobile connection faded in and out. Although the vicar sat at the top of the crypt stairs, reception was bound to be poor.

'I didn't mean it to happen but it didn't hurt anyone.' It hadn't. A little more money in the church's all but empty coffers had been the only result. Until now. And if the contribution he'd originally asked for hadn't been refused he would never have felt cross enough to insist.

'Blackmail always hurts someone. In this case,

118

me. But all you have to do is keep your mouth shut and carry on. This doesn't have to be anything to do with you. The donations will keep coming. Now stay there till everything dies down at the rectory.'

'So you admit you—'

'Shut your mouth, you frickin' stupid old man. There's nothing to panic about. We'll talk. Wait and I'll be there as fast as I can.'

'I can't go on like this, I tell you. We have to—'

Reverend Restrick heard the connection click off and climbed down the stairs, the many-times capped heels of his shoes clicking on ancient stone.

Under the oldest part of St Aldwyn's, this crypt had been left untouched over the hundreds of years when sporadic renovations had gradually turned the main part of the building into an imposing enough but commonplace Victorian edifice. At that point the rebuilding had stopped but the church was left as a solid building in good repair.

Or it had been until the roof showed problems.

Muscles in his jaw jerked rigid. And that was when he had started down a path he had never expected to tread. But it hadn't been blackmail, never that. He hadn't threatened anything if he wasn't given big sums to get the roof done.

Sinking to his knees on the cold stone, Evelyn Restrick clasped his hands together. The threat had been implied, or had been taken as implied, and he'd never put the impression right.

Tears squeezed from his closed eyes. 'Dear God, I would never have hurt anyone with what I knew.'

But he had made a terrible mistake and allowed that mistake to perpetuate.

119

The spiral steps leading down here were wide enough for only one to pass. Candle in hand, he had taken refuge among the long dead, their sarcophaguses lining the windowless tomb.

At any moment the police might scour the church above him. That good man should not have died as he had, alone in a stranger's rectory. He could help the police shed light on what had happened – he was sure of it. If he went upstairs now and started his story from the beginning, they might follow all the threads leading back to a hot afternoon when no clouds marred a cerulean July sky. An innocent sky. An innocent day when his life changed forever.

A faint, musty breeze made the candle flame flicker. It was as if what was foul about him breathed up around cracks in the flags.

He thought of the man killed in the woods, his body left to freeze. Fumbling, he set the candle on a ledge beside him, covered his face and sobbed aloud. It could have been stopped on that July day.

Air brushed his cheek and the faint candlelight he saw through his eyelids flickered out.

Evelyn welcomed the total blackness.

He heard his skull crack.

Sixteen

Lily had come to fetch the dogs from Tony's clinic. She gave some long looks but when she got no explanation, other than they needed her to keep the dogs for them, Lily nodded grimly and took off for Corner Cottage where they all decided fewer questions would be asked than at the pub, particularly about Katie.

It was from Lily that Alex got her habit of keeping information to herself.

Alex and Tony had grown up playing in the lanes and byways of Folly-on-Weir and they knew how to get most places without using the obvious, if usually shortest, routes that took them through the village.

Since the clinic was at the furthest end of the area from their destination, Leaves of Comfort, they set off through what would be Tony's vegetable garden later in the year, behind the cottage next to Paws Place. This also belonged to him and he rented it out to tourists in spring and summer. Alex had never been inside Streamside, formerly owned by a single lady who spent most of her life there, but understood it was 'quaint' and much in demand by holidaymakers.

Past the higgledy-piggledy canes and sagging string from the previous year's pea crop they went. The earth had been turned at the end of the season but still lay in large clods to be broken down when the time came. Alex was grateful that despite a day that had cleared up from a rainy start to show some sunshine through the clouds, it was still too cold for the ground to be running with liquid mud as the last of the snow melted.

In most places the dry stone walls were backed by overgrown hedges, leafless but dense enough to make them impenetrable to casual eyes, other than those of the odd, blanket-draped horse that ambled over to push a hopeful nose through a gap in search of carrots or an apple.

They had decided not to mention to the sisters either the cincture or where the lace came from, other than it having been found among scraps. 'Those two are so sharp, y'know,' Alex said. 'If they get an inkling we aren't on the up and up, they'll shred us until they get answers.'

'No answers possible at this stage,' Tony said. He pulled her to a halt and peered around the next bend. 'How do you feel about O'Reilly?'

The question surprised her. 'Feel? I think he can be overbearing and a bit arrogant. But maybe that's a police thing – I haven't had much experience, although he goes out of his way to be charming most of the time. He wants our co-operation – one hundred per cent – but he's quick to tell me to back off if I ask the simplest thing. He had another go at whether or not I saw anything in the woods. Keeps saying, "the smallest thing", as if I won't work it out that he literally means something small. I'd love to find that ring.'

'If there is one.' He helped her over a stile and, single file, the two of them hugged two long expanses of hedgerow, the first to a corner where a conifer known locally as Big Twin for its double trunk marked where the narrow road outside turned sharp south-west. 'Don't suppose you asked this Brother Percy about it?'

'Oh, blast!' Alex stopped in her tracks and threw up her arms. 'What a blithering idiot. I was going to at the pub but I held back, then forgot. How could I be so stupid?'

122

'Whoa,' Tony said. 'Enough with the self-flagellation. If I'd been in your shoes I don't think I'd have thought of it, either. The circumstances would throw anyone off.'

She crossed her arms tightly and muttered, 'Twit.'

He shook his head and carried on. 'You are so hard on yourself.'

Eventually the square tower of St Aldwyn's showed in the distance with the jumble of thatch, stone and tile roofs just barely visible at that end of the village. If they followed the wide lane they would eventually come to a dip that led into Underhill.

'I should just have let him go,' Alex muttered, slowing down. 'Or done what O'Reilly says I should have and called him as soon as I realized Brother Percy's connection to the dead man.'

Tony looked at her over his shoulder. 'I would have done what you did. Trying to get him to talk to O'Reilly today was logical.'

'That's not what he said. According to the detective I'm trying to interfere in his case. I ask you, why would anyone want to get muddled up in a horrible murder case?'

A large, slightly rough hand closed around hers and surprised Alex but she smiled at Tony and let him pull her along beside his longer strides. 'Who's that Agatha Christie character?' he said. 'The woman who solves all the cases for the inept police?'

'Miss Marple,' Alex said, pretending to frown. 'She's about a hundred years old and wears ugly little hats with flowers. Is that who I remind you of?'

123

He chuckled. 'We're not talking about my opinion,' he said, and left it there.

Alex's mind started to race. She remembered Percy's sweet smile and his discomfort over the second glass of wine, although he did drink it.

And this morning, as O'Reilly heaved the man's weight to make room for Alex to cut the cincture. He'd let him down on the bed and immediately started making calls while she stood there, unable to do anything to help other than straighten Percy's habit.

She had pulled the hood around his throat to cover the ugly bruising above his collarbones. That was when O'Reilly warned her away.

Her heart hammered and she concentrated on walking.

Another few minutes and they picked their way through a stony passage beside Leaves of Comfort.

'We'd better not let them think we can settle in,' Alex said. 'I want to find O'Reilly and get rid of this knife. I don't like having it.' Harriet had answered the phone when she called and sounded delighted to welcome visitors.

Tony cleared his throat. 'I'm a bit surprised our Detective Inspector let you go so quickly.'

Her stomach squeezed. 'I'm sure he didn't realize I'd gone. When all those people of his started pushing in I walked out. No one said anything, so that was that.'

She didn't need a response to know what Tony was thinking. 'That wasn't clever, was it?'

'It'll be all right.'

'But we're taking the back way so I don't get picked up before we can talk to Harriet and Mary.'

124

Tony didn't answer.

Two ladies who worked for the Burkes were in early and busy setting tables in the tea shop. They nodded to Tony and Alex when they came in.

The door at the top of the stairs stood open and the new boy, Oliver, met them there. He sashayed back and forth, his exceptionally long tail straight up and flicking like a flag. He already looked sleeker than the first time Alex saw him.

'There you are,' Mary said from a spot by the windows. 'We thought you were lost. They're here, Harriet,' she added loudly in the direction of the kitchen. There was no sign of her 'illness' of the prior day.

Before either of them could say something, Mary carried on: 'Harriet's finishing the tea. Come and see this. It doesn't look good. What do you suppose is going on?'

With a quick glance at Tony, Alex joined Mary and peered in the direction of the churchyard and the church beyond. Somehow an ambulance had been maneuvered along the narrow path between graves and backed up to the church. The door wasn't visible but a uniformed officer stood, partly in view, his hands behind his back.

'Do you suppose someone collapsed in church?' Mary asked. 'I heard sirens but that was earlier.'

'Let's hope it's nothing serious,' Alex said, although she tried to piece together why these people were going into the church for something that must be tied in with Brother Percy's death.

'It reminds me of being up on the hill after Brother Dominic was killed.' She clamped her

125

mouth shut and kept looking out the window, hoping Mary hadn't noticed what she'd said.

'Brother Dominic?' Mary said.

'Brother Dominic?' Harriet echoed from behind them.

Slowly, Alex turned around and gave Tony an embarrassed little shrug.

'That's right,' Tony said, winking at Alex. 'The man Alex found was a monk. But we're not supposed to talk about it. Not that the whole village doesn't already guess it was someone religious after the parish hall meeting.'

That reference made Alex feel better, but Tony had to explain all about what had been said at the parish hall meeting and finished by saying, 'Weren't you at the Black Dog last night? Someone must have discussed it.'

'They didn't know his name,' Mary said defensively. 'You were talking to a monk, too, Alex. That's what people said. I didn't see him myself.'

'Yes, I was.' The sadness that swept into her yet again was overwhelming.

'We came looking for your expertise,' Tony said quickly, raising his brows at Alex. He didn't want her to talk about Brother Percy.

'Tea first.' Harriet dispensed four steaming cups and passed them around. 'The pastries are late but I made these Bakewell tarts myself. Not my best effort, but they'll have to do.'

The flaky little golden tarts with their currant mincemeat filling entirely enclosed in glazed and sweetened pastry made a fibber of Harriet. Some seconds of silent munching attested to that. Alex ate, although all she could concentrate on was the need to get to O'Reilly.

'Any luck finding this cat a new home?' Mary said abruptly and at least she had the grace to blush.

'Ignore her,' Harriet told them. 'She won't be giving my Oliver away.'

Oliver bypassed Harriet, went directly to Mary and brushed himself around her legs, purring all the time.

Digging in the pocket of her old parka, Alex pulled out the lace edging, being sure not to disturb the knife again. 'Is it true that lace is distinctive?' she asked. 'Can anyone recognize someone's work, someone in particular?'

Harriet held out a hand and said, 'Of course. A few people and some are better at that than others, but if a piece is either famous or local it can be identified.'

This could be from anywhere, Alex quickly decided. But it was worth a try.

Mary and Harriet sat on a little couch. They ended up shoulder to shoulder as sagging springs gave way in the middle of the seat cushions. They bent their heads over the strip of badly stained lace and murmured together.

'Can you tell anything?' Tony asked, clearly impatient.

'It's not as old as it looks,' Harriet said. 'But it's been abused, so to speak. Not treated with adequate respect.'

Alex rolled her eyes. Mary caught her and gave a pinched little smile and shake of the head.

'But it is old,' Harriet said. 'Water got to it, I

think. Where's the rest of it?' She raised her face to look at Alex.

'We don't have it.' She thought about the possible implications but added: 'It could be really important.'

'In the murder?' Harriet asked at once, her eyes bright. 'I'll tell you right now, I think these policemen are an arrogant lot and if we can solve the crime without them we could put them in their places.'

Alex almost groaned at the 'we,' and the sound Tony made couldn't be anything but a groan.

Harriet set the scrap on her lap and curled fine old hands into fists with which she gave little, excited pumps. 'All right, all right. Don't look like that. We're not about to make fools of ourselves but if we can do anything to help, we will. Won't we, Mary?'

Enthusiasm set Mary into a bounce on the couch. 'You can bet your boots on that,' she said.

'But do you know anything about the lace?' Tony said.

'All right, all right,' Mary said again. 'Don't get your knickers in a twist.'

Over Alex's laughter, Harriet tapped the miniscule balls fashioned with such fine thread. 'I've seen this and I'm sure Mary has.' Her sister nodded emphatically. 'But not recently and we'll have to call on some of our friends who make lace themselves and know the history of some of the old patterns, particularly the ones invented by individuals.'

'The silver filaments,' Mary began, but Harriet shushed her.

'We mustn't jump to conclusions. I'll call you if and when we have something useful,' Harriet said. 'And don't bother to ask us to guard this with our lives. No one will know we have it.'

Tony said, 'Not even over a glass of your favorite Sandemans sherry?'

'No,' Mary said. 'But if we advance this case for you we'll expect a whole bottle.'

Seventeen

'I didn't know you collected children's books,' Tony said when he walked from the cottage with Alex. As they made to leave, Harriet had handed over a large bag she said were for Alex's collection.

She didn't respond.

'Books?' he said, holding up the bag with one hand and closing the door behind them with the other.

'There are a lot of things you don't know about me,' she said shortly.

That stung but he was sure she was right. He wished there was nothing she ought to know about him.

'First editions, mostly,' she added. 'A lot of them aren't worth anything but they make me happy.'

She said it as if not much made her happy, but he could be looking for these things.

'Oh, hell, I should have thought of that,' he said, and stopped walking. 'O'Reilly's going

129

to be browned off about Harriet and Mary having the lace. He . . . This is going to give him one more reason to make digs about interference. He'll go roaring over there and shake them up.'

'They haven't done anything.' Alex's chin came up. She prodded his chest with a forefinger. 'And he won't be going anywhere near them. When I get the stuff back, I'll take it in and tell the truth: I found it in my pocket.'

'I don't think that's—'

'Such a good idea?' she finished for him. 'I've had worse ideas. This one isn't hurting anyone. C'mon. Let's get this over with.'

They turned right out of the path leading to the tea shop and went in the direction of the church. 'Are you OK?' Tony asked. 'I can feel your mood going down – not that I expect you to be singing and laughing.'

'There's nothing wrong with my mood,' she told him sharply. 'There's nothing wrong with me at all.'

He glanced sideways at her. Of course she was upset, but he sensed something else. He'd felt it before – sadness that ran deep. When she had first returned to Folly she'd avoided conversation almost completely, but there had been a gradual thaw and he had hoped they were closing in on the easy friendship they'd once had.

Several police vehicles were parked in the driveway to the church and another could be seen squeezed into the small parking area in front of the rectory.

Alex touched his arm. 'I'm not being very nice,'

130

she said. 'It's nothing to do with you. Thanks for being with me.'

When she smiled at him he warmed up more than he should.

So be it. He was human and he was a man. 'Forget it. Do you want to go in here now, or not?'

'O'Reilly's car is unmarked,' she said. 'A navy blue Volvo saloon. It's not here.'

'Should we call him?'

She shook her head. 'He said something about setting up an incident room at the parish hall. Let's take a look there.' Putting a hand on his arm again, she said, 'You don't have to come, Tony. I've taken up enough of your time.'

'I think we're in this together,' he told her. 'Which is the way I want it to be.' And he approached the side of the parish hall without checking for her reaction to that statement.

'No cars in the parking lot,' she said.

But there were a number in front of the hall, including a dark blue Volvo. 'Is that O'Reilly's?'

'Yes.' Alex dragged her feet even slower. 'I've got to do this but I don't want to. What was I thinking when I ducked out like that this morning?'

It hadn't been a good idea but she was going back in now. 'Let's just do this. He didn't tell you not to leave, did he?'

She shook her head, no, and they approached the hall. Another vehicle arrived, a van, from which two men emerged, carrying in computer equipment.

'Have you ever wanted to run, Tony? As far and as fast as you can?'

'I know what you mean,' was all he said, but

131

he thought considerably more. He had run from Australia the moment he'd been free to leave.

'Did you think they *would* just tell you anything you wanted to know?' O'Reilly's voice reached them from somewhere to the left of the open doors. 'You know better than that.'

'We can get the rest when we need it,' Lamb said. Tony could see the man leaning back in a chair, his sandy crew cut as thick and neat as ever.

'If there's any point to it,' O'Reilly said. 'I'm not sure there is.'

'She attacked her husband,' Lamb said, letting the front legs of his chair slam to the floor.

'Where did you get this from?' O'Reilly asked.

'Witnesses. She was hysterical and said it was her husband's fault their baby was dead. She went for him right there by the grave. Then she went for the minister when he tried to stop her and just about scratched his eyes out.'

'Grief can make people irrational.' O'Reilly didn't sound too sure of himself now.

'I'm just telling you, boss. Maybe it doesn't mean anything but it's out there. Alex Bailey-Jones ended up having what they called a nervous breakdown and she admitted herself to some sort of loony bin.'

Eighteen

Fight or flight?

One of a number of useful things she'd figured out in the 'loony bin', known to her and thousands of others as a stress recovery spa, was how to deal with her automatic reaction to threat.

Running away only made you look weak.

'That does it,' she said, not trusting herself to look at Tony, or anything other than the back of Lamb's head. 'I'll call you later, if that's OK.'

She was on her way into the parish hall by the time she heard him say, 'I'm right behind you.'

'Hello, gentlemen,' she said evenly to O'Reilly and Lamb, who faced each other across the pock-marked folding table someone had requisitioned from the Women's Auxiliary supplies to use as a desk. 'I thought I'd check in. With all the commotion at the rectory this morning I decided to get out of the way, but I'm sure you'll want some sort of statement from me.'

Lamb drew down his brows and gave her a closed look but – and she could have imagined it – she thought O'Reilly smiled slightly before wiping his expression clean.

'Leaving the scene this morning wasn't a good idea,' he said to Alex. 'You've slowed us down.'

She heard Tony mutter what sounded like, 'Is that possible?'

'We've wasted manpower looking for you,' Lamb said.

'You're joking.' She widened her eyes. 'I haven't left Folly. If you can't find someone in this little village—'

'We just came from the Burke sisters' place,' Tony broke in, not particularly smoothly. 'We saw all the palaver still going on by the church from one of their windows. We wondered how things were going.'

133

She wasn't ready to skate past what she'd heard a few minutes earlier. 'Have you heard of the East Anglia Stress Recovery Center, Detective Sergeant Lamb?'

O'Reilly reached absently for one of his lumpy bags of sweets, this one from beneath a stack of unpleasant-looking photos. Alex tried not to look too hard but saw enough to know they were of Brother Percy – after his death.

'Have you heard of it?' Alex pressed.

'No,' O'Reilly said for both of them, dislodging a bright yellow sherbet lemon from its sticky partners and putting it in his mouth. A bump appeared in his cheek.

'Well established,' Alex said. 'Emphasis on healthy living. Diet, exercise, rest, meditation, massage – the holistic approach. You get the picture? They definitely do not cater to loonies. I imagine the other paying guests would take a dim view of loonies wandering around. I'm not sure that's an appropriate term for anything these days, by the way. But that's where I went after a bad time in my life. Have you ever had a bad time in your life, Detective Lamb?'

His gaze slid away from her face. There was a stain of color over his cheekbones.

'We all have,' O'Reilly said. He made an attempt to shuffle the photos under a folder. His dark eyes weren't happy and his naturally soft Irish voice got even softer. 'You do know you shouldn't have left this morning?'

'Of course I do.' Her mother used to tell her to reason unreasonable people into submission. 'It's not every day I'm asked to help cut down

134

hanging people. I couldn't do anything to help him and I didn't want to stay there. And to be completely honest, I panicked. I'm not proud of that but it isn't unreasonable.'

'No, it isn't,' Tony said.

She was grateful to have him at her shoulder. Even his presence felt solid.

'Did I hear you say you'd spoken to people about me, Detective Lamb?'

'That's right.' At least he had the grace to sound slightly subdued. 'That's a normal part of an investigation. You do seem to be involved in what's been happening here.'

O'Reilly cleared his throat.

'What the hell does that mean?' Tony said. 'Involved? She's been unlucky enough to come upon two dead men. Does that give you the right to go digging for dirt in her past? You won't find any. Take it from me.'

Alex began to feel warm. Tony was a good man to have around when things got tough – at least for her. She gave him a quick smile.

'You may walk on puddles around here, Dr Harrison,' Lamb said, heavily sarcastic, 'but what you think won't go far outside your little village.'

'Bill,' O'Reilly said, 'could you get back to the other thing we talked about? Did the search team arrive?'

Lamb said, 'Yes, boss,' stiffly, and gathered up his gloves and notebook from the table. 'They're combing the hill. They've got dogs too, which may not be useful but it can't hurt.' He nodded and left.

'I'll get another chair,' O'Reilly said, hopping up.

135

The hall looked foreign to Alex. Transparent panels had been hung from an overhead beam and these already had a smattering of photos on both sides and a lot of undecipherable notes, arrows, rough charts and diagrams drawn in glaring orange.

Two other tables stood, one behind the other, with uniformed police working at computers. Phones rang intermittently. She hadn't realized what a lot of activity there was, but hearing about reinforcements coming in to help with the investigation alerted her to just how much activity there was in the hall.

Tony took the second chair from O'Reilly and they all sat down.

'So they're searching the hill?' Tony said. 'What are they looking for?'

O'Reilly's secret little smile returned. 'That's what we're hoping to find out. Unfortunately we haven't had any useful information from anyone who might know.'

Alex sighed. 'Brother Percy could have been able to help with that.' She didn't elaborate and Tony avoided adding anything. 'Too bad he wasn't taken seriously when he tried to talk to a policeman yesterday.'

'More than too bad,' the detective said. 'But I still wish you hadn't run off this morning. It didn't look good when we realized you'd gone. Why do you think darts from your pub have been used?'

The swift change of topic startled Alex. 'How would I know? It doesn't make any sense.'

'I had to ask. I don't want to scare you but it

136

does seem that someone wants to connect you to these crimes.'

'There wasn't a dart this morning,' Alex said.

'How do you know that?'

'I . . . well, I don't know. But I didn't see one. Do I need a lawyer?'

'This isn't an official interrogation,' he said, 'but you're entitled to representation whenever you want it. Not that I have more questions at this point. I remind you that you came to me and initiated this conversation. That's a good thing.'

'Would I leave darts from my pub lying around at crime scenes?' Alex said and heard Tony clear his throat. She met his eyes and saw a warning. She was saying too much.

O'Reilly propped his elbows and steepled his fingers. 'I might be able to think of a reason why you'd do that.'

She was more rattled than she wanted him to see. Having to listen to Lamb trot out the things she wanted to forget had unbalanced her. Now she wanted to get away from here and not think about what O'Reilly was suggesting.

'The first victim didn't kill himself,' he said. 'The pathologist has demonstrated that there appears to have been a surprise attack and the victim couldn't have had much chance to defend himself.'

'That's what we expected,' Tony said.

Expecting to be stopped, Alex reached for the top photo of Brother Percy's body. O'Reilly let her pull it in front of her. She stared at the full-color horror of it. At least the monk's face was turned from the camera.

Without looking away, Alex pulled the kitchen knife from her pocket and placed it on the table. 'I took that without knowing what I'd done,' she said. 'It's what I used to cut him down.'

The man didn't say a word.

'Why are there bruises down there?' Alex asked, pointing at marks above Brother Percy's collarbones. 'Shouldn't they be up here where the cincture tightened . . . around . . .' She covered her mouth.

'Since this is going to get out anyway, you might as well get it from a reliable source,' O'Reilly said. 'He didn't kill himself either. He was strangled then strung up. I'll want to talk to each of you more later on. Please make sure we know if you decide to leave the area.'

Nineteen

'You're not going up there.' Will Cummings' raised voice carried through to Alex before she'd had time to close the front door to the Black Dog. 'She asked you to go riding with her? Why would Heather Derwinter want you to go anywhere with her, did you ask yourself that? That woman's nothing but trouble. If she wants you up there she's got some motive we haven't figured out.'

'You're hard on Mrs Derwinter.' This sounded like Kev Winslet. 'She's all right. She treats the people who work for them well.'

Cathy said, 'Excuse us, Kev. Will's decided to

138

have a domestic in public. In case you've forgotten, Will, I went to the same school as Heather Derwinter.'

'Toffee nosed, aren't we?' Will said. 'So you think she'd want you as a member of any club she belongs to? Wake up, Cathy. How long d'you think it was after you left the school before she even got to the place? It was years. She found out you went there and now she's pretending that's a reason to be your friend. What a load of tripe.'

This didn't sound like Will, who usually treated Cathy with respect.

'What school was that then?' Kev Winslet asked.

'Drop it,' Will said. 'That was before Cathy's parents decided I wasn't good enough for them and—'

'Shut up!'

Alex hurried into the bar before things got any more out of hand. She glared at Will, who still had his mouth open from being barked at by his quiet wife. She was relieved there weren't more customers.

'You and Cathy used to live up there,' Kev said to Will. 'Heather would have known Cathy.'

'That was probably before Heather was born. Leonard was just a little nipper. By the time Heather and Leonard got together we were long gone. And by the way, Cathy, you didn't even finish at the academy so you and her aren't sister alumnus or whatever rubbish you're spouting about.'

'That's mean,' Alex said, going to stand beside Kev Winslet at the bar. 'Whatever's going on here is none of my business – or anyone's but yours and Cathy's.'

'Sorry,' Cathy muttered. 'I used to love to ride when—'

'When you lived with Mummy and Daddy and had your own horse?' Will broke in. 'Know what I think? I think that woman wants to find out if there's any gossip down here about the murder and she knows you're in the middle of things. She just wants to use you.'

Cathy was pale but seemed resolute. 'Thanks for the advice, Will. Maybe she's got a right to be interested in anything that happens right now. She did get thrown from her horse and nobody's said much about it but there was a dart involved. Heather said that.'

'Good excuse for a so-called wonderful horse-woman taking a fall, if you ask me.' Will threw down a tea towel and crossed his hefty arms. 'Maybe she stuck it there. Have you thought of that?'

'Oh, Will.' Cathy shook her head. There were tears in her eyes.

'You worked for Cornelius Derwinter,' Kev said. 'You had a good cottage on the estate to bring Cathy to after you were married. The Derwinters were good to you. Old man Derwinter even paid for you to take courses when you wanted them. And you used to say how cushy it was. Whatever the old man wanted, you did, and gladly. But it wasn't enough for you, working for other people. You couldn't wait to get to this place and run things. What was that all about – impressing Cathy to try to show you were as good as her and her family? Anyways, I didn't intend to interfere. None of my business.'

'What's the harm in wanting to better yourself?' Will said, clearly past caution. 'We were only managers to begin with but I came into money. This was a good investment.'

'Cathy, could I have a Britvic orange juice,' Alex said, just wanting to stop this back and forth. 'It's been a difficult day.'

'Now you're back to being managers.' Kev nodded around the bar. 'You couldn't hang on to this. You lost it. You're lucky to be here at all. At least you've still got a chance to dig yourself out of debt.'

'Kev!' Alex shoved her face in front of him so he had to give her his attention. 'Stop. Now. That's history. We're all very happy with the way things are.'

While Will continued to fume silently, Cathy emptied a bottle of Britvic orange into a small glass and put it in front of Alex.

Kev turned his back on Will. He nodded toward the front of the building. 'Flies on a jam pot up on the hill,' he said. 'Never saw so many plods in one place.'

Alex had seen the swarm of police fanned across the hill, searching, and dared to hope they'd find something to make all this go away. 'I wish them luck,' she said. 'I don't see how they'll find anything new, though.'

'If we knew what they were looking for we might be able to help,' Kev said, his florid face thrust forward and pugnacious. 'Too much secrecy. It's not as if we aren't all involved – or our lives, anyway. Has anyone said what it is? The man's wallet, maybe?'

141

'They're not saying anything. We probably won't find out until it gets leaked to the press.' This wasn't a conversation she wanted to continue. 'I'll take this upstairs with me, Cathy. See you later.'

'The coppers were by earlier looking for you,' Will called after her. 'I didn't know you were out so I sent them up. It's too bad you found that body.'

Alex raised her glass and said, 'I think so, too,' without turning around.

First she wanted to go to her rooms, take a bath and change her clothes. She had been a bit short with Tony when she said she was coming here before picking up Bogie from her mother. He hadn't deserved that, but he'd heard what she'd heard before they'd gone into the parish hall and she owed it to him to give some sort of explanation. She wasn't ready for that yet.

Halfway up the stairs from the closed restaurant, Alex paused. If she never said another word about her baby, or Michael, Tony wouldn't ask. Darn it, if he didn't have other plans already she'd invite him for dinner although it would have to be at her mum's, which would probably thrill Lily.

Carrying on slowly, she balanced the glass against her chest while she punched in the number on her mobile. 'Hey,' she said when he answered on the first ring. 'We need some downtime. I thought I'd ask my mum if I could have you to dinner at her house this evening. Sounds funny but I think O'Reilly would have a cow if I went back to the lodge at this point. Mum'll be here working and she likes me at her place anyway.'

142

'Sounds great,' Tony said. 'What time?'

Her key locked rather than unlocked her door. Alex reversed the process and went in. 'Around seven?'

She didn't hear his answer. Impotent rage threatened to choke her. 'Tony,' she managed to say, 'they've bloody well turned my room upside down. They've searched it.'

Twenty

The policeman who tapped on her doorjamb looked about eighteen, if that. His helmet under his arm, he showed his warrant card and said, 'Constable Smith. You called in about some trouble.'

Alex walked toward him, deciding what to say. She gave a shaky cough. 'I take it your people did this? Ransacked my room?'

His brown eyes got very round. 'Excuse me?'

'This.' With one arm she took in sheets tossed on one side of the bed, the mattress thrown off so it came to rest against an easy chair missing its cushions and a chest from which all five drawers lolled open and the innards were scattered and trailing.

'It's a good job I don't have any more personal things here than I do. If you'd waited until tomorrow, I would have made a run up to my house for more supplies – then it would have been more fun for you. What did you people think you were, kids in a sandbox?' As seconds passed she became more furious. 'What were you hoping to find?'

'Fuck!'

Tony's arrival and opening salvo struck her momentarily dumb.

He didn't apologize. 'What a damn nerve. And the police did this?'

He advanced on the much smaller copper.

Katie, grinning as only she could, turned her ears into pointed wings that stood straight out to the sides of her head and started sniffing around the room.

'Sir,' said the red-faced young man, his blush quite fetching on dark skin. He sounded very Welsh. 'I don't know what any of this is about. I came in response to this lady's request. I'm on loan, out of Broadway. We're helping out. If you have any complaints about the department, I suggest you contact them. Under the circumstances, I'm calling for back-up.' He worked a police radio from beneath the heavy yellow slicker he wore over his uniform and pressed buttons.

'*Back-up?*' Tony sputtered. 'Is that because we're so bloody terrifying? Do you think we're going to beat you up? Look at this place. Why throw the few bits and pieces off the desk? It's just vandalism. You broke a bottle of perfume. Yes, that's what we've got here, Alex, *vandalism.*'

Constable Smith had stepped past him on to the landing and continued talking without apparently hearing a word Tony said.

The mentioned perfume, the Je Reviens she favored, overwhelmed everything.

'Right then,' Smith said, facing them again. 'Someone's coming right away. They'll be here quick enough. I'm sorry you're upset. You should be, of course. I expect you'll want to check for anything missing.'

'Police,' a very recognizable and officious voice said from the stairs. Detective Sergeant Lamb came into view, two steps at a time. 'What's all this, then, Constable Smith?'

'Room break-in is what it looks like, sir. Lady came back and found it like this.'

Alex began to have a nasty feeling she was making a fool of herself. She cleared her throat, half watching Katie curl up on the pile of discarded bedding. 'I was told you – or some of your people – came up here looking for me earlier,' she said. 'Why would you do this? If you'd asked to look around I'd have let you.'

Glancing at the room, Lamb smirked and, from the corner of her eye, Alex saw Tony make fists. She rushed to stand beside him and hold his arm.

'When you ducked out of the rectory early this morning we wanted to know where you were. A couple of our officers checked here. I assure you they were never in this room. We would have needed a search warrant for that and we hadn't had time to get one – even if we wanted it. You can get back to the parish hall,' he told the constable, who left without another word.

'Maybe I made a big mistake,' Alex muttered. 'It seemed so obvious. But someone's been in here. Why, Sergeant? Can you think why someone would search *my* room?'

He rolled from his heels to his toes, not settling

his baby blue eyes on anything in particular. 'Whoever it was could have made pretty certain you wouldn't even know they'd been here,' he said. 'But this was done so it would be obvious.'

Tony muttered something under his breath and got the detective's full attention. 'You have something to add, Doctor Harrison?'

'I said, no shit, Sherlock. Seemed appropriate given what I'm looking at.' He showed no remorse. 'I think you should be thinking about who's trying to frighten Alex. So many things point to an effort to scare her off. The darts from her pub. What happened up at Lime Tree Lodge when she was on her own. Now this. Don't you think someone wants to frighten her?'

'Could be. Could be they even want to make her decide to leave.' A flicker in his expression suggested Lamb hadn't intended to say that much.

Alex wandered past him to the landing and held on to a railing over the stairs. Her legs didn't feel steady and her heart beat too fast. 'Why?' she asked herself more than the men.

'That's what it's all about, isn't it?' Lamb said. 'An endless string of why questions. We shall just have to keep on asking. For now I don't want you to touch anything until our people have had a look.'

'To check for fingerprints?' Alex said.

'Among other things. Someone may be along today but more likely tomorrow. This room will be taped off and someone stationed here to make sure it stays off limits. That needs to be taken out of here.' He pointed at Katie.

Before Alex could tell Sergeant Lamb how much she disliked him, Tony picked up Katie and carried her out of the room.

Hurrying footsteps came up the stairs behind them and Lamb said, 'Hello, boss,' at the same time as Alex and Tony turned to watch O'Reilly, an unexpected smile on his face, coming to join them.

The instant he saw the room, he said, 'This needs to be taped off.'

'It will be,' Lamb said.

'You have residents or guests at the moment?' O'Reilly said to Alex.

'Two rooms occupied tonight,' she said. 'It's slow in winter.'

'Get someone up here with that tape,' O'Reilly said, and paused while his second-in-command made his way down for reinforcements.

'Don't you wonder what happened to Reverend Restrick?' O'Reilly asked without preamble, addressing Alex. 'He just about ran into you leaving the crime scene this morning. Didn't you tell me that?'

She rubbed her forehead, trying to unscramble her thoughts. 'I forgot,' she told him honestly. 'It's been a weird day. Did something happen to him, too?'

'Wouldn't it be reasonable for him to just come back when he recovered from the shock?'

'Of course.' Relief flooded Alex.

'But you immediately think of something happening to him.' O'Reilly didn't sound aggressive but he was a master at planting seeds of doubt – at least about her.

'Wouldn't that be a reasonable assumption, Inspector?' Tony said. 'From the way you phrased your question.'

O'Reilly gave a short laugh. 'Next you'll be accusing me of leading the witness. Everyone watches too much TV. This isn't a court of law and you're a vet, not a barrister.'

A nasty feeling intensified in Alex. 'The reverend – is he all right?'

'No, he's not all right. He was plainly upset when he ran out of his house. He must have gone to the church looking for some sort of sanctuary, I suppose. Then it seems he fell down the stone steps into the crypt. He's in hospital with a serious head injury. He may not live.'

Alex's hands felt frozen. She clasped them together and stumbled to sit on the top stair. 'I don't believe this.'

'May I take Alex somewhere more comfortable?' Tony asked.

'In a moment. I want you to take a look at this first, Mrs Bailey-Jones.' He had been holding a plastic bag behind his crossed forearms and he gave it to Alex. 'Don't open the bag. Just tell me if you recognize what's inside.'

She squeezed her eyes shut and opened them again. Here it was. It did exist. A man's heavy gold ring, dulled by mud and with sundry pieces of debris stuck to it.

Tony crouched down behind her and muttered, 'That has to be it. Looks expensive. Even under the mud.'

It was a signet ring but larger than would fit on most men's small fingers the way they were usually worn. She held it up to the light and pulled the plastic tight against the flat side so she could see any engraving.

She heard Tony's indrawn breath behind her and shook her head.

'This can't have belonged to the monk,' she said. 'It's got the Derwinter crest on it.'

Twenty-One

Corner Cottage was as inviting on the inside as it was on the outside, but tonight Tony was most aware of tension in the small sitting room.

He stuck his head out of the door to look into the kitchen where Alex was clattering among pots and dishes making them 'something easy' even though he had tried to insist she let him drive them into Bourton-on-the-Water to eat.

After a horrible day, she needed to catch her breath, but she wouldn't hear of going back on her invitation.

Katie and Bogie were in front of the fire he'd lit when Alex brought him in. With their noses to the warmth, they anchored a blanket to the floor, one each side and as far from one another as they could get without giving up occupation. The temperature was plummeting again and there was talk of more snow – not a cheerful thought for hill dwellers.

'Coming through, Alex,' he called and joined her in the kitchen. 'I don't need to be waited on.

I'm not used to it and this is one time when someone should be looking after you.'

'I'm almost done.' Her face was tight, the mouth a straight line. 'Mum said to finish the Oxtail soup she made. You get reheated soup but fresh bread from George's and cheese and apples. Comfort food tonight. Here.' She took a bottle of Pinot Noir from the counter. 'Please open this for us.'

Her movements were too quick and too jerky. A tiny dining room opened off the kitchen with just enough room for a round table covered with a red cloth, four chairs and the row of shelves that adorned all four walls of a lot of these small cottages. A couple of feet from the low ceiling, books crammed every inch, and Tony had the thought that daughter had followed mother in a love of reading.

He carried the opened wine and two stubby, stem-free glasses to the table, poured and set the bottle in the middle. 'I'll lay the table,' he said, and did just that with the cutlery, placemats and napkins she'd already heaped there.

'Please, sit down,' she told him. If she got much stiffer she was likely to stop speaking at all.

'I was thinking you might like to run up to Lime Tree Lodge,' he said. 'After dinner? You must want to get more of your things.'

She mumbled under her breath and when she felt his eyes on her repeated, 'I'd like to burn everything at the inn.'

Old blue willow plates reminded him of some his mother had used. The soup bowls Alex placed on top were big with wide rims, the way soup bowls used to be. He remained standing and held his glass, waiting while she loaded food on to the table.

Alex looked at him and he said, 'Don't mess with us,' and touched his glass to hers.

At least she smiled a little. 'It's all unbelievable,' she said, sitting down and clasping her hands in her lap. She popped up again and drew the heavy, red linen curtains.

'The big question is whether or not that ring was on Brother Dominic's finger. If so, where did he get it?'

'Someone could have dropped it at any time,' Alex said, playing with her soup. 'It doesn't have to be anything to do with him.'

'Eat,' Tony told her and dug into his own food. 'Your mother makes a mean soup,' he said. He tore off a hunk of bread from a braided, glazed multigrain loaf and slathered it with butter. 'Start eating, Alex. Seriously, it's so good you'll get an appetite once you start.'

They carried on in silence. Tony cut big helpings of Cheshire cheese for each of them and cut up an apple.

'Wouldn't the Derwinters have reported a missing ring?' With a piece of apple halfway to her mouth, Alex had a distant look. 'I know the crest for the same reason you do, it's on everything at the manor house on the estate. Not that I've been there more than a couple of times. I never noticed any rings. That's the coat of arms over the door, right, not the crest?'

'Right. I recognized the crest, too. A man's hand in armor raising some sort of mangled bird claw. Never saw anything like that before. I don't think I'd want it on anything of mine.' He grinned at the thought. 'I'll have to ask my dad if the Harrisons ever had a crest. Probably a shovel and a pickaxe – that'd be in keeping with my serf stock.'

'Serf stock?' Now Alex actually laughed.

'How about you? Anything interesting in your family?' He managed not to either turn red or clamp his mouth shut. *Idiot.*

With raised eyebrows, Alex said, 'I'll have to ask Mum about her family. She never said anything. I think she came here after I was born. And although I remember your heroic defense, I really am a bastard.' The little jerk at the corners of her mouth showed what it cost her to say it.

Moving right along. 'Leonard wears a signet ring on his right small finger. I don't think I remember one on Cornelius. He was around the horses a lot and I can see his hands in my mind. Leonard's always been low key but I think Heather likes being lady of the manor. She'd probably want Leonard to wear his.' He ate more soup.

'That ring they found had nothing to do with Brother Dominic,' Alex said. She sounded convinced. 'But I do think he had a ring on his finger and the police were looking for it. The pathologist would work out what happened to that finger even if we hadn't. It was obvious. I think the police were looking for it in my room before they knew one would be found on the hillside.'

'They insist they didn't search that room,' he pointed out. 'Don't you think they'd admit it if they did?'

She nodded miserably. 'I can't find out anything

152

about how Reverend Restrick is either and I can't contact Charlotte Restrick. I don't know where she is.' Her voice clogged. Tears began to course her cheeks but when he made to go to her she waved him away. 'I'm going to sound sorry for myself, but I've been doing well since I came home. It wasn't easy, but I got it all together again.'

'You do so well.' He put a hand over hers on the table and she didn't pull away. 'Give yourself a break for being human.'

'You heard all that stuff Lamb said about me.'

'Lamb's an ass.'

'I lost it when I saw Michael looking as if he was devastated by the baby's death.'

He doubted she could see through the wash over her eyes.

'And at the same time I kept wondering if I could have done anything different that would have saved her.'

This wasn't a good time to feel inadequate. Scooting his chair close to hers, he put an arm around her shoulders. 'There aren't too many absolutes in medicine. You can only guess at another outcome and that won't help you.'

He wanted, badly, to tell her his own story, to get it into the open, but it would feel like piling on tonight.

She sobbed now. 'It was a placenta first – placenta praevia, I think it's called, where the placenta comes before the baby. I was at home on bed rest. I went into labor and then I haemorrhaged. Everything seemed to move in slow motion. The ambulance probably came really fast, but it seemed like it took forever. I should have been in the hospital earlier. I didn't feel good all day but I kept thinking it would pass.'

Her breathing grew shallower and sweat sprang out on her brow.

'I'm so very sorry,' Tony said. And how stupid it sounded – he was so sorry her little girl died. Sheesh. 'It's a horrible, senseless loss and I don't think you could have done anything to change it.'

'I kept waiting for Michael to show at the hospital.' Her tone rose and she held her mouth open to grab breath. 'And I knew he wasn't coming but I hoped. They couldn't reach him, Tony. He wasn't where he said he would be. I thought – dreamed things would get better after the baby. I don't think he liked being around me when I was pregnant.'

'Alex—'

'When the placenta is at the bottom like that it doesn't have to mean the baby will die. Women get through it all the time now. But it wasn't found until I went into labor. They couldn't stop the bleeding. They set up for a caesarian section but it was too late for my little girl.'

He didn't want to ask where Michael had been. He wanted to take the man by the throat and throttle him.

'Michael . . . was . . . with . . . another woman.' She choked between each word. 'But I knew that in my heart. I just didn't want to admit it.'

'You were the normal one – he was a monster,' he said, desperate and angry. He went to his knees beside her chair and pulled her into his arms, settling her head on his shoulder.

'I blamed him.' She was starting to

hyperventilate. 'That's what happened at the funeral. I had my first panic attack.'

'Hush,' he told her. 'Take a deep breath. Do it, Alex. Let it out slowly. Now again.'

'Panic again now,' she managed to say. 'Sorry.'

'Alex, you've got guts. Look what you've worked your way through. And you don't have to be sorry around me. I . . . I care about you. Now, another deep breath. Deep and slow, all the way to your toes. Let me help you up. Make some more room for that diaphragm.'

When she hiccupped he was relieved, and took a glass of wine with him while he guided her into the sitting room and on to a couch.

She pointed. Both dogs stood in the middle of the room with their tails between their legs.

'See. We all care about you. Sometimes we aren't so strong we can't use some help from a friend.' He kept shoving thoughts out of his head. He did care about her but he couldn't let what that might mean intrude now. His own history with relationships hadn't left him confident about trying again. And since his father warned him he'd better come clean about Penny or risk any chance of Alex trusting him, he had thought of little else.

'Fine doctor I am,' he said as lightly as he could. 'I'm going to follow instinct and make you drink some of this. Don't you choke on me, or tell me your heart's doing crazy things. It should quieten you down.'

He sat beside her and held the glass until she took it herself and drank. 'Feels good,' she said, breathing easier. Glancing up at him, she held the wine to his lips until he let her tip some into

155

his mouth. 'You don't look so good yourself. Harrison and Bailey-Jones, private eyes, aren't at their best. I wouldn't hire them today.'

With a smile, he eased the glass back in her direction. 'I admire you, Alex. I always have and never more than now.'

'I'm glad you're with me, Tony.'

Twenty-Two

The Gloucester Mortuary dealt with most coroners' cases in the area. O'Reilly paced the lobby. He had visited Leonard Derwinter the previous evening and asked him to meet here at noon.

Derwinter was already half an hour late. Another ten minutes and they would have to track him down. Understandably, he had been shaken, confused even, to a point where O'Reilly wasn't sure how much the man understood of what he'd been told.

Snow had started lightly enough that morning but now it splatted in fat blobs against the glass doors. O'Reilly could feel the temperature going down.

'Getting your exercise there, Detective?' Steven Runcie was one of those pathologists who subscribed to the lighthearted approach, although he didn't buy into the black humor some of the police used during post-mortems.

'Hello, Doc,' O'Reilly said. 'I'm hoping to reduce your John Doe load by one.'

'His place won't have a chance to get colder,' Runcie said with a grimace.

O'Reilly was glad to be left alone in the lobby once more. A lot of digging among the residents of Folly-on-Weir had finally revealed that there had been two Derwinter brothers. Edward, older than Leonard, went away to a boarding school in Yorkshire when he was seven or eight. No one knew much about the kid except that he never returned home to live.

Leonard should be able to fill in the blanks about his brother, who was rumored to be dead. Lamb was on the trail of when and where this had become the case, but there was what appeared to be deliberate vagueness on the topic.

'Inspector? Sorry I'm late.' Leonard Derwinter entered the lobby looking ruffled. 'The roads are getting bad again and it'll be worse tonight.' His dark hair must have been raked through by his fingers many times and purplish scoring under his eyes suggested he hadn't slept much.

They shook hands. Compact, fit-looking and wearing a well-cut tweed jacket and cavalry twill trousers, almost the uniform of the Englishman of his class, he nevertheless had a Latin appearance. Lightly bronzed skin, a narrow face and generous mouth. Harassed, about summed up the impression he gave.

'Before we do this—'

'Let's get it over with.' Leonard, sliding his hands in and out of his jacket pockets, looked anxiously around the lobby. 'I don't see what help I can be, but of course, I'll do whatever I can.'

'I do need to ask you a few questions first,'

157

O'Reilly said, nodding to a corridor. 'We can talk in private down here.'

A small waiting room, mostly never used, provided the chairs O'Reilly wanted. He waved Derwinter into one of them and remained standing out of habit.

'First, there may be no connection between you and the corpse.' He almost winced at the bluntness of it.

Derwinter shook his head but lost color beneath his tanned skin.

'As I told you last night, this is the man who was found dead in the woods above Folly-on-Weir. There was nothing to point to his having anything to do with you until late yesterday when the hill and woods were searched. A ring was found in the woods. We still have to make an absolute connection between the body and the ring.'

Leonard rubbed his hands together until the palms squeaked. 'You didn't say anything about a ring. What ring?'

'I thought you had enough to process last night, sir. Take a look at this but don't take it out of the evidence bag, please.'

He took that bag from a Manila envelope and gave it to Leonard, who took it as he might a grenade minus its pin. O'Reilly sat on the edge of a chair that brought their knees close.

After as close a look at the ring as the plastic would allow, Leonard covered his eyes. 'Where was it?'

'Buried in brush in the woods.' He noted the ring Leonard wore on the small finger of his right hand. 'Is the crest yours?'

Leonard nodded. 'But I don't understand. Do you think the murdered man was wearing this?' He looked up sharply. 'Or the murderer? The only other one I know of, apart from mine, is the one my father wore. He took that off, oh, when I was in my teens, I suppose. He used his hands a lot and the ring annoyed him, he said, so it must be in with some other bits and pieces of his.'

This announcement caused more hope than it probably should. 'In that case I'll have you find that for us. We wondered if it had been stolen by the dead man.'

'You can't be sure he ever saw it.'

'True. But in case you have seen him, and remember him, it could help a great deal.' He had decided to save his questions about the brother, Edward, until after the viewing. It did appear that this family had a few unexplained details from the past. Hitting Leonard with too much all at once might be counterproductive. 'Let's do this.' He led the way from the room.

The body had been taken from storage and wheeled into an area without any distractions. The folded-down sheet exposed Brother Dominic's face, neck and upper shoulders but covered all but the start of the Y incision made by the pathologist.

O'Reilly watched closely as Leonard approached the gurney. Sadness wouldn't have been the first expected reaction but it was clearly there. He pointed to the gaping wound in the throat. 'That was made with a dart?' he said.

'We think so. The killer worked at it to make

sure his victim wouldn't be coming back from the dead.'

'He was a monk, right?'

'Yes. We have some confirmation of that from a reported conversation with the second monk, the one who talked to Alex Bailey-Jones.'

Derwinter shook his head. 'Pointless.'

'Do you know him?'

Silence fell and stretched. Leonard stared at the body and kept on staring.

'What did your brother Edward call you when you were boys, Mr Derwinter?' O'Reilly asked.

Leonard straightened. He stared at O'Reilly and frowned. 'Edward? Why would you ask me that? I haven't seen him since I was just a little kid. He's been dead for years.'

Conjecture was right up there with leaps of faith, O'Reilly thought. He'd better step carefully. 'Did he call you Lennie?'

'Everyone did,' Leonard said, his voice rising. 'My family, or what there was of it. So what?'

'Probably nothing. Do you recognize this man?'

Leonard looked uncomfortably close to breaking down. 'I don't know.' He made as if to touch the face but drew back. 'I want to see his hands.'

Without responding, O'Reilly left the room and found a technician who came and slid Brother Dominic's arms from beneath the sheet. He crossed them over the waist. 'Call me when you're done,' he said, and walked out again.

Leonard went to the left side of the gurney to look at the right hand, the hand where the ring finger was distorted into an awkward angle.

160

He took the hand in both of his and O'Reilly didn't try to stop him.

'I must have seen it but I don't remember. I was too young. Father said Edward's finger was broken when they closed the lid of our mother's casket on it. He didn't make a sound and no one noticed for days. Edward said he'd run away if they broke and reset it. He wanted it that way. Could it be like this if he grew up with something like that?'

O'Reilly shook his head. Either this man was one hell of an actor or he was devastated by the possibilities in front of him.

Twenty-Three

'Edward was the oldest,' Kev Winslet said, his jaw thrust out as if daring someone to challenge him. 'I'm just tellin' you, that's all.'

'Hardly necessary, old chap,' Major Stroud said. 'We all know as much.' His feet were planted apart in damp brown suede brogues and his scalp sparkled through carefully combed back hair.

Alex was busy putting out clean beer mats and greeting customers. Then she went to add wood to the fire. Apart from what Kev Winslet was reporting – supposed facts overheard at the Derwinters – she hadn't heard anything about Leonard's visit to the mortuary in Gloucester. She knew he had gone there to meet O'Reilly because Constable Smith had let it slip when he stopped by to remind her to stay out of her room upstairs.

'You're an incomer,' Winslet said suddenly, glaring at Major Stroud and getting red, as expected. Steam rose from the shoulders of his waxed jacket as it started to dry out from the storm. 'You 'aven't lived here all your life like some of us.'

The major's guffaw was genuine. 'I was born here. I served my country for a long time. Takes a fella away from time to time, as you might remember – or perhaps not. The Vines was my father's home and his father's before him. Not that we're discussing my right to be in this village and have an opinion.'

The Vines was the largest house in Folly proper. There was a Mrs Stroud who didn't mix much, and two grown children, both males. One son had followed his father into the army; the other did something in the capital. From the look of the Maserati he drove down from London some weekends, he did something very well in that financial maze that was the City.

Will worked behind the bar while Cathy flitted in and out of the kitchen with snacks. Liz Hadley, who ran a struggling dress shop in Broadway, filled in as barmaid three nights a week. This was one of her nights. The regulars obviously liked her even though she didn't say much.

Harriet Burke beckoned Alex. When she got close the woman said, very low, 'Mary and I have some interesting news.'

'Better tell her it's a bit fantastic,' Mary said.

'In the hard to believe way. I'm not sure someone isn't pulling our legs.'

'I promised Tony I'd wait for him to get here,' Alex said. 'He's going to go up to Lime Tree Lodge with me so I can get more clothes. They won't let me into my room here.'

'We heard about that,' Harriet said. 'Nasty business. It's nice you've got Tony looking after you.'

With a sigh, Alex raised her eyebrows and said, 'He isn't looking after me, just being a good friend. Mum's loving me staying at her place and Tony has appointed himself chauffeur until I'm settled down there, for however long it takes. I just hope it won't be long before I can get back to my own place permanently. Can you stay here and let Tony and me drive you home? It's bitter out there, and dangerous to walk in. Then you can tell us what you've found out. Is it about the lace?' she finished, so quietly both women leaned toward her.

'Yes,' Mary whispered back. 'And some other things we wonder about.'

'Later, then,' Alex said, bursting to find out what they knew.

'You can't go around accusing people of things like that,' Will Cummings announced in his best bellow, the one usually reserved for, 'Time, gentlemen, please. Drink up!' when he'd already said it twice or so at closing time.

Alex glanced at the sisters. Mary had her glasses on to see her knitting and the irises of her eyes resembled tadpoles in Petri dishes.

'Loud-mouthed little boy, loud-mouthed man,' Harriet murmured. 'Not that he spent much time in school.'

'I can say what I bloody well want to,' Kev Winslet hollered. 'I'm only repeating what's on everyone's mind. They reckoned the older brother was dead, so everything went to Leonard. The old man liked the young'un best so that would have suited. But if that wasn't really the way it was then it'd be a bit inconvenient for our lord and lady of the manor to have the real lord show up. I'd say Edward Derwinter would be the last one they'd want to see.'

'Why is he saying that?' Harriet asked.

'Don't know.' Alex's stomach jumped around and she hurried from her spot by the fire.

Will and Kev faced off across the bar. Liz Hadley, tall, dark-haired and as serene as if nothing had happened, continued to serve staring customers.

'Are they talking about little Edward Derwinter?' Mary said, stopping Alex as she passed. 'His father packed him off somewhere up north as a young lad, Yorkshire, I think. Never came back.'

Harriet sipped her sherry and put the glass down slowly. 'That was a disgrace. Poor little boy. They said he wasn't right – whatever that means. Seemed fine to me, even if he was very quiet. The father never had any time for those boys. Edward saw the Cummings' boy drown. Stopped talking altogether after that.' She glanced around the bar. 'It can wait till we go home, though. There's too many ears waggling in here. We only found out what Cornelius Derwinter wanted put about anyway, but none of what happened to that boy was right. It's a miracle Leonard's as normal as he seems to be. You go on, Alex, you'll be wanting to referee those fools.'

164

She made straight for the bar and stood between Kev and Major Stroud. The latter stood his ground but only, she thought, to have a front-row seat on the flap between Kev and Will.

Kev turned all his attention on her. 'Was the one on the hill a monk?'

Alex assumed everyone must know that by now anyway. 'Yes.'

'And some other monk came looking for him? You were talking to him the night the dart match got cancelled?'

She waited so long to answer the sound of fruit machines in the next room became deafening – at least to Alex.

'Ah,' Kev said sagely. 'That's right, then. And now that one's dead, too, isn't that right? That's what all the fuss was about at the rectory yesterday.'

'I say, old man,' Major Stroud said, his back ramrod straight and his well-mown mustache bristling. 'Alex isn't on some sort of trial here. She doesn't know any more than the rest of us.'

'Doesn't she?' Kev drained his beer and pushed the glass back to Will. 'Same again. Reckon there's a lot you know, Alex. The other monk was found hanging at the rectory and the vicar was so shocked he ran into the church and fell down the steps into the crypt. Beaned himself good enough to just about finish him. He's in a hospital somewhere in London, only no one knows which one because the police aren't sayin'. Why would that be?'

'Oh, my God.' Liz Hadley tuned in on Kev's last comment. 'Reverend Restrick got hurt? Nobody said a word.'

'Nope,' Kev said. ''Cept me, and I waited to

165

hear if anyone else would say something before I opened my mouth. Seems to me there's a lot going on around here that's not being talked about. I reckon we got a lot more trouble on our hands than we know about and it's time we pushed that O'Reilly and his mouthy sidekick for some explaining.'

Some assenting grumbles started.

'Don't you think we can move things along best by just keeping our eyes and ears open? That and taking care of ourselves?' Alex smiled hopefully. Surely these were all reasonable people.

A woman from Underhill, Gladys Lymer, scraped her chair back. 'Take care of ourselves?' she said. She and her husband had been coming in fairly regularly lately. 'If we're in danger, the police should be taking care of us.'

So much for her peacemaking attempts. 'They're doing their best,' Alex said. 'Let's allow them to do their job.'

'What about Charlotte Restrick?' Liz said. 'She was away, wasn't she?'

Caught between feigning complete ignorance and giving information that seemed only right to give, Alex said, 'The reverend told me Charlotte was staying with her sister. I'm sure they've contacted her. We'd have been asked where to find her if they hadn't.'

'Why would that monk hang himself?' Major Stroud mused. 'I would have thought that was against his religion.'

'Reckon I know about everyone and everything around here,' Kev said vaguely. 'I hear most things. Could be that monk didn't hang himself.'

166

Alex cringed.

'How would you know that?' the major said. 'Damnably difficult to hang a man who doesn't want to be hanged unless he's unconscious.' He looked away, frowning.

'Or already kicked the bucket,' Kev said. 'Not that you wouldn't have to be as strong as a horse to lift a dead man like that.'

Twenty-Four

The night had turned treacherous. After he shepherded Alex and the Burke sisters outside, Tony all but lifted Harriet and Mary Burke into the back seat of the Land Rover, which he'd parked behind the Black Dog. When he got in himself he glanced anxiously at Alex, who had greeted him with an expression that suggested the end was near. Her apprehension was palpable.

'Let's sit here and talk,' he said. 'The car's still warm and we can add some heat if we have to. I doubt it'll be so easy to get close to your front door, ladies.'

'We're used to it,' Mary said in a determined voice that reminded him how important independence was to these two. 'We walked down. It's not far and we've had plenty of experience. We stand or fall together.'

She and Harriet laughed.

Alex kept her face turned from his and stared through the window. The yard behind the pub

167

was dark except for the faint glow from steamed-up windows on to the snow.

'Mustn't leave Oliver too much longer,' Mary said, and when Harriet gave a muffled chuckle, she added: 'You have to accept what you can't change, like that wretched cat someone foisted on me.'

Snuffling called attention to Katie in her crate. Bogie was still ensconced in Lily's care and seemed happy enough, although Tony had seen the dog's eyes following Alex, who had become his lifeline.

'You notice young Tony doesn't leave his dog all alone for hours,' Mary said. 'Knows it's not good for them.'

'Bring Oliver with you, then,' Harriet said shortly. 'You can pull him along in that wheeled grocery bag of yours and take him everywhere you go like that batty Prue Wally and her smelly little poodle.'

Alex did look at Tony then, with a smile he couldn't miss even in the murky light. He patted her hand and she briefly used her free one to give his a squeeze. Just as quickly, she pulled away to fiddle with her scarf.

'I already told Alex that some of what we've been told sounds peculiar but it does tell us about the lace handkerchief. Or it seems to.'

Tony swiveled toward Harriet. 'Handkerchief?'

'This is a bit from the edge of an old handkerchief,' she said, passing him a folded piece of tissue. He could feel the scrap inside. 'It was made by Violet May, Winnie Hawker's mum. Winnie recognized it because Violet invented the

168

pattern. She liked it so much she put it around the handkerchiefs she gave to brides as gifts to use on their wedding days. Something new.'

'See?' Mary said. 'I told you the story gets a bit deep in places.'

'I think it's interesting.' Alex broke her silence.

'That pattern's really intricate,' Harriet said. 'Violet is in her nineties now. She still makes lace-edged handkerchiefs but they're much more simple.'

Mary harrumphed and said, 'If her eyes are like mine she's got my sympathy. Before we go on with this, I want to ask something about Reverend Restrick. Kev said the police won't say which hospital he's in. Don't you think that sounds as if they're afraid someone will get in and kill him?'

Tony smiled to himself. In this village everyone was a budding detective. 'I suppose it could, but it could also be a big leap to think that. Could be the man's so injured they don't want a lot of visitors showing up.'

Alex put a fist to her mouth. 'We shouldn't talk about what we think too much. You heard the way they were going on in the Black Dog, Mary. You, too, Harriet. If they could settle on a culprit they'd have him in the stocks by now. Then we'd have to make sure they threw rotten fruit and veg at him, not darts from the Black Dog.'

'Unfortunately our village stocks are missing the top bit,' Harriet said with a smile in her voice. 'But you're right. They were . . . well, to be honest it was mostly Kev Winslet who was ready to convict the first likely candidate.'

169

'Did he have anyone in mind?' Tony asked.

'Just a lot of stuff about how he heard the police were saying the man on the hill could be Edward Derwinter, which is silly when he died years ago. And how Edward coming back would mess things up for Leonard and Heather, because of the inheritance.' Harriet sniffed. 'We still don't understand why that boy was sent away. He had a terrible stutter and sometimes he didn't talk for weeks on end, but that shouldn't have been a reason to hide him away like that. First he lost his mother and he'd been like her shadow up till she died. He turned very quiet then. And after he saw the little Cummings boy drown, he shut up altogether. If he did try to talk, you couldn't understand him. We all think old man Derwinter was ashamed of him.'

They were all quiet until Mary said, too loudly, 'Kev should know better than to sneak around his employers' place listening for things that are none of his business. Those people have been good to him – they're good to anyone who works for them.'

Tony could sense Alex's distress. The past days had been too much for her. His father's warnings about not waiting too long to tell her about what happened to him in Australia weighed heavily. When was the right moment for something like that? He was almost sure she would believe his side of the story, but he couldn't be completely certain.

'Is there more about the lace?' Alex asked. She swiveled in her seat to look at the sisters.

Neither of them answered, just gazed out of the windows.

170

'Is there?' Alex pressed.

'Don't say we didn't warn you. It sounds outlandish. There's a little edge of the bride's initials still on the lawn. Just the very top of the first one, and the second one, but a bit more of the third one. The letters M, then O, then S. There's a bit more of the S but we're all sure the first two are M and O from the very top shape.'

Alex shocked Tony by abruptly resting her forehead on his shoulder. 'How will we ever make something out of that?' she said.

He stroked her black curls. Alex glanced down, then straightened up quickly. What he felt was more than the reaction of a friend.

'Any ideas?' he asked the sisters.

'Violet's sure she knows. Maria Olivia Scaduto. Says she could never forget anything that unusual.'

'And Violet's in her nineties?' Tony said.

'We don't all go dotty past the fine age of thirty-five, young man,' Harriet said.

'Absolutely not,' Tony said diplomatically – if a little late.

'She was Cornelius Derwinter's wife,' Mary said. 'That's where Leonard's coloring comes from. Italian. Beautiful girl. Only saw her a few times.'

Tony watched ever fatter flakes of snow fluff the windscreen and slide to join the thickening heap on the Land Rover's bonnet. Inside, the temperature had dropped.

'That doesn't make any sense,' Alex said. 'Where's the rest of the handkerchief?'

Mary leaned forward and lowered her voice as if afraid of being overheard. 'According to Violet, the whole thing was put in Maria's coffin.'

Twenty-Five

She would probably get hell from Tony. Alex whistled and leaned forward to peer through the windscreen, trying to keep a steady speed on the hill leading to her house. If she slowed down she could slip to a halt.

When they had walked Harriet and Mary safely into their cottage, Tony got a call to come to his clinic and set a sheepdog's leg. He left Alex at Lily's and she told him she'd wait for him to come and take her up the hill to get fresh clothes and supplies.

He had been gone a long time, called and said he'd be even longer, and she became afraid they wouldn't get up the hill and back again if they didn't go now. She stopped over at the Black Dog to tell her mother where she was going, collected Bogie and took off.

No one would be fooling around the lodge in this weather. It would be safe. With luck, she could do what she had to in record time, not that she owed Tony any explanations for her actions. Even if she had come to like being with him more than without him . . .

The Land Rover scrunched to a stop. Alex could already make out the turn to the right that came before the driveway at Lime Tree Lodge. Not that she felt like trying to go the rest of the way on foot. Letting the pedal up slowly, she slid back a little and made another attempt.

It didn't work, but the next try did.

Bogie sat close, leaned against her and swayed with every jolt. And managed to get in a lick to her jaw from time to time.

In this manner, creeping forward and sliding back inches, she reached the lodge, where inches of virgin snow covered everything. Winters were getting more extreme. Last year there had been sub-freezing temperatures in late April.

Rather than risk getting on an unplanned downward roll in the driveway, Alex stopped a little distance away from the front door. The outdoor lights came on and she got out of the Land Rover with Bogie trying to push past. It was funny how quickly a place looked deserted. This time she would leave more lights on inside the lodge.

She let herself into the house and shivered, even in her parka. The rush of air that met her felt more chilling than it was outside. It shouldn't be so cold in here. She hadn't turned off the heat, but a hand on one of the space heaters installed deliberately because they looked like antique radiators confirmed it was cold, and felt as if it had been for a long time.

The pipes will freeze. Several descriptive words came to mind but she swallowed them all. These were the joys of owning a home and having no one to share thinking about the upkeep – not that she needed anyone, she reminded herself.

Bogie bustled around familiarly. She was glad to have him. That thought warmed her up and brought a grin to her face. It was amazing how quickly she'd become accustomed to her little sidekick.

Suitcases were kept in a cupboard under the

main stairs. The space was finished and very dry so made a good storage area. Her mother said that in the Second World War that's where the occupants would have hidden during bombing attacks, not that Lily had actually been around for that. This area was just far enough from London not to have experienced much wartime activity, but Alex always got a funny feeling when she opened the door and thought about those who might have run under there to take cover. There were still several well-made cupboards that must have been used for supplies, and the area was reinforced.

Deciding on two small bags rather than a big one, she took the wheeled duffels into the hall but stopped before going upstairs. She needed to find out why the heat had gone off. In the morning she must call Simpson Brothers, who were actually father and son these days, and get them up here if possible. The Simpsons were the kind of family do-all firm that also did everything well without overcharging.

The heat ran on electricity and since the lights were working, there could not be a general failure. She looked at the circuit box and threw the breakers. She really didn't know enough to work out what might be wrong.

The lights were on. Nothing else looked unusual. The problem had to be peculiar to the heating.

Another check of the heaters showed they were still cold.

The only thing she could do was turn the heaters all the way up and hope at least some warmth came through.

Alex rubbed her hands together. A breeze,

strong and icy, was coming from somewhere. She turned the nearest control and kept turning and turning. Frowning, she looked closer, then moved to the next heater. It was turned all the way off, as the first one must have been.

A rapid survey of the living room as she walked round revealed the same situation. Someone had turned off every bit of heat and it hadn't been her.

What she had been too preoccupied to notice were open drawers. The room wasn't turned upside down but there was no doubt someone had been in there searching for something. Cushions remained on couches and chairs but they were pulled out and untidy.

Alex stood still in the middle of the room and listened. What she heard was the beating of her heart.

The house sounded and felt silent, still.

Alex had a problem squishing a fly but these were serious circumstances. She picked up one of a group of antique walking sticks she'd collected in a polished brass umbrella stand.

The beat of her heart in her throat hurt, but she followed the perishing current of air back into the hall and through to the kitchen. Running out the way she'd come in wouldn't help. If someone was around, they'd get to her no matter where she went.

The door from the kitchen stood wide open. She could see the stone wall at the side of the grounds and how snow heaped on every surface.

Again, someone had made a perfunctory search. Unlike the room at the Black Dog, nothing was broken here or scattered about. A single dart with a yellow flight stabbed a small square of printed paper, pinned it to the table.

She didn't want to cry but tears squeezed from the corners of her eyelids and burned. A few steps took her to the table and she read a copy of a simple announcement outlined with a single black line. Alex had never seen it before.

In Loving Memory
Of
Michelle
Infant daughter of Michael and Alexandra
Bailey-Jones.
Taken before she drew breath.
We will never forget.

Bogie leaped up and barked wildly. An instant later the front doorbell rang.

Shaking, Alex stopped breathing. She called her baby Lily – but only to herself. She pulled out her mobile phone.

The bell rang again before loud hammering sounded. And the outdoor lights blacked out.

Alex screamed. The sound erupted before she could contain it. She punched in 999 and held the phone to her ear with both hands.

A disembodied voice at the other end asked the questions she had hoped she would never have to answer again. 'Lime Tree Lodge,' she started. She heard meaningless questions but she talked over them, trying to keep breathing deeply. 'I need the police. I think someone's been in my house. And now they're outside trying to get in.'

While she spoke a tall shape materialized from

the darkness and faint white glow outside, approached the door and rushed toward her, arms outstretched. His head and lower face were wrapped in a black scarf.

Alex dropped the phone, raised the ivory head of the walking stick and braced her feet apart.

Twenty-Six

Bogie stopped barking.

'Dammit, Alex, why didn't you wait for me?' Tony caught her arms as she raised them, a stick held in both hands. He couldn't remember this sensation of frustration and protectiveness hitting him at the same time before.

She struggled against him until he took away the stick. 'Tony?' Taking in short, shallow gulps of air, she pushed him away and sat down hard in a kitchen chair.

'Alex? I talked to Lily and she said you'd only left a short time before. You said you'd wait. Look what you've done. You've scared yourself half to death – and me.' Bogie panted and jumped up to get his attention, ignoring Katie who had followed him in.

'The snow was getting heavier all the time.' Her pallor, and the sheen on her face – and her obvious fight to breathe – could be the start of another panic attack. 'Who would be up here in this kind of weather if they didn't have to be? I just thought . . . I could get a few things and be back in the village without any problems. I was afraid that if I waited another hour or so it wouldn't be so easy to get up here.'

Katie gave a thorough, whole body, almost levitating shake, showering Alex, who flinched.

'Down,' Tony told his dog. He propped the cane against a counter. 'Alex, why did you leave the back door open?'

'I didn't.' She bent over the table. 'Thought you were . . . I don't know.'

Tony rubbed her back. 'Take a deep breath and hold it. Let it out slowly. Everything's OK now.' He saw a piece of copied newsprint on the table and reached for it before pulling his hand away. One of those darts pinned the paper to the table. The police wouldn't want it touched. 'Breathe,' he told Alex, reading the announcement.

Crazy bastard.

'I'm so sorry,' he said quietly, crouching beside her. At her other side, looking doleful, sat Katie, and Bogie muscled in to share the space. 'Whoever's doing this is sick. And he really doesn't want you around here.' *Probably not the best thing to say.*

'I would have called her Lily, not Michelle,' Alex said quietly, her breathing slower. 'I never saw that announcement before. I don't even know what paper it was in, or whatever. Who would put it in?' She leaned back in her chair. 'Why does someone want me to leave – that *is* what they want? Tony, is what's happening to me really something to do with these deaths?'

'We've got to try to figure out answers for all those questions. First we decide whether to start looking for connections from the present and work back, or figure out a starting point in the past and come forward.' He paused to unwind the scarf from his neck. 'Let's call the police. We should have done that right off.'

'I called them just before you got here – I think.'

'What do you mean, love?' He noticed what he'd called her but it was OK, she wouldn't be aware of it. 'You think you called?'

'I think I did. I went into that silly screaming fit. I must have hung up.'

'They would still have logged the call. And probably traced it.' He wondered why the police hadn't called back. He picked up her phone. It appeared to be still connected. 'Hello,' he said into the mouthpiece.

'Just hold the line, sir. A unit is on its way. Stay inside and don't attempt to confront the intruder. Stay calm and don't move or touch anything.' The voice sounded like a recording, or someone accustomed to repeating herself frequently.

'They're coming,' Tony said, starting to take closer notice of the kitchen. Apart from a couple of open and sagging drawers, he didn't see evidence of more than a cursory look around. 'I can hear sirens now. Whatever happens, we don't give them any reason to start getting stroppy.'

A siren arrived and cut out. Seconds later the doorbell rang but, before Alex could move, they both heard footsteps scrunching around the outside of the house, coming toward the kitchen entrance.

'Attacked on both flanks,' Tony said with a grin, but Alex didn't crack a smile.

179

A uniformed constable arrived cautiously at the open door.

'It's OK,' Tony said. 'Come in, please. I'll answer the front door.'

He left Alex staring dully at the policewoman and strode to answer the bell with two barking dogs at his heels.

'Harrison? You get around.' O'Reilly sounded mild enough but his dark eyes were sharply appraising. 'I look for Alex and you're never far away.' He stamped snow from his shoes and brushed at his coat.

Before Tony could invite the man in, he stepped past him, searching in every direction. 'Where's Alex?'

'In the kitchen.'

Walking in that direction, O'Reilly said, 'You were here with her the whole time?'

Tony followed. 'No . . . I got here just after she called you people.'

'Were you expected or do you really make a habit of following her around?'

If this was the charming side of Detective Inspector O'Reilly, Tony hoped he wasn't around if the man got nasty.

O'Reilly paused before going into the kitchen. He looked back at Tony. 'Did Alex know you were coming?'

'We originally planned for—'

'I asked if you were expected.'

Tony clamped his back teeth together and breathed deeply through his nose. 'Not exactly,' he finally said.

'Right you are,' O'Reilly said. The dogs beat

him into the kitchen. 'Hello, Alex. Another rough arrival on the home front? What's your name, Constable?'

'Bishop, sir.' With shiny blonde hair pulled back at the nape and her young face scrubbed, Bishop had the glow of an outdoorswoman.

'Keep your ears open while you make us some tea, would you?' O'Reilly told her. He closed the door to the outside and stood facing them, his hands in his coat pockets.

Alex made a move toward the constable, filling a kettle, but O'Reilly shook his head. 'Stay where you are. You look shocked. Don't worry about noises outside. Your grounds are being searched.' He frowned. 'It's very cold in here.' Even as he spoke, he fixed on the pinned announcement in the middle of the table and went straight to it, bent over with hands behind his back.

'The door was left open,' Tony began. 'Before Alex got here.'

'Someone turned all the heaters off,' Alex cut in. She felt the tension between O'Reilly and Tony.

'And you found this when you got here?' O'Reilly said, still staring at the copied cutting. He glanced back at Alex.

Her throat jerked when she swallowed. 'Yes,' she said quietly. 'I never saw it before. It's to frighten me, right?'

O'Reilly's incline of the head was noncommittal. He pulled surgical gloves from one coat pocket and plastic bags from the other, but he went to the door and outside, returning with an officer carrying a camera. 'Get that,' O'Reilly said, pointing to the dart and paper.

After photos from every angle, O'Reilly bagged the dart and the paper separately. He handed them to the photographer, who went back outside.

'You didn't touch those?' O'Reilly said, and when she shook her head, no, added: 'Good. We'll see if we get anything from them.'

'I haven't been upstairs,' Alex told him. 'I almost missed that they searched downstairs. They definitely aren't thieves or they wouldn't have left things that are worth a fair amount – things that are in plain sight. What are they looking for? Do you know?'

D.I. O'Reilly's smile probably appealed to women. 'I think all three of us know. You want to go first, Harrison?'

'Call me Tony,' he said, deliberately cloying. 'Everyone does. Even my patients. I imagine they must be looking for that ring you've already got. What do you think, Alex?'

She didn't look amused at his sarcasm. 'Right. But I think I want to hear I'm wrong about everything I've started thinking. Biscuits are in that tin, Constable.'

'Why don't the three of us sit down and think about this. And while we're at it, I've come up with a few questions for you.'

'Alex has been through a lot,' Tony said. 'Let me bring her in to see you in the morning.'

That earned him a long, steady look from O'Reilly. 'We should do this while things are fresh,' he said. 'Unless you really don't feel up to it, Alex.'

'I'm fine.' She waved Tony into a chair and O'Reilly joined them.

'Do you think anything's missing?' he said.

She shook her head, no. 'There are a couple of good vases and a decent little painting in the living room. They're still there.'

The kettle boiled and steam hit the cold air in a stream of white vapor. Rivulets ran through haze on the windows.

'Here we are.' Bishop slid a floral melamine tray on the table. Three mugs of milky tea, the bags still inside, added more damp to the atmosphere.

'Please take one of these,' Alex told Bishop, but she shook her head, pulled a chair to a corner and sat down. She drew out a very new-looking leather notebook and waited with pen at the ready.

While they dispensed with the teabags, more vehicles turned into the driveway and squidged their way through the deepening snow.

'Isn't all that a bit of overkill?' Tony said, inclining his head toward the slam of car doors. 'Sounds like an army. What are they going to find in weather like this?'

'The sooner they look, the better the chances they'll find *something*,' O'Reilly said. 'You remember what was around Brother Percy's neck when we found him, Alex.'

'You think I could forget?'

'Rhetorical question,' O'Reilly responded mildly. 'It was the cincture from his habit. You managed to cut it through with a kitchen knife. Was there anything else you noticed when you were doing that?'

Tony waited to see if Alex would speak. When she didn't he snapped his fingers and said, 'The

183

shred of lace. What you found stuck in your pocket later, remember?'

The look she gave him was a reminder not to mention the Burke sisters.

Keeping his mouth shut cost Tony a lot of control. He hoped the omission wouldn't come back to haunt them in some way.

'Alex,' O'Reilly prompted, so gently Tony had a crazy impulse to hit him.

'Yes, in my pocket.' She looked at Tony and her worry showed. 'I didn't find it till afterward. It's not much. It's wrapped up so it won't fray any more.'

'Good,' the detective said. He took out another evidence bag. 'Your fingerprints will be on it, so you might as well go ahead and drop it in here.'

'You can get fingerprints from material?' Tony asked, and sensed it had been a mistake.

O'Reilly gave him a measured look. 'Times change,' he said. 'The answer would be yes.'

If Alex took any note of the fingerprint exchange, she showed no sign, but when she glanced at Tony again he knew they were both thinking how odd it might look if the police could tell the fabric had been pulled off the knife. 'It's at my mother's,' she told O'Reilly. 'I didn't want to carry it around. I'll give it to you tomorrow.'

'We'll collect it as soon as we get back down,' O'Reilly said.

He sat quiet. Bishop's biro had a scratchy nib which sounded as if it were tearing up the paper.

'Did Leonard identify the body?' Tony said, not expecting a straight answer.

'What makes you ask that?'

184

'We heard he went to see the body. The ring you found on the hill was a Derwinter ring. There can't be many like that. It would be natural to see if Leonard knew the man. Something had messed up the poor devil's finger – something like a very tight ring being pulled off. Whoever took it off must have dropped it and not been able to find it in the dark.'

'All very logical,' O'Reilly said evenly. 'But I imagine you're a very logical man, Harrison.'

And that, Tony thought, is as much as I'll get on the subject.

'If it were Leonard's brother, wouldn't you be able to find that out through DNA?' Alex leaned toward O'Reilly, picking up her mug at the same time.

Tony had stopped himself from suggesting the same thing, expecting the detective to resent any more questions from him. He already knew the answer but should have assumed Alex was just as likely to ask.

O'Reilly took advantage of the door opening to avoid answering the question.

A blast of cold air rushed in with Lamb. Without acknowledging anyone, he went to stand behind his boss and handed him a folded slip of paper.

O'Reilly read it. 'You don't say,' he remarked, his expression showing nothing, and put the paper in his pocket. 'Anything outside yet?'

'Could be,' Lamb said. 'I'll take over here, Constable. They need all the help they can get out there. Time's against us – and the weather.'

'I don't expect to find anything, but we need to check the house,' O'Reilly said. 'You look as if you're done in, Alex. I'll have someone drive you and Bogie to your mother's and you can give the lace to the driver. We'll talk more early in the morning. Harrison, I'd like to see you, too. You'll be told when. I'll be staying at the Black Dog until we can wind things up. We'll meet there. Ask at the desk and they'll tell you where to find me.'

'I'll drive myself down,' Alex said. 'But thank you for the offer.'

Tony got up and looked outside. 'It won't be easy for anyone to get down that hill without putting on chains,' he said, looking over his shoulder at her. 'If you'd be comfortable with it, you could stay at my house tonight. I parked my car outside your gates and it's almost flat between here and there. Give Lily a call so she doesn't worry.'

He turned back to the window without checking either O'Reilly's or Lamb's reaction.

'Our units are already chained up,' O'Reilly said. 'We won't have any problems.'

'Thank you,' Alex said, 'but no. I'll take you up on your offer, Tony. Come on, Bogie and Katie, let's get moving.'

Twenty-Seven

Tony's house was warm.

He scooped the post from the hall floor and flipped through envelopes as she passed him with

Bogie. 'Hot toddy in order, I think,' he said, taking her by the arm. 'Have you been here before?'

Katie bustled by with proprietary importance and disappeared inside.

'I've only seen the house from the outside. What a relief to be warm. It's cozy in here – particularly for such a big house.'

'A lot of it is closed off,' he said. 'No reason to keep up extra rooms you don't use. If I hadn't been so smitten with the property in general – and the house – I might have thought twice about getting something so large.'

'How long have you been back in Folly?' She knew it had to be considerably longer than she had but wasn't sure when he'd returned.

Tony looked up from the envelopes he had riffled through and set them aside on a demilune table. 'About five years,' he said, but showed no interest in discussing the topic of returning prodigals. 'Let's go in the breakfast room. I keep the fire ready in there. It's not a breakfast room any more but that's what it was supposed to be.'

The wide hall showed off an impressive dark wood staircase with a carved newel post and balusters. Stretching toward the back of the house before opening right and left, the hall continued and they took the left fork.

The breakfast room, as Tony called it, was a small room with waist-high wainscoting painted a deeper cranberry than the walls above, dark oak floors and a soft old Chinese carpet. Several wing chairs upholstered in dark, striped velvet faced a fireplace where he soon had logs crackling.

187

'This is so comfortable,' she said, smiling at him and hunching her shoulders appreciatively.

He took her coat and shrugged out of his as he pushed open sliding doors that led directly into the kitchen. 'Odd layout, really,' he said. 'But it appeals to me. Do you like hot port?'

'I've never had it but it sounds wonderful. And I really like this place – the way it's designed, too.'

'Sit by the fire. This won't take long.'

She chose a chair from which she could see him moving beside a butcher block kitchen island with copper pans hanging from overhead hooks.

Weighted down by the fatigue that intensified by the minute, Alex curled back into the chair with Bogie on the floor beside her. Automatically, she kicked off her boots and pulled up her feet.

When she and Tony had been together at her mother's cottage, she had been a mess and they had spent the time discussing her issues. She had made it easy to let him draw her out. But they hadn't talked about Tony's life, or why he'd returned to the village and bought a home here – alone. All she knew was that he didn't appear to be married any more.

When he used to bring Penny Cowan home, their connection had been obvious. They had moved in a private, shiny aura.

Tony had been a quiet fixture when Alex returned. The one time she asked Lily about him, she said Doc James had never volunteered anything about Tony's personal life and she had never asked him.

Alex watched flames shoot up from the logs. The sound they made comforted her. Sights and sounds, memories that brought back snatches of good times. Her mother reading stories by the fire in their tiny Underhill cottage. Decorating a tree, the same tree they kept growing in a tub outside, for Christmas. That tree was planted in the garden of the cottage in Folly-on-Weir.

Her eyelids wanted to close.

Colored wrapping paper saved and cut into strips for paper chains.

Holly sprigs collected from the woods and tucked along behind the old-fashioned picture rail in each room. And snowflakes cut from folded paper to stick on the single-paned windows Jack Frost painted with icy patterns in the early mornings.

Magic.

'Mummy, where is our daddy?'

Her own child voice, high, clear and ingenuous, sounded as clear as if she had spoken in this room.

Alex didn't hear her mother's response, or remember what it might have been, but she never got an answer to any questions about her father.

She jumped and her eyes opened sharply. Tony stood beside the chair, looking thoughtfully down at her, a small glass mug in each hand.

'Hello, sleepy. As soon as you've had this we'll find you a comfortable bed. You're wiped out, kiddo. Use the handle – the glass gets hot.'

'Mm. Sorry to drift off on you. Thank you.' She took the mug and sniffed hot, spiced port appreciatively. 'You need to take it easy, too.'

They sat quietly, sipping companionably – until Alex heard the soft, snow-laden sweep of a branch across a window. She could see the branch and a scatter of falling snow on the glass, but darkness cloaked whatever lay behind.

This was an illusion. At any moment the peace could pop like a soap bubble and droplets would sting her eyes with reality.

'What is it?' Tony watched her. 'No poker for you, my friend. You have the most expressive face I've ever seen.'

She nodded, but made no attempt to enlighten him. 'I hope it's OK to ask, but you know quite a lot about me and I don't know anything about your life since we left Folly. You and Penny did marry?'

'Yes. I thought you knew that.'

'You never really said.'

'I'm a widower.'

The cold in her belly had nothing to do with the temperature this time. 'I . . . Oh, Tony. It sounds so trite to say I'm sorry, but I am. I'm more than sorry. I'm horrified. I don't understand why I didn't know about Penny.'

He set his mug aside. 'It was a long time ago. You know how people are here – they don't talk much about certain types of things. Of course they gossip, but not usually about everyday tragedies. It's like an unwritten rule.'

'Everyday tragedies, Tony? Oh, it's fine to get through and get on, but it's also all right to admit you've been hurt.' She swallowed hard. Her throat was dry. 'Sorry. I don't mean to judge how you deal with things. I didn't expect you to say something like that.'

He looked straight into her eyes and gradually smiled. 'You're OK. Do you know that? I like you, Alex Duggins – I mean—'

190

She interrupted him with a laugh. 'I know who you mean. After seeing that announcement about . . . After tonight I may go back to Duggins and try to forget as much of my marriage as I can. But thanks. You're OK, too. When you're not trying to be masterful.'

They both laughed, and abruptly stopped.

Katie was exercising her impressive bark. Bogie popped up to sit on her haunches, her floppy ears twitching. Moments later someone hammered the front door, waited a second, perhaps two, and swung the knocker with vigor.

'Bloody hell,' Tony said. 'Now what?'

He hopped up and strode from the room, the mug still in hand. A minute or so, and a lot of murmured male conversation later, he returned with Dan O'Reilly.

Fatigue shadowed the detective's face but his stance, and the way he assessed his surroundings, were alert. 'I didn't realize you two lived so close,' he said. 'This is another nice house. People who don't know the area never guess how many big places are hidden away in these hills.'

Alex wasn't sure how to answer, so she didn't.

'It's you I mainly came to see,' he said to her. 'Thought you'd want to know immediately if we found anything significant.'

'Can I get you a drink?' Tony said.

O'Reilly declined. His intense stare, the suggestion that he was poised to pounce, made sure Alex was wide awake.

'At least sit down,' Tony said, and went back to his own chair.

'Thanks.' Without removing his coat, O'Reilly

took a seat where he could look directly at either Alex or Tony. The confrontational position, she thought, her spine stiffening.

Katie-the-traitor went to the man's knees and rested her big head there. He stroked her square muzzle and scratched her ears. 'Did you know the motion sensors at your place can be turned on and off from the outside, Alex?'

She blinked several times, thinking about what he'd just said. 'They can't,' she said at last.

'They can. There's a switch mounted in an insulated box under what looks like storm grating, only the runoff's been diverted and the grate has a liner mounted under it.'

'That's senseless,' Tony said, shifting to the edge of his chair. 'It defeats the purpose.'

'Depends on your purpose,' O'Reilly said.

'It could have been included in the system in case it malfunctioned,' Alex said.

'Smart girl.'

Alex pressed her lips together hard rather than make a 'smart' comeback at O'Reilly. A glance at Tony showed he was amused. No doubt her 'poker face' said exactly what she was thinking about O'Reilly's verbal pat on the head.

'Unfortunately – or fortunately at this point – that switch is a recent addition. In other words, it hasn't been there long.'

'But I haven't had any work done lately,' Alex told him. 'I'd know about a thing like that.'

'Would you? How much time do you spend at the lodge versus in the village? Anyone who knew what they were doing could have dealt with this little job in no time and you're away for hours at a time, Alex. The good news is that we now know how the lights were turned on and off, and we know you weren't imagining things.'

'That's a bit bloody much,' she snapped. 'If you think I'm making things up that's your business, but have the decency not to tell me to my face that you thought I was lying.'

O'Reilly sighed. 'Forgive me. I didn't mean that to sound the way it did. It's always a relief when we can tie up an end or two, sure. Not that there aren't plenty of ends still waving in the breeze.'

'Is that all?' Tony asked brusquely. 'If so—'

'It's not,' O'Reilly responded. 'And this is for both of you.'

'Twenty questions,' Alex muttered, not caring that she was easily heard.

'Yes,' O'Reilly said. 'Could be more than twenty. Are either of you aware of a path that runs behind both of your properties? It's extensive, or we think it is. The snow makes it impossible to be sure exactly. It hugs the walls but we already saw places where it probably branches off.'

Tony shook his head, no. 'I've lived here, either in the village or up here, most of my life but I didn't know of a particular . . . what did you call it? An extensive path?'

'Lane. Footpath. Whatever. It runs past here and on up the hill and down behind Alex's back garden, close to the wall, then close to hedgerows. It's not maintained but it's been used enough. It's easily passable. Or it would be easy for anyone who knew it was there. We're waiting for morning

193

to see just where it does go. But someone used it last night. We've got one footprint – which could be useless now – in a sheltered patch by a spot where someone's pushed through a hedge at the corner of the property. We went ahead and got a cast. We could still get lucky with evidence from where our boy, or girl, has been getting in and out.'

Alex got up and stood behind her chair. Bogie picked up her ears. 'So someone's sneaking on to my property and getting into my house when I'm not there,' she said. 'I more or less knew that but it's creepy to have proof.'

'So far it's been when you're not there,' O'Reilly said. 'Fortunately.'

Tony also stood. 'Frightening people won't help, will it?'

'Making them wary could.' O'Reilly got up. 'Would you like me to stop by and let your mother know where you are, Alex?'

The kind of anger he aroused made her feel like a stranger to herself. 'Thanks for the offer, Detective Inspector, but I've already called her.'

O'Reilly grunted. 'Frightening you isn't my intention,' he said. 'But I want you to think twice before you spend time at the lodge again until all this is cleared up. We won't be surprised to find out the nice, easily missed little access network may even be a shortcut to the village. Someone knows the way very well.'

The detective's mobile rang. He answered, listened and left the room.

'This has to be over soon,' Alex said. 'It's been three days. It feels like weeks.'

'Coffee?' Tony asked. 'I don't think we're going to get much sleep tonight.'

'I think I'll have more port,' Alex said, deliberately giving him a bright grin. 'Don't bother to heat it this time – just bring the bottle.'

He laughed and did as she asked, returning from the kitchen with a big bag of crisps as well as the bottle 'Eat some of these, too,' he said, tearing open the package.

O'Reilly returned and stood with his feet planted apart. He pushed his coat back and sunk his hands in his pockets. He watched them but seemed lost in thought.

'Well, now,' he said finally. 'It would probably be better if we all sat down again.'

Hesitating, Alex looked to Tony for his reaction. He nodded. 'We're both tired, O'Reilly. I hope this won't take too long.'

They both sat and O'Reilly followed suit.

Alex worked to calm down. She sipped port, picked up the bag of crisps and crunched several. When she offered the crisps to O'Reilly, he gave her one of his askance stares and shook his head, no. Tony scooped out a handful and munched steadily. 'They're salt and vinegar,' he said with his mouth full.

'That's grand,' O'Reilly said without interest. 'We've had some information of interest tonight. Sure, it could be nothing important, but under the circumstances we have to be cautious. Alex, are you aware of what happened to Tony's wife in Australia?'

She frowned at Tony, who clamped his mouth firmly shut. Muscles in his jaw jerked.

195

'You don't know?' O'Reilly pressed.

Alex sat on her hands while Bogie nosed her thigh and made soft, troubled sounds.

'Why don't you say your piece,' Tony said. 'Alex knows I lost my wife, if that's what you mean.'

'Does she know what *lost* means? Alex, stop me if you've heard any of this before. Apparently Penny Harrison went missing but her husband didn't think it was worth reporting for a week. The story goes that she died while diving, but her body was never found. Of course, this doesn't mean that Tony here had anything to do with the death, but it's certainly worth a thought or two.'

Tony didn't say a word. He sat back in his chair and settled his hands on the arms. He kept his eyes on Alex's face.

No, she didn't believe Tony had done something horrible to his wife. They must have a conversation but she wouldn't have it in front of O'Reilly.

'What does this have to do with what's happening in Folly-on-Weir?' she said, clearing her throat every other word. 'What point are you making?'

Tony rested his elbows on his knees and scrubbed at his face.

She wished he would say something.

'It probably has nothing to do with our case, but we're bound to make sure you know everything that could affect you.'

Why hadn't anyone talked to her about this? Why hadn't Tony told her? 'I'm afraid I don't understand why it's your job to spread other people's troubles around.'

196

'You're not looking at this with your eyes open,' O'Reilly said. 'We'll move on. It did occur to you that we've started on a second box of darts, didn't it?'

'Yes,' Alex said. 'That makes it even more important for you to get to the bottom of all this, doesn't it?' She hadn't thought too much about it but she would now.

'It would have made it easier if you'd known how many actual darts you had down there.'

'Well, I don't,' Alex said, surprised by Tony's complete withdrawal from the conversation. 'They were there when I bought the pub. Anyway, how do you know they came from the Black Dog? There must be thousands that look like they do.'

'Batch numbers,' O'Reilly said shortly. 'They're from the same one.'

'You've made your point,' Tony said. 'Now tell us why anyone would use a weapon – or something as a weapon – when it leads right back to a place like the Black Dog.'

'Because none of this has a thing to do with the pub,' Alex said defensively. Did O'Reilly want her to feel trapped and guilty for some reason? He had to know she wouldn't point a finger to herself.

'True enough,' O'Reilly said. 'But could be at the start it was a snap decision, then the killer was stuck with it so he or she carried on. Those darts were easy to get at when someone decided to use them.'

'That could be any one of dozens of people,' Tony said. 'They come and go all the time.'

'You'd know that, Alex. I never had you picked out as a crack darts player.'

She realized her mouth had dropped open and closed it. This had to be the most irritating man she'd ever met. 'You learn something new every day,' she said, smiling tightly at him. 'I bet I started out younger than most. When my mum worked as a barmaid at the Black Dog, I got into passing the time with darts. Unfortunately other things filled up my time soon enough and there was no more of that for me.'

'You never fill in if they're a player short.'

Her palms shouldn't be sweating. This was ridiculous. 'I've been known to do that, but not if I can help it.'

'Hey,' Tony tossed aside the crisps he'd been about to eat. 'For crying out loud, is this another of your wild goose chases? Now you find out Alex has thrown some darts in her time so she's a suspect. That would be smart on her part, wouldn't it? To kill with a dart and risk someone making the connection.'

'Just making conversation.' O'Reilly stood again. 'There's no need for either of you to involve yourself in this case unless we find out we need you.'

Apparently it didn't bother the man to feel intense dislike aimed at him.

'It'd be a simple thing for me to take you down to your mum's, Alex,' he said. 'I'm sure she'd feel better to have you with her tonight.'

'You obviously don't know my mother,' Alex said. 'She brought me up to be self-sufficient and she doesn't hover.' Her mind seemed to almost

198

touch something, but not quite and she couldn't make sense of what she was thinking. She had missed something. They'd all missed something.

O'Reilly wasn't giving up. 'You'd make everyone more comfortable if you were in the village,' he said.

'I'll be staying.' She was damned if some policeman would turn her against someone she believed in – or tell her what to do in any case.

'Perhaps it would be best if you went,' Tony said, leaving his own chair. 'For everyone.'

Cold slicked over Alex and goosebumps followed in its wake. 'Everyone?'

'It would be more comfortable for me,' he said.

Her cheeks actually stung.

Twenty-Eight

When they were in O'Reilly's car and he started the engine, he turned to her and said, 'You've made a wise decision.'

'The decision wasn't mine.' She sounded curt but that was fine with her.

He steered from Tony's driveway and set out for the downhill drive. 'Harrison knew you were just being a loyal friend. He helped you do what you knew you should.'

She didn't answer. What Tony had said hurt. But leaving him like that hurt more. As soon as she could, she would call him. And she'd make sure she saw him within hours.

Bogie sat on her lap and stared straight at the detective. His little body was rigid. He'd made it clear he wasn't interested in coming back out into the icy night.

If she let the man goad her, she'd lose her temper. That could be exactly what he wanted. Out of control people often talked too much. She let it go, closed her eyes and pretended to rest – not that he'd be fooled.

What felt like an interminable time later they drew to a stop and Alex saw they were in front of Corner Cottage.

'I'd appreciate having that lace, now,' he said. 'It's late, sure enough, but it would be a good thing if we could talk some more. Just the two of us.'

She shrugged and got out of the car with Bogie in her arms. O'Reilly managed to reach the gate in time to hold it for her.

Lily opened the door before Alex could knock and she raised her brows. She obviously hadn't expected to see her daughter, and certainly not the detective.

'Detective Inspector O'Reilly drove me down, Mum. He wants to ask me a few more questions.' He wouldn't see how she wrinkled her nose with distaste for her mum's benefit.

'I was just off to bed,' Lily said. 'I'll leave you to it, then. Unless the detective has questions for me, too.'

'Not at the moment, thank you, madam,' O'Reilly said, excruciatingly polite.

Lily took Bogie from Alex. 'I'll put him on your bed,' she said and went quickly upstairs.

'In here, please,' Alex said, opening the door

to the tiny front sitting room for O'Reilly. 'I'll get that material.'

When she returned from the kitchen where she'd put the folded tissue in a drawer reserved for manuals they never used, O'Reilly was looking carefully at one of her mother's much-loved pieces of Belleek porcelain – the shapes of two fish formed into a pale lemon vase.

'This is an old one,' he said. 'Back in County Wicklow my own mother has a glass-fronted cabinet filled with little pieces. She says it's patriotic for the Irish to collect Belleek. Do you know why they started making it?'

She didn't, but she did recognize a tiny alarm. O'Reilly wasn't above using a tried and tested method to get her to relax with him. Chatter about simple, unthreatening interests could do wonders to break social ice.

'Y'don't, do you?' And now he really sounded Irish. 'It was a brainchild to get some people work after the potato famine. Too bad it took so long to get going, but it happened in the end. You can see through the stuff. I used to sneak a bit and look at it in the light.' He held the vase to a nearby lamp to show how transparent it was.

'Pretty,' she said. 'Mum's been buying bits and bobs since I was little. I hope you never broke anything at home.'

'Aw, no. I'm still here, aren't I?' He laughed, and looked young and appealing.

O'Reilly, giving her an open and so charming smile, could have swept her into his cozy corner. But this wasn't the night for cozy anything.

'Here's what you're looking for.' The simple

201

hospitality her mother would have expected shamed her into adding: 'Can I offer you something? There's Glenlivet unless you've an aversion to Scots whiskey. Or tell me your poison and I'll see what I can do.'

'Glenlivet will do nicely,' he said and grinned again, pulling on a pair of blue latex gloves. 'I'll count myself not officially on duty.' He sat at the end of the small damask-covered sofa to unwrap her tissue packet.

She poured the amber Scotch into two glasses, her own just a half finger. O'Reilly got half a glass. She needed all the help she could get.

When she was seated across from him he took a healthy swallow and set the drink aside. The tissue he spread open on his thigh before gently straightening the lace-edged lawn.

Satisfaction. It gleamed in his dark eyes when he looked up at her. 'Have you a magnifying glass? No bother if you don't.'

'I do,' she said, knowing instinctively that somehow he had already learned about the initials.

The glass was in Lily's sewing basket. Holding it close to the specimen, O'Reilly didn't make a sound, but this was one time when his face didn't don his practiced blank expression quickly enough.

Alex wanted to ask what it meant to him but passed her whiskey back and forth under her nose instead and watched intently.

Finally he sat back and there was nothing of the smile left. She got the full force of how cold he could appear.

'There's been a lot of violence in this village,'

he said abruptly. 'Far more than most think we're looking into. Do you understand what I'm talking about?'

So much for Belleek. 'No, I don't.'

'Well then, Alex, what do you know about this little lace exhibit, other than where it came from? We've been looking for it, by the way – to complete the whole piece. We've got the rest of it.'

The less squirrely she appeared, the better. 'It was inside the cincture, wasn't it? When I cut it I must have cut through that, too, and caught a little bit on the edge of the knife.'

He looked at her for a long time but she wouldn't let her eyes move from his. 'Didn't you have to pull this off the knife? You could have given them both to me at the same time.'

'No, I couldn't.'

Again the extended stare. 'We can go into the station and do this as officially as I should. I thought we could be friendly about it but I expect you'd prefer to have your solicitor with you.'

Her stomach flipped, just as he'd intended. She crossed her arms and gave him back some of his own silence.

'All right. Is there anything you think you want to tell me? About anything?'

Thinking, turning over possibilities of what he did and didn't know and what he wanted her to say, she looked at her hands in her lap. If she could make him feel she wanted to help him – not that she didn't, but she would not drag dear friends into this. She could help without harming, couldn't she?

When he moved she thought he was getting

up, but he picked up his Scotch again and savored another mouthful.

'There's an old story in the area,' she told him hesitantly. She could mess this up so easily. 'About a bride's handkerchief being placed in her coffin after she died. That would be some years after her wedding. Have you heard anything about it?'

She heard the breath he took in through his nose, slowly. 'Something. Yes, I'm thinking I did.'

'It's probably just a silly tale that's hung around for years. You know how those things go in places like this.'

'A bride's handkerchief? Like this one?' He set a forefinger on the tissue.

'So you think that's what it is?' Her chest bumped hard.

'Do you?' he asked.

'Could be.'

'How do you think it came to be inside Brother Percy's cincture?'

She frowned at him.

O'Reilly didn't blink. 'Doesn't make any sense, does it? But if that were, say, a handkerchief that belonged to Cornelius Derwinter's wife and it was put in her coffin? Who took it out?'

'Edward Derwinter?'

O'Reilly leaned toward her. He didn't look tired any more. 'That's the story you heard, is it? Did you hear it a long time ago, like some kiddies' ghost story? Or is this being talked about now?'

When she didn't answer, he went on: 'Are they saying something happened to Edward Derwinter because of this?' That steady forefinger remained

204

on the tissue paper – beside the handkerchief scrap. 'Concentrate. Did they do something to the boy that could have a bearing on this case?'

Alex stood abruptly and jerked her arm, forgetting the Scotch. Droplets of pale gold liquid arced through the lamplight and glittered as they fell.

'What?' O'Reilly said, scrambling to get up and protect his precious evidence at the same time.

'Was Brother Percy . . . no, I was thinking for a second that Percy was actually Edward. That's not right. But Percy was wearing Edward's cincture. He said he had something he wanted to give back to him.'

Twenty-Nine

'*This is Tony Harrison. Please leave a detailed message. I'll get back to you.*'

Alex was finished with leaving messages.

'Don't do this, Tony.' She spun away from the phone on her mother's hall table and stood, staring the wall. 'Damn, damn, damn. This isn't going to help you – us.' He ought to know she trusted him and that they'd come too far not to keep on working together.

But did his reaction mean he *didn't* trust her?

She had started trying to reach him as soon as she woke up early that morning. He had turned his mobile off. By this time he should be at the clinic but, if so, he was screening her out.

205

O'Reilly would be pleased. He wanted to drive a wedge between her and Tony. Divide and conquer – or at least see what contradicting information he could worm out.

She already regretted her outburst about the cincture. That idea should have been kept to herself until more pieces of the case fell into place.

Now she was even thinking like a plod, as Will would say.

Her mobile rang and she slapped it to her ear, 'Tony?'

The clearing of a throat at the other end let her know she should have waited. 'Hello, Alex.' The very English voice was held low. 'Major Stroud here. Your good mother gave me your number. I'm calling on her behalf, and mine. She's tied up. We've got a bit of a shindig in progress at the Black Dog, m'dear. Hate to disturb you but it shows signs of getting nasty. Of course, I'll make sure nothing gets too out of hand, still . . .'

'Oh, f-iddle.' She collected herself, but couldn't do anything about the thumping headache that began. 'Thank you, Major. Not even lunchtime and someone's fighting?'

'Not exactly. Not yet. Usual suspects but I regret to report that Mrs Winslet set it off. Unexpected arrival. Not that I think she intended to cause this.'

Alex sighed, having difficulty imagining the diminutive Fay Winslet causing a row. She rarely appeared at the pub and more rarely had anything to say. 'Thank you, Major. I'm on my way.'

With Bogie behaving as if he was on his way

to a canine carnival, she clipped on his lead, put on the black woolen coat and a green scarf she'd retrieved from Lime Tree Lodge and left Corner Cottage. This time she locked the door and she would be insisting her mum did the same in future.

The snow had finally stopped. A white-blue sky dazzled her but the wind was still cold enough to make sure she was wide awake. She paused for a pair of toddlers, the Graham twins, and their mum to fuss over Bogie, but didn't tarry any longer than she could help.

O'Reilly was staying at the Black Dog. She'd only partially taken it in when he'd told Tony to meet him there. Hurrying across the snow-packed street, she scanned the road for his car. No sign, and she hoped fervently he wasn't hearing whatever was going on in the bar.

The sound of raised voices met Alex as she walked into the entryway. This was getting to be a nasty habit. She went straight through the door into the public bar but apart from Major Stroud who raised a hand in acknowledgement and grimaced, the disagreement raged on as if she hadn't arrived.

'Enough's been said.' Will caught her eye. He gave a half-hearted wave and let his arm fall heavily to his side. 'Let's pack it in, boys and girls.' Cathy attempted to continue serving but seemed to have withdrawn into herself.

The place was too crowded for the time of day. Alex wondered how many had arrived in response to the village person-to-person system.

'If Kev spent more time at work than 'e does

proppin' up that bar, none of this would have happened.' Another Derwinter worker, this one Colin Best, was too close to Kev. A burly, dark-haired Welshman in his thirties, his naturally ruddy complexion was the color of beets and veins stood out at his temples and in his neck.

'And if you weren't propping it up right now, we wouldn't have to listen to your foul mouth,' Kev said.

Colin narrowed his eyes and put more distance between them. But he didn't stop muttering.

'I haven't said anything the rest of you aren't thinking,' Kev said.

Alex had the thought that anyone passing by should be able to hear him. Gladys and Frank Lymer from Underhill stayed close to the door as if ready to escape. *Wonderful.*

'Let's go, Kev,' Fay Winslet said. 'Don't say any more.' She didn't match her husband. Small and fair – and usually quiet – she had big brown eyes and pointed features. In the village, if she was mentioned at all, it was likely to be in reference to her church work.

When Kev looked at her his regret showed, but he was too wound up to just walk away.

'You started this,' Colin said. 'You shoot your mouth off. If you didn't want to be the center of everything, we'd all be better. There, now I've told you.'

'And I'm so hurt,' Kev said, sneering. 'A man telling a bit of truth doesn't mean others who don't know what they're talking about can blab a lot of rubbish and make trouble. But now you want to blame me and back out of it, don't you?

208

Without the Derwinters, where would we all be? They keep this village alive – as much alive as it's likely to be.'

'If you hadn't talked out of turn, repeatin' what you shouldn't be listening to, no one else would be any the wiser. You sowed the rotten seeds here. And what does it matter now, you say?' Colin warmed up to full pitch. He'd set down his glass, propped his elbows behind him on the bar and made large white-knuckled fists. 'Who cares who that man on the hill was? You tell me that.'

'I say—'

Alex cut Major Stroud off. 'I should think anyone who cared about him before still does, Colin. That's an awful thing to say. I, for one, would like to be sure who he was and why he was there. He must have had a reason.'

'You've got that right, Alex,' Will said. 'I reckon that's the most important thing the plods have got to ferret out. If they knew that they might get somewhere.'

'And people might stop being killed or hurt,' Fay said, hugging herself in a red down coat. 'And we could all stop jumping at our shadows. Poor Reverend Restrick – we haven't got a word about his progress. Charlotte hasn't come back here. I don't know what to think.'

'The question that matters,' Kev said, 'is whether that was Edward Derwinter who died up on that hill. He was the older brother, remember.'

'So you keep saying.' Will gave the bar a vicious swipe with a cloth. 'What's your point? Whoever he was, that man is dead now.'

'His point,' Colin said, 'is that he's angling toward it being all a made-up story that Edward died years ago. And that if he was still alive, it would mean Edward was the next in line for the Derwinters, not Leonard. The money would be Edward's.'

'So? A fat lot of nothing it means now. If it was Edward and he was alive, he's gone now so nothing changes,' Will said.

'Ah, but there's more, isn't there?' a man called out. 'Why don't you explain proper, Colin?'

Will slammed up the flap and came from behind the bar. His was the second pair of fists in evidence and Alex closed her eyes. She took a deep breath and opened them again. 'I want this to stop now. Or take it somewhere else.'

'That's the way, Alex. Ms Bailey-Jones has told you how it's going to be, fellas,' the major said, but Will's fists were in evidence again.

'Alex Duggins,' Alex said loudly and with no prior intention of doing so. 'Remember that, please. I'm not married any more.' And she wanted to forget everything about Mike and his name. If she ever saw it in print again it would have nothing to do with her.

Major Stroud pushed his lips and mustache out in a thoughtful pout. 'OK, old thing. As you will.'

The slightest pause was followed by Colin saying, 'Stop shilly-shallying, Kev. What do you want to hear someone else say – just so you can pretend to the Derwinters that your own nose is clean.'

Will grabbed the man's arm and gave him a mighty shove, knocking him off balance. Colin

210

staggered but managed to stop himself from falling. 'This is too much for Alex,' Will said. 'It would be too much for most people but you've all piled on and it's enough.'

'Out!' Alex cried. 'Get out until you can be civilized.'

'For crying out loud,' Kev exploded. 'They'll be wrong, but don't tell me the police won't charge Leonard Derwinter with killing his brother. And they will say it was to keep his hands on what he's used to having.'

With a hand over her mouth, Alex sagged. She'd started to feel sick.

The solid feel of Will's arm surrounding her shoulders was a comfort. 'Look, Alex,' he said, 'why don't you get out of the village for a break? You're wearing yourself down, girl. I can run this place for you – I've had practice. We're all worried about you.'

She gave him a grateful smile. 'Thanks, Will. I may have to think about that seriously.'

Thirty

O'Reilly hovered at the top of the stairs, hidden by a wall, until Lily Duggins left her reception desk and went into the kitchens. Only two lunch-time diners were seated and they had listened in silence to at least part of the argument in the bar.

He had heard the entire thing.

Swiftly, he went downstairs and slipped outside.

One of the early comments hurled by Winslet had been that there were plenty of people in the village who knew more about the Derwinters than they were saying. Someone else had chimed in that 'you can't bite the hand that feeds you'.

O'Reilly and his team had interviewed all the villagers, but that had been when the case wasn't as advanced as it was now. And it made sense that what amounted to a feudal village would be tight-lipped.

He turned his collar up against the wind. A grayish cloudbank on the horizon taped white land to blue sky.

The oldest, sharpest candidates he could think of for a little early history of Folly-on-Weir and the Derwinters were the Burke sisters. They might know very little, and they were canny enough to keep secrets if they thought it was to the advantage of a friend, or themselves, but approached in just the right way they could decide they'd like to help him. Particularly when, thanks to Constable Bishop, who had visited the old ladies' shop, he'd thought of an opening. Constable Bishop was still finding excuses to haunt the place for tea and a host of cakes, scones with jam and clotted cream, and other goodies she listed regularly and with a look of bliss on her healthy country girl face.

He knew the sisters lived over their café and it was called Leaves, or something similar. For tea leaves, he supposed. And the place was on Pond Street off Mallard Lane, close to St Aldwyn's.

The local school continued to operate. Not too many snow days for the children of Folly-on-Weir, but there were more teenagers than usual about, which meant he passed a group of four. For all he knew these were the only four in the village. They must travel to school by bus and few things on wheels were moving today.

He'd grown up where winters were mean and he walked on treacherous ice and snow with sure feet. He liked to see the occasional horse and rider ambling up the lanes and along the roads, but there were none of those today, either. A pristine quiet flattered the sparkling air.

Pond Street – more of a wide pathway than a street – was easy to find, as was Leaves of Comfort. A simple sign stuck up on wooden posts showed above the hedge in front of a pair of semi-detached cottages with doors painted a rich indigo. Bow windows on either side displayed what seemed to be more books than anything else, except handcrafts. A pile of books with a teapot on top. A row of books held up by jars of jam used as bookends. Hand knitted dolls and teddy bears artfully stretched on their stomachs around a large, open book. In what seemed an original blue carrying case open to display three sections stood a surprising collection of antique Matchbox cars he fancied a look at himself.

And lace tablecloths, lace-edged guest towels, lace doilies, lace antimacassars like the ones his ancient granny still used, lace-embellished every-thing. He smiled to himself, but straightened his face at once and raised the doorknocker. It barely fell, making one solid echo to the inside, when a window opened over his head. 'Hello, down there,' a firm voice called.

O'Reilly stepped back, his warrant card already out of his pocket. 'Detective Inspector Dan O'Reilly,' he said to the woman he recognized as Harriet Burke. 'We met before, Miss Burke. Sorry to interrupt when you're probably taking a rest before opening up, but could you spare me a few minutes of your valuable time?'

'Hah,' she said. 'When you get to my age, the fewer rests, as you put it, the better. You never know when you'll forget to return from a rest altogether, if you see what I mean. And I can't afford time wasting anyway. I need to pack in as much as possible.'

He was tempted to ask if she risked sleeping at night but smiled instead and gave what he hoped was an understanding nod of agreement.

'Come on up, then. Door's open. Stairs straight ahead.'

Another nod and he followed her instructions. Inside he met the fragrant aromas Officer Bishop rhapsodized about. She had even given it away that Lamb had made a sneaky personal visit to the shop. Freshly baked goods tickled his nose. And again he was surrounded by books, teapots, and lace, lace, lace – and embroidery. His mum would love the place, although she'd love it more if it were in Ireland.

'Tea's brewing,' came Harriet's announcement from the top of the stairs.

A long-legged, extra-long-tailed tabby cat met him before he got all the way into the Burke sisters' flat. 'That's Oliver,' Mary said from a plump chair. 'He lets us live here.'

214

Harriet laughed, such a sudden, high trill that O'Reilly cocked his head inquiringly.

'Listen to Mary,' she said. 'That pretty boy's only been here a few days and she didn't want to keep him.'

'Poppycock,' Mary said. 'I had to test you, sister, to make sure you could seriously care about him.'

He entered a comfortable if old-fashioned sitting room with a fireplace at one end. Doors in two walls must lead to bedrooms, kitchen and the rest of the flat.

Harriet left and returned quickly with a large teapot covered with a quilted tea cozy. She set it on a tray beside floral, fine bone china cups arranged across the top of the kind of tea trolley he hadn't seen in years. From a cupboard underneath she took a two-tiered cake plate already piled with cakes.

'Sit down, Inspector,' she said. 'The sofa's comfortable enough as long as you don't sit in the middle. You're likely to get stabbed by the springs if you do.'

He accepted a fragile cup and saucer and sat down. Harriet balanced a plate on one of his knees and held out the cakes. Gaining trust was essential and the tea ritual made for the right atmosphere. He took an almond tart, and when the display continued to hang in front of him, smiled up at Harriet and helped himself to a lemon curd slice. 'You'll fatten me up,' he said, praying the goodies would stay balanced, and took a sip of milky tea.

While she made her selections, Mary put on

one of the thickest pairs of glasses he remembered seeing.

When both women sat facing him, he got the impression they could communicate without talking.

Intelligent faces, both arranged in questioning mode.

'I'll have to eat these before I do another thing,' he said, biting into the tart and making appreciative noises. 'One of my people, Constable Bishop, has told me how wonderful the food is here. I have to say, she's told the truth.'

'Now, now, Inspector, surely everyone tells you the truth.'

He expected Mary to smile but she didn't, just continued to watch him through the distracting lenses of her glasses.

'You'd be surprised.' Until he decided whether this pair was as harmless as they appeared, he'd keep things very light.

They ate and drank in silence with the cat swishing around their legs.

'No scraps,' Mary said archly. 'He's a piggy. Human food is bad for cats.'

O'Reilly gave a sage nod, but he did stroke the sinuous cat.

When he could, he set the teacup and plate aside.

'You can manage more than that,' Harriet said, already on her feet. 'Have you had your lunch? I forgot it's a bit early. I could pop a steak and kidney pie in the oven for you. No rabbit pie, I'm afraid.' She chuckled.

With barely a pause, he laughed, too. 'What I

had was enough, thank you.' Funny how many people assumed all Irish liked rabbit stew or rabbit pie. Never a favorite of his – the meat was too slimy. In fact he wasn't particularly tempted by any meat.

The front door opened, ringing a little overhead bell, and slammed shut again. 'It's Tony. All right if I come up?'

'Of course,' Harriet called out. 'Tea's already made.'

Damn, damn, damn.

O'Reilly watched Harrison come into view and the way the cat leaped into his arms. Fair enough. He'd carry on as planned rather than look as if he was keeping something from the vet.

'Inspector O'Reilly,' Harrison said. 'I'm interrupting. Just wanted to stop in and see how my favorite ladies were doing. I can come back.'

'No need,' O'Reilly said. 'There's nothing I wouldn't say in front of you.'

'Join us,' Harriet said, already pouring a fresh cup of tea. 'Sit by the inspector.'

O'Reilly would rather be able to see the man's face but there was nothing to be done about it. Harriet piled cakes and biscuits on to a plate for Tony Harrison.

O'Reilly took a good look at the man's expression and decided he looked entirely too comfortable with the situation.

The couch sagged when the vet sat down at the far end from Dan. At least Alex was more on her guard about the man than she'd been before last night's announcement. The two of them together didn't make O'Reilly happy, not

217

that he knew how seriously to take the Australian story.

He would see how comfortable Harrison was in a moment or two. From his jacket pocket he took an evidence bag with the piece of lace inside and held it out to Mary. 'Have you seen this before?'

Mary held the bag at the end of her nose. 'Mmm.' She turned the bag over, and back. 'We've seen this on something, Harriet. Take a look. Tell me if it's that Violet Knot pattern. I don't think it's made any more.'

The two women literally put their heads together over the bag.

Looking for Harrison's reaction was irresistible but the man chewed on part of what looked like a ginger toffee biscuit and looked disinterested.

'Looks like it,' Harriet said. She pulled out a drawer in a tall chest and removed several white items. 'These laces can be so intricate, Inspector, and so beautiful. You don't often find the kind of antique collection we have. This one is a table doily.'

She held a circular piece that was all lace and embroidery.

'Mmm,' he said.

'See that,' she pointed to the center. 'That's stag and bird. What's called a figural piece. Imagine working that.'

'Oh, my ears and whiskers,' Mary muttered reverently. 'Do you have the Pointe de Venise there? I know the inspector would be fascinated by that.'

'Right here,' Harriet said and whipped a fragile

white lawn blouse, all tucks and fine embroidery, across his knees. 'At the bottom of the right sleeve and around the neck. That's the Pointe de Venise. It's missing from the edge of the left cuff.'

'I had no idea.' O'Reilly made sure he looked admiring. 'You didn't say where you saw the . . . Violet's Knot, was it? Anywhere in particular?'

A thoughtful vagueness overtook them both. Finally Mary said, 'I do know it was used on brides' handkerchiefs. See the fine thread of silver in the knots? And . . .' She held the lace to the lenses of her glasses. 'I think there might have been initials. That's what they do for brides' hand-kerchiefs. You look, Harriet.'

Harriet looked, holding the piece almost as close as Mary had. 'Yes,' she said. 'You're right.'

'We think we've got the rest of this handker-chief,' O'Reilly said, watching for any giveaway reactions but seeing none. He sighed. 'We'll have to take a closer look now we know what it might have been.'

The only response he got was purring from the cat curled by the fire.

O'Reilly wished, fervently, that Tony Harrison would just disappear.

'Would you say you were long-time residents of the village?'

That got him scrutiny that questioned his sanity. 'We were both born in the village,' Harriet said. 'We left when we went away to school but apart from that, this has been our home.'

'Well now, and that's wonderful,' O'Reilly said, trying to make sure his smile wasn't obviously condescending. 'So there's not much you don't know about major events during your lifetimes.'

Both women shook their heads, no.

'You must have known Edward Derwinter when he was a child.'

He felt Harrison turn to him but when their eyes met, Tony's were interested but untroubled.

'We knew Edward,' Mary said. 'Nice boy. Edward was always very quiet – silent even. He had a severe stutter and I don't think his father had a lot of patience with that so the child rarely spoke at all.'

'How do they say he died?' This was a shot in the dark. 'They do say he's been dead for years.'

He felt the sofa sag even more as Harrison settled himself more comfortably. Damn the man, observing and filing away anything he decided was useful. O'Reilly cleared his throat. Why should any of this be useful to the vet?

'After the accident he went away again.' With a piece of shortcake halfway to her mouth, Harriet paused, her expression far away. 'He'd been at school somewhere up north since he was little. By then he'd have been about . . . eight. There were rumors about why Cornelius Derwinter would pack off a motherless boy, then never have him home even at the holidays, but they were only rumors. Not one of us knew the truth. Leonard stayed close to home.'

'Cruel,' Harrison said under his breath, and both women nodded, yes.

'What accident would that be?' They were skating on the edge of something useful, O'Reilly could feel it.

220

The sisters glanced at one another and shrugged.

Lavender was a scent that could become oppressive, O'Reilly decided. He had an urge to stand up and throw open the window – and walk around the room. He had an equally strong – and he knew, wrong – urge to get tough.

'You said Edward was sent away after *the* accident.' This pair was sharp, but would they deliberately withhold important information in a murder enquiry?

If they think protecting someone is more important than the truth. The realization served to harden him. 'Either of you?' he said sharply.

'A child drowned in the Windrush,' Harriet said. 'At Bourton-on-the-Water. Four or five, he was and he was playing around on those flat rocks. So was Edward. Children have always done that. From what we heard, the younger boy slipped and drowned.'

O'Reilly frowned. 'The water's so shallow there.'

'He hit his head. No one noticed until it was too late. There was talk about Edward being – well, it was wrong of course – but the suggestion was that he was too stupid to help the other boy. And some even said it was Edward's fault.'

Mary's hands fluttered and she turned slightly pink. 'Unfair. Totally unfair. He wasn't stupid and an accident like that happens quickly and easily. But Cornelius shouldn't have been so protective of the Derwinter name that he packed Edward off rather than risk more open talk.'

'I think my dad mentioned that,' Tony Harrison

221

said suddenly. 'He hadn't been here more than a few years. He went to help.'

'Who was the boy who died?' O'Reilly asked him.

'Graham, I think, was the first name.' Harrison rubbed the space between his eyebrows. 'He was the Cummings' boy.'

'Will and Cathy Cummings?' New possibilities clicked over in his mind. This had never been mentioned before, but these people were as closed-mouthed as their reputations suggested.

'That started more talk afterward,' Harriet put in. 'It wasn't that long afterward when Will and Cathy were put in as managers of the Black Dog – although they were too young. It belonged to the Derwinters but it was some time later before they could buy it from Cornelius.'

The need to move was too strong now. 'Well, thank you for your time.' Getting up, O'Reilly smiled at the women and nodded to Harrison.

'It was all lies, you know,' Mary said. She couldn't keep her hands still now. 'No one really blamed Edward for Graham's death. But the whispers didn't stop. The job at the pub was to keep the Cummings quiet, that's what they insisted. Because Cornelius was so proud he didn't want anyone to keep on suggesting Edward was responsible in some way.'

Harrison made a disgusted noise. 'That's the kind of rubbish that comes from people not having enough to occupy their minds. Couldn't the man have been reaching out in kindness to people who had lost so much? It was a very decent thing to do.'

Thirty-One

'I've been expecting this,' Doc James said when Alex led him to the small conservatory Lily had added to one side at the back of Corner Cottage. 'But I thought the questions would come from the police.'

A portable electric fire with glowing artificial coals kept the space warm. Several cane chairs clustered around a table painted free-hand with fanciful begonia blooms in oranges, reds and yellows. Potted plants thrived in built-in troughs on the three glassed-in walls. On this evening, snow covered the roof and hung in frozen swags where it had slid down the windows earlier, but inside was warm and cozy.

'Thank you for coming,' Alex said. 'Tony called and told me what Harriet and Mary said to O'Reilly while he was there.' She'd been surprised but also glad to hear Tony's voice.

And afterward she'd been disappointed he had so little to say.

'He's on his way,' James commented. 'Hope that's all right with you. I thought it would save a lot of repetition.'

Alex's heart gave an extra thud but she said, 'Of course,' and did her best to look unconcerned.

Doc James made the rounds of her mum's plants, making admiring sounds as he went. 'Your mother has two green thumbs.'

223

The front door knocker cut off any reply and Alex went to bring in Tony. 'Where's Katie?' she said. Her throat was dry.

'She wasn't about to come out in the cold again,' he said.

'Clever girl. Bogie's in his favorite place on my duvet. Doc James is in the conservatory.' She led him to join his father. 'What can I get for the pair of you?'

'Nothing for me,' Tony said without looking at Alex.

Doc James immediately said, 'Scotch, please.'

'I'll get it.' Tony left quickly.

Doc James coughed into a fist and jigged up on to his toes. He was about to speak when Tony returned and handed him a glass. Only the GP sat down. Tony and Alex stood, one on either side of the room, both facing the back garden.

'You know I have to consider patient privilege?' Doc James said. 'I didn't really go into that with you on the phone, Alex.'

She glanced at Tony, who was already watching her. They both gave tight smiles.

'Before we get to your interrogation, are you two going to get over whatever's eating you?'

Tony crossed his arms. 'Alex and I hoped you would help us understand some things, Dad. We don't have any standing when it comes to interrogating anyone. You've been through these last few days the same as we have. Don't you get the feeling the police are running in circles and getting nowhere?'

'I was talking about *you*,' Doc James said. 'What's going on with you . . . and Alex?'

224

'Let's just deal with the serious stuff,' Tony said.

His choice of words annoyed Alex. 'I thought it was pretty serious when you told me to get lost last night.' She turned hot all over.

'You exaggerate,' he said. 'I think I said we'd all be more comfortable if O'Reilly brought you down here. Given that he'd just more or less . . . scratch that. He'd just suggested I murdered my wife. Even if you've nerves like Margaret Thatcher, that would have to make you a tad edgy. I wanted to help everyone out.'

'Damn fool,' Doc James said, barely parting his lips. 'I warned you to tell Alex the story before someone else did. He had nothing to do with whatever happened to Penny, Alex. If and when you two can be reasonable with each other, I hope you'll air it all out – as far as anyone can.'

'Thanks, Dad. You deserve your "told you so" moment.'

'Let's leave it, please,' Alex said. 'O'Reilly must have thought he could get any information he wanted out of two silly old women. Only they aren't silly.'

Tony breathed in deeply. 'I don't think he did believe they're silly, but he may have decided they aren't worldly enough not to trot out blithe answers to whatever he asked.' His chuckle startled Alex. 'You should have watched the show they put on. They really ran him around. Examples of old lace . . . he went to ask about the lace scrap. I didn't interrupt and they behaved as if they hadn't actually seen it before. They did give some name to the lace pattern. O'Reilly said they've got the rest of the handkerchief.'

Tired of standing and growing more tense, Alex sat in the chair next to Doc James but Tony remained where he was.

'It's about time they did find the rest of it. We knew it had to be in the other part of the cincture where I made the cut. Did Harriet or Mary show any surprise when it was mentioned?' Alex asked. 'I wouldn't blame them. The police keep everything so close to their chests.'

'He might as well have told them it was cold outside. Their expressions never changed.'

'Bless them,' Alex said. She had to get to the real reason for asking to see Tony's father. 'Did you see the little boy who drowned, doctor? When the accident happened years ago?'

Doc James didn't seem surprised by the question. 'About forty minutes afterward. I was on my rounds and they had to find me, but it would have been too late anyway. He'd been dead longer than that.'

She took her own deep breath. 'Could Edward – the older Derwinter boy – have done anything to save the younger child?'

'I wasn't a witness and I'm not a policeman.'

Alex rested her elbows on her knees and rubbed her fingertips up and down on her brow.

'But you've got opinions, Dad.'

'Isn't all this for the police?' Doc James said.

'If they're getting anywhere, they aren't telling us,' Alex said. 'Where's the harm in trying to put the pieces together? Tony and I have had some pretty pointed questions put to us and meanwhile there's been another death and Reverend Restrick

226

has been spirited away with some sort of horrible injury. Why did he fall down a flight of stairs he's been using for years? Why can't the police move faster? This is a small place. That should make it easier.'

'Let's not get carried away,' Doc James said. 'If there was anything we could do to help things along, that would be one thing. But I'm not putting myself in a position to be accused of meddling.'

'In other words your reputation comes first.' Embarrassed, Alex shook her head. 'I'm so sorry. That wasn't called for. I understand your reticence.'

Doc James took a thoughtful swallow of Scotch. 'Some things are best left unsaid if all they'll do is cause pain.'

'How do you decide what things those are?' Tony asked. 'Rather than details that could help right a wrong.'

'Sometimes you have to be patient, son. If it becomes obvious that you ought to speak up for the general good, you do it. Not otherwise.'

Alex took the risk of asking, 'Did you ever see Edward as a patient?'

'A few times. Usual childhood ailments.'

'What about his speech difficulties.'

Doc James snorted. 'A stutter made worse by his family's ignorance. And there was nothing stupid about the boy although that was the story circulated. I never understood Cornelius's attitude. Sending Edward away seemed cruel.'

'Dad, do you think Edward was the sort of boy who might grow up and want to be a monk?'

'How could I possibly know?'

'You couldn't,' Alex said. 'You saw the man I found in the woods. Was there anything familiar—'

'I'd have to be clairvoyant, psychic, whatever, to make a connection there. But they've got to find out who did that. There's someone very sick running around.' The doctor got to his feet and put down his glass. His agitation showed. 'That poor man couldn't have had a chance. He didn't even put up his hands to try to save himself.'

'Tony . . .' Alex turned to him. 'The story about the coffin.'

Looking as if he expected to be laughed at, Tony began, 'It's just some twaddle about Edward's hand getting caught when his mother's coffin was closed.'

'It did.'

They all fell silent. For the first time Alex noticed the slight hissing sound the artificial flames of the electric fire made. Still wearing his Barbour coat, Tony flexed his shoulders.

His father said, 'Where did that come from? How did you know about it?'

'Harriet and Mary mentioned it. They said Edward supposedly had his hand in his mother's coffin and they closed it without noticing. Broke his finger and it was never set.'

Doc James turned his face away. 'It was the only time I heard him speak clearly. He didn't want the finger touched because it was special, he said. It was between him and his mother or some such thing. I told his father that setting it would take more out of the child than it was worth. It would be a bigger job, but bones are broken again to get them properly set all the time. I expected Cornelius Derwinter to fight me about it but he didn't. Edward was a nice boy. Very deep and in a lot of emotional pain.'

'Do you think that's Edward's body in the morgue?' Tony asked.

'If it's Edward and he's Leonard's brother, DNA will prove it. That shouldn't be much longer now. They'll have taken a swab from Leonard, you can be sure of that. You may think nothing much is happening but I'd put money on this investigation getting a fair amount of attention from the police. They'll be in a hurry for that DNA. They'll also know if there's an old break to a finger.'

'Would whatever you don't want to talk about help clear all this up?' Alex said softly. Her eyes felt gritty and she longed to be somewhere completely quiet.

'No. If that were the case I wouldn't wait. What I do think is that the answers will turn out to be close to home. I only hope there isn't anyone else who could be a threat to the killer. They wouldn't be safe.'

Thirty-Two

'You're going to love the latest,' Bill Lamb said as O'Reilly buckled himself into his partner's car outside the Black Dog.

They pulled away rapidly and set out for the road up the hill and toward the Dimple. This morning the sky was clear enough to outline Tinley Tower on its vantage point in searing blue. 'The tooth' fitted its pointed, up-thrust, slightly leaning shape well, but O'Reilly wondered just why the earliest villagers had made the folly their settlement's namesake.

'You in a coma, Guv?' Lamb asked.

'I'm bloody tired, if that's what you mean. Sleep and this case don't go together. OK, spill the news. You're dying to.'

One of the good things about Lamb was that nastiness ran right off him. 'For once we've got a break. It's going to turn out to be a break, or else.'

'Or else?'

Lamb stuck a cigarette in the corner of his mouth, lighted it and squinted ahead through acrid smoke. 'Heads will roll,' he intoned, managing not to grin. 'The obit for the baby came from the announcements in some uppity small-circulation society rag. *Our Kind*, if you can believe that. One of our eager beaver boys went after their circulation list and got no joy. But the sheet of copy paper used for the obituary left on Alex's kitchen table turns out to come from a batch in use by the library system. Apparently a bunch of London libraries – in appropriate areas – carry the magazine, and the Home Counties, of course. No breaks for several hours but then he hit on a branch in Gloucester where a librarian remembered someone asking for an old copy of *Our Kind* in the last few days.'

O'Reilly gave the man his whole attention. 'Go on.'

'They've got CCTV. The Gloucester boys are going through the surveillance films and the librarian is helping. She thinks she might remember the man if she saw him.'

'But—'

'I know.' Lamb cut him off. 'We've got to be sure he wanted to look at the same copy with the obit. But the one he wanted was the right one – according to the librarian.'

'Don't suppose he was a regular, or she got his name?'

'No, but if he's on film and identifiable, we've got him.' Lamb negotiated the hill with the familiarity of one who had done so a few times before. 'You heard they put a rush on the DNA?'

'Yeah, I know. Could get it any time.'

'So what's the drill for this fishing expedition, Guv,' Lamb said.

They were on their way for an informal interview with Leonard Derwinter.

'Just that. I can smell a break and if these people aren't in the mix up to their necks, someone wants us to think they are. There's the entrance. Stags on the gateposts, huh? How high would you say those were? Twenty feet?'

'Conservatively.'

Impressive was an understatement for the Derwinter estate. It had to cover hundreds of acres and the pale honey-colored stone house itself, set a mile or so back from the road, stood in Georgian splendor amid sloping lawns, and pools more properly classified as lakes, where sculptures rose out of the water and stone urns of evergreen vines interrupted low walls at intervals.

O'Reilly had decided to have Lamb drive them there in the new gray Ford Fiesta which made Bill a happy man. The two of them worked well as an interview team and he wasn't in the mood to soft pedal anymore. He could feel facts tightening around them. Too bad he had yet to find some strong connecting pieces between the revelations.

'Will you look at this lot?' Bill said. 'Conspicuous consumption, or what?'

'That about covers it. See the workers' cottages in the distance. Good for a bit of pastoral color. Not close enough to mar the landscape but visible to prove how important it all is.'

'A lot of it will be farmland, right?' Lamb said. He inclined his head to numerous sheep huddled together around the trunks of great beech trees. 'Just sheep, you think? Or other livestock?'

'They're known for their stables and there's bound to be more. You can only see a sampling of what they've got from here, I shouldn't wonder.'

'This is only a sampling?' Lamb made a disbelieving sound and stopped the Ford at the bottom of the steps to the main doors. 'I'd like to see what the whole thing looks like then, boss.'

O'Reilly looked at him sideways. He'd never liked the 'boss' bit. 'None of this is what it once was,' he said. 'If it wasn't a working farm they'd probably be holding tours for the public and have a theme park.'

'A petting zoo,' Lamb said and laughed. 'Miniature train? An iced lolly and floss stand?'

'Down to business,' O'Reilly said, but he grinned. 'I think it'll work best if I'm Mr Sympathy.'

'Be my guest. Nice Guy was never in my MO.'

O'Reilly glanced thoughtfully at his second in command and partner. Here was one who hadn't had it easy, but under the hard crust everything wasn't completely without a shred of compassion.

They climbed out of the car and started up the steps, steps brushed clear of snow and coated with grit. Before they arrived at the top, one of the double doors opened and the sexy Heather Derwinter emerged to greet them. O'Reilly had never seen her without a tight high-necked jumper – this one white – and skin-tight jodhpurs. He was grateful there was no sun or the sheen on her boots might blind him. She no longer wore a sling, but held her left arm protectively against her ribs.

'Welcome,' she said, smiling and showing off beautiful teeth. 'We're expecting you.'

O'Reilly and Lamb automatically flipped out their warrant cards and introduced themselves, although they'd both met Heather Derwinter following her encounter with the dart in her horse's rump. She still had healing scratches on her face. They entered the house and O'Reilly nodded to a servant, a man in a dark suit, who hovered nearby.

The portraits that lined dark green silk-covered walls were of horses rather than ancestors, although the most prominent painting, large enough for small details to be more or less discernable at the top of a first flight of marble stairs, had to be of Heather Derwinter mounted on a handsome gray. Derwinter House was in the background, and the richness of rolling land.

'I didn't want Leonard to put it there,' she said, and O'Reilly realized she knew what he was looking at. 'He wouldn't listen. *Men*. Really.' She giggled and he didn't think she made that particular sound often. The message he got was to treat her gently, as Leonard's charming but uninvolved pet.

She led the way beneath lofty ceilings and through towering gilded doors into some sort of receiving room. The place was huge, furnished with elegant-looking antiques, although O'Reilly was no expert on that subject, and smelled heavily of the large floral arrangements on tables, desks and mantel.

Leonard rose from a straight-backed chair in an alcove where he had been reading – or holding a book open – and showed none of his wife's cheery countenance. 'Detectives,' he said, shaking hands with each of them. 'You must have news for me. I admit I've been edgy – more than edgy, waiting to find out what you know.'

'I'll ring for coffee,' Heather said. 'Elliot's nose is out of joint because I took over his duties at the door. Serving coffee will mend his ego.'

Mrs Derwinter had definite ideas about what assuaged the egos of the served and those who served, O'Reilly noted. 'We just had coffee,' he said, avoiding catching Lamb's eye. Bill would drink coffee whenever he could get it, which was most of the time. O'Reilly didn't want the interference of niceties.

Leonard didn't sit. He remembered the book he held and tossed it on a sofa with spindly legs that reflected in polished wood floors. 'So?' His raised eyebrows underscored the question.

'We'd like to talk more, Mr Derwinter,' O'Reilly said as if he didn't know the man was asking for DNA results. 'There have been some developments. Informal would be acceptable to us but you might prefer to have your solicitor. If that's—'

'Hell, no,' Leonard shot back. 'You're not accusing me of anything. Why would I need my solicitor? What did the test show?'

'Anxious about that, aren't you?' Lamb said, producing a notebook. 'What difference will it make one way or the other? The man's dead.'

Leonard stared, swallowed hard enough to make his throat jerk, and a flush spread over his olive skin.

'That's really not very nice, Detective,' Heather said behind them. 'Wouldn't you like to know if a man who was found dead was your brother or not?'

'Given that Mr Derwinter supposedly thought his brother had been dead for years he must be used to the idea.'

Time for the sympathy. 'Those results aren't back yet,' O'Reilly said pleasantly. 'Could we sit down and go over a few things?'

Leonard closed his eyes for an instant and let his hands fall to his sides. 'Of course.' He waved them to a pair of red velvet chairs and sat at one end of a facing loveseat.

This was just one of half-a-dozen potential conversation groupings in the room, which seemed like a lot of redundancy to O'Reilly.

Heather joined her husband on the couch and the girlish ingénue had left. The woman glared steadily at Lamb, who could always find a smile in such moments.

235

'Your brother, Edward, was older than you,' O'Reilly began. 'That would have made him your father's heir.'

'Correct.'

'Hypothetically, why would your father invent the death of a son?'

'He didn't,' Heather said reflexively. 'That couldn't have been Edward's body.'

Without turning to her, Leonard found his wife's hand and said, 'Shh, darling. I . . . I don't think that's what Father did but we'll have to wait for those results, won't we?'

O'Reilly switched his attention to Heather. 'I'm glad to see you're getting better, Mrs Derwinter. Would you hazard a guess about the reason why someone would want you to take a fall like that?'

She looked startled. 'No, how could I?'

'It ties you to the case. Since your husband's family is already heavily implicated – or potentially so – surely you have some thoughts about why you were singled out like that.'

She blushed. Heather Derwinter wasn't a blusher but he'd clearly caught her off guard. With a finger and thumbnails on her right hand, she traced the seams in her jodhpurs.

He saw inspiration clear her expression. 'Someone wants you to think we're involved,' she said, falling over her words. 'Why didn't I think about this before? They did it as a . . . what do you call it? A smokescreen. You know, they took a chance. Whoever stuck that dart in poor Shiny Boy had to do it while I was taking that hedge. If anything had gone just a little bit wrong, I'd have seen them – only I was too busy flying over Shiny Boy's head. Wretched nuisance.'

Unfortunately she might make perfect sense. He didn't respond.

'I bet the horse wasn't thinking it was a nuisance,' Lamb said. 'Poor devil.'

Bill was very good at setting people's teeth on edge.

'Could we go back to the death of Graham Cummings?' O'Reilly asked. He could still enjoy watching shock tactics work and Leonard fell against the back of his chair, his eyes haunted. 'You were very young at the time, Mr Derwinter.'

'And he wasn't there,' Heather put in. 'He couldn't have been more than six. Six-year-olds don't remember that sort of thing.'

A glance from Lamb reflected O'Reilly's own thought that Heather might need closer investigation herself.

'I remember,' Leonard said quietly. 'Afterward, anyway. Edward was in a terrible state. He didn't say anything, just muttered and stuttered while father raved.'

'But he was just a boy, too,' O'Reilly said. 'Eight or nine.'

Leonard nodded. 'Yes, and Doc James said it was an accident. Graham was playing in the shallows. He slipped and hit his head on a rock just under the water. How was Edward supposed to fix that?' He frowned and started to speak again, but closed his mouth.

'Yes, Mr Derwinter?' Lamb said. 'What else?'

'Nothing,' Heather said. 'Stop pushing him. Can't you see how painful this is?'

'We're dealing with a murder investigation,' O'Reilly said evenly. 'We have to pursue every angle.'

'Well, it can't have anything to do with a kid who drowned because he was fooling about in the water,' Heather said.

'Don't,' Leonard told her. 'My father thought it best for Edward to go where he could get a lot of peace and care, so that's what he did. Father was still grieving for my mother and he wasn't equipped to bring up two young boys on his own.'

O'Reilly pivoted again. 'Have you found your father's signet ring?'

Leonard put his face in his hands and shook his head, no.

'No, well, I'm sorry for all your troubles but would you look at this again.' He took the evidence bag containing the ring found on the hill from his pocket. It had been thoroughly examined for trace evidence and he slid it into his palm. 'Take a close look, sir.'

Reluctantly, Leonard picked up the ring and turned it this way and that, then he looked on the inside of the shank and grew quite still.

'What do you think?' O'Reilly said.

'Was this taken off the dead man's hand?'

'Possibly.' He didn't admit the ring might have been dropped by someone who did pull it from the corpse, and subsequently found in a patch of gorse and stones.

'It was my father's.' Leonard's lips were colorless.

'But they didn't find it on the body,' Heather said, all urgency. 'They've just admitted that. For

238

all they know, your father lost it on the hill years ago. He loved to ramble all over the place. He used to turn the ring around and around because it was uncomfortable. What if he did that when he was out walking, lost the thing, and never did anything about it.'

'You've a neat train of thought, madam,' Lamb said with a slight smirk. 'Orderly thinking, as it were.'

She scowled at him. 'You're on a fishing expedition.'

O'Reilly almost laughed.

'Who was there when the Cummings boy died?' He liked to keep the subject off balance. 'Your father?'

'I . . . I can't think why he would have been.'

'But Edward was there. Why was that?'

'Edward liked the river. Father took him into Bourton-on-the-Water with him sometimes so he could be by the Windrush.'

'So your father was there when the other boy died.'

'Perhaps he was. I don't know. I wasn't there, was I?'

'So you say.' He didn't want Leonard to get his feet under him. 'How did the Cummings boy come to be there with Edward?'

'Will Cummings was there, too,' Leonard said and turned his face away. 'He'd have had to be. Graham was too small to be on his own.'

'But you don't know if your father was there or if he just left a young son to wander by the river on his own?'

'Will could have been watching both of them

239

if Father was seeing someone about business. But Father was there after Graham had the accident. I remember that. He was distraught . . . angry. Damn it, what does this have to do with a dead man on that hill – or another man dying at the rectory – only days ago? Graham Cummings was nothing to us – the child of an employee – and he's been dead for years.'

'Leonard!' Heather looked over her shoulder. She stood and took several steps away from the couch. 'Cathy, how lovely to see you. I was going to call you when I could ride again.'

Cathy Cummings hovered on the threshold of the room, a bunch of paper-wrapped flowers in her hands. She seemed unable to move and her face was stretched into stricken agony. 'I brought you these,' she said finally, her voice breaking. She looked at the flowers. 'Because you had an accident.'

Elliot hovered behind her, all but wringing his hands at having let her arrive on the scene without warning. She turned and thrust the bouquet at him, already running from the room.

Lamb's mobile rang and he answered. He said, 'Yes,' twice and clicked off. 'Results are in,' he told O'Reilly.

'And . . .'

'Mr Derwinter here and the dead man were related.'

Leonard choked. He bent over to rest his face on his knees. He didn't make a sound but his back heaved.

Thirty-Three

He didn't have to be with Alex to see her face. All he had to do was think about her. Tony went into the inn entrance at the Black Dog and walked through to the public bar. He stopped to watch her sliding the stems of clean glasses into racks above the counter.

His life was a bloody mess. Oh, on the surface he had it all together, but there was major unfinished business and he couldn't do one thing to tie it up.

Did that have anything to do with what had become a complicated connection with Alex?

She had to stand on tiptoe to seat those glasses but she didn't have the look of a lot of small women who managed the impression that a good wind would blow them away. Alex was compact. When she forgot herself she could be vivacious and he'd seen that come peeking through. And he liked her looks, those tilted-up eyes the kids called 'witchy' back when they were all running the fields and getting into trouble. Like scrumping apples and making it away, pockets bulging, arms flying, laughing madly, and with yelling voices behind them.

It was a long time since they had been children.

'Good morning, Alex,' he said, and smiled when she saw him. 'It's quiet in here.'

241

'Probably a good thing. I'm on my own. Cathy and Will both asked for the day off – or Cathy did, then Will got in a mood and said he needed to get away.'

'I can help if you tell me what to do.' He knew how unlikely that sounded. 'Katie thinks she's a pub dog anyway.' Katie was already beside Bogie in front of the fire.

'That's sweet of you,' Alex said. 'I've got extra staff coming in shortly and Mum's in the kitchen if I need her. But right now it's just you – my one and only customer. What can I get you, Dr Harrison?' She grinned and that vivacious girl came out to play again.

'Coffee, me darlin',' he said and stood with his forearms crossed on the bar and a boot braced on the brass foot rail. 'And I wouldn't say no to a nice Tesco's digestive biscuit.'

She poured a mug of coffee, paused, and poured a second mug. That was all it took to make him feel warmer. Alex coming to join him and drink coffee. He didn't mention that she'd forgotten the biscuits.

'Have you seen O'Reilly today?' he asked.

'No. I assume he left very early. I feel as if there's a huge shoe hovering just out of sight, waiting to give all of us one big kick in the posterior.'

Tony snorted into a fist. 'Posterior? Now there's a word I don't often hear.'

She frowned, set her mouth in a line and suddenly said, 'Arse. Is that better?'

They both sniggered into their coffee and Alex held up a finger before grabbing a package of digestive biscuits from a shelf. Coffee, biscuits and sporadic sniggering had the expected result, and they both caught sprays of crumbs in napkins.

She sobered first. 'I think I'm getting hysterical. If some sort of religious person – the official kind – walked through the door, I'd faint. Early this morning I was on the internet searching for anything I could find about gyrovagi. Nothing very complimentary was said about them, at least not a century ago, or even ten. They were persecuted. I don't think Percy or Edward were wandering charlatans likely to whip out the odd potion for getting rid of evil spirits, or wooden dolls for warding off whatever. They just didn't have a need for a group. They didn't need to belong. And they liked being free.'

'So you're sure it was Edward?'

She looked thoughtful. 'I called him that, didn't I? Don't you think that's who it was?'

'Probably. But the idea of some anti-religious zealot knocking off men of the cloth doesn't cut it for me. I believe there's a history to all this and the Derwinters are tied in somehow.'

'They have to be,' Alex agreed. 'But not, you know . . .'

'No, of course not,' he filled in for her. Neither of them wanted to even mention murder in the same breath with Leonard and Heather.

A phone rang and Alex went to answer.

Liz Hadley walked in behind the bar, glancing around the empty room with a frown on her face.

'Business will pick up,' Tony told her.

'It better,' she said. 'I closed the shop early when I heard Alex needed help – not that I had any customers either. I think all this trouble is starting to keep people home.'

She might be right but he didn't want to say so. 'It's been cold a long time. We all get tired of braving it eventually. How's the shop doing?'

'Not too bad,' Liz said. 'It's always a bit quiet in Bourton at this time of year but Christmas was really good and it's light now, but not dead.' She raised her shoulders slightly and grimaced at him.

Death had become an avoided topic.

Four people who looked like businessmen came in, talking and chuckling their way to a table. One of them came to the bar to order drinks and food. Liz went busily about her own business and looked more cheerful immediately.

The coffee was good. Getting a little cool but still good.

With the phone still to her ear, Alex pivoted slowly toward him. Her eyes downcast, a deep furrow between her brows, she spoke quietly. When she glanced up their eyes met. He knew real concern when he saw it.

She put down the phone and went directly to Liz, then almost ran through to the kitchen. Lily came back with her, wearing a similarly worried expression.

Tony's gut clenched. He took a deep breath, watched Alex, and waited.

Finally she hurried to him and leaned close. 'I'm not supposed to say anything in case someone else gets the idea to follow me.'

'Follow you where?' He realized he'd all but shouted and lowered his voice. 'What are you talking about?'

'That was a nurse at St Mary's Hospital in London.' She spoke so close to his ear; her cheek brushed against his. 'Reverend Restrick is there and he's asking to see me. She said Charlotte asked them to call me.'

'His wife?' He caught her by the shoulders. 'Does that make sense? That he'd ask to see you? Why didn't Charlotte Restrick call you herself?'

'I don't know but she probably couldn't leave him for long enough.' Alex closed her eyes. 'I've got to go. Now. If anyone asks, make an excuse for me. I've picked up a bug – anything. I haven't told anyone but you about the call. All Mum knows is that I have to leave.'

'I'll come with you.'

'No.' She shook her head emphatically. 'I think he's going to tell me more about what happened to Brother Percy.'

'You don't know that.' He could tell she wasn't really listening to him.

'Why else would he ask to see me in particular? I trust you not to tell anyone, Tony. Back me up with this, will you? I'll go straight there and call you after I've seen him. If we went together and O'Reilly heard about it, he might suspect we were *meddling* – which is what he thinks we're up to anyway.'

'I don't want you to go on your own.' He cast about for something to back up his case. 'The roads are bad.'

'And I'm a damn good driver. I'll call you on the way.'

Thirty-Four

Alex warmed up the Land Rover thoroughly, hovered at the exit from the yard behind the pub until she could be sure of getting out without being seen, and gunned the engine.

She hoped no one looked through a window to see her slide, half sideways, on to the road.

Tony's opinion of this trip had been obvious – he didn't want her to go. Her mother had looked anxious when all she'd been told was that Alex would probably be gone the rest of the day and possibly night. But Lily made a habit of not asking for information that wasn't offered, so didn't know where Alex was going.

Mixed rain and snow in the early morning had reverted to steady, light snow a couple of hours ago. The roads were covered with a layer thin enough to allow the heavy vehicle to sink straight through to the crunchy, frozen remains of the last fall that had frozen there.

Her route was the same old B4068 until she could cut off toward Bourton-on-the-Water and the A429. Then she hadn't far to go before she passed within a couple of miles of Upper and Lower Slaughter toward the A road.

Alex had only traveled a couple of miles between dry stone walls and frostbitten hedgerows when a farmer ventured from a gate, signaled with his crook, and a herd of sheep like puffed up marshmallows on dark sticks came pouring across the road. A sheepdog raced, belly to the ground, from one side of the group to the other, disappearing back into the exit field for stragglers before shooting out to funnel his charges to their destination and a good feed.

When her breath started making clouds of vapor, Alex remembered to turn on the heater. With her thick coat she hadn't felt the cold before. Alex Duggins had been watching sheep herded across roads, paths and tracks since her earliest memories.

Duggins. Yes, she liked being Alex Duggins again. It felt right and it was who she was. Her marriage, or most parts of it, seemed far away. She was starting to heal in some ways.

At last, the gates were closed and the roadway clear. She drove fairly slowly, on the lookout for more obstacles, until she made the final turn toward Bourton.

As she got around the bend she saw a familiar red vehicle up on the left verge. Will Cummings' panel van with the bonnet up.

Will's head and upper body emerged from the innards of the Volkswagen and he immediately jumped up and down and waved his arms.

Smiling, she ran the Land Rover on to the verge and stopped in front of him. He arrived at her window as she got it rolled down. 'Didn't you think I'd see you?' she chuckled. 'Jumping jacks on a day like this will give you a heart attack. Or they'd give me one.'

'That thing was just serviced,' he sputtered. 'I called the mechanic and his wife said he's out and there's no one else to come. Ah, that's the way it is these days. Used to be a man's work was his pride and he'd want to get here any way he could. Not now. They all feel too sodding important – beggin' your pardon, but truth be told he's probably in front of the telly watching *Coronation Street.*'

'Let me help, Will.' Alex was anxious. She wanted to get into London as quickly as possible.

'Well—' He looked her in the eye, then settled his attention on the distance where only snow-covered fields with a white pall hanging above them could be of interest. 'Hmm. P'raps I should try myself a bit longer.'

'That's silly, Will. Lock it up and I'll drive you until we can find someone to come and get it going – or give you a tow.'

His gray woolen hat sat atop his head as if it would pop off at any second. Despite the cold he was perspiring and his face shone. His agitation was catching.

'Not all of them work on diesel,' he said. Finally he added: 'Thank you, I'll take you up on your offer,' slammed down his bonnet and ran around to the passenger side of the Land Rover.

As soon as he was buckled in, she took off again. 'Shall I go into Bourton?'

His sigh was huge. 'To tell the truth, I'm in a pickle. I've got to get to London. Fast.'

She glanced at him. 'Where in London?'

He drummed his fists on his thighs. 'Any Tube station will do. I can get where I want easy enough.'

Could he be going to Reverend Restrick, too? She dare not ask.

'I'm going into London. I can take you where you need to go.' She smiled. 'As long as it isn't Wapping or somewhere. I'd only get lost there.'

He took a while to respond, then said, 'Whereabouts are you going?'

This wasn't her strong suit, making things up on the fly. 'I'm meeting some old friends from art school. They're in Notting Hill.' That wasn't so far from Praed Street and St Mary's but it wouldn't give her real destination away.

'I'll be glad of that then, lass,' he said, sounding as he had when she was a girl. 'You're an old hand at the drive but I bet I can show you a shorter way to the A429.'

Thirty-Five

Beer wasn't Tony's drink of choice. He nursed a pint of local Ambler – which he could probably learn to love – afraid that if he drank the whiskey he preferred he'd go through too much, too fast. He could be sitting in the Black Dog a long time, repeatedly checking his watch and meeting Lily's anxious glances.

Each time he looked in her direction, she stared back while she rubbed at the same area of the bar.

He needed his wits about him.

Alex had only been gone . . . thirty minutes. With the roads the way they were she wouldn't be moving fast. But she'd promised to call and that could be at any moment.

249

It was too soon yet.

He took out his mobile and put it on the table.

Cathy Cummings arrived. She didn't greet him, or seem to notice him, didn't even greet Lily behind the bar, just got to work serving the straggle of customers making it in for lunch.

The noise level was rising and Lily remembered to put some music on. One of the customers whooped, 'Dirty Hat Band, yeah.'

Lily was good at assessing a crowd.

The inn door opened and Bill Lamb came in with Constable Smith. The younger man sniffed appreciatively at the lunch smells and was obviously pleased to be out of the cold.

Lamb made straight for Tony but searched the whole room while he came. He nodded at Tony's dad, who arrived and sat at the table.

'Where's Ms Bailey-Jones?' Lamb asked, standing beside them. Smith got a little closer to the fire and Bogie got up to give him a sniff and a tail wag.

'Not here at the moment,' Tony said, chewing the side of a thumb, a nervous habit he'd forgotten years ago.

'Where is she?'

For once, Lamb's pushy approach raised more pit-of-the-stomach foreboding than irritation. The man expected him to know where Alex was?

'You aren't usually here if she's not, or so I'm told. Why did you come now?'

'To have a drink.'

'Don't be smart with me. Is Will Cummings here?'

Tony ran a hand around the back of his neck.

Lily had brought his dad a coffee. 'No, he isn't. Alex said he was in a bit of a down mood and took off for the rest of the day. Cathy's here.' Although he couldn't see her at the moment.

'Damn.'

Tony raised his eyebrows but his heart started to do odd things. 'Where are you going with this, Lamb?'

'You haven't seen Alex today? She isn't at the lodge, or her mother's cottage. And you don't have a clue where she is? You expect me to believe that?'

Pushing his half-empty glass away, Tony struggled to keep his voice even. 'I already said I saw her earlier. She isn't here now, and I don't know anything else.'

Lamb stared him down.

'What's going on?' He'd promised not to tell anyone where Alex had gone but he wasn't feeling secure about any of his decisions right now.

'Come to the parish hall, please. Now.' He gestured to Smith and said something to him that Tony couldn't hear. The constable went to the bar.

Tony was instantly on his feet. 'Something's badly wrong, isn't it?' he said in a quiet voice, staring from his dad to Lamb. 'You're looking for Alex . . . and it sounds as if you're looking for Will Cummings, too.'

'I'll come with you.' The unmistakable loss of color in his father's face did nothing for Tony's confidence.

'We'll be back,' Tony called to Lily, deliberately cheerful. 'We aren't done with those.' He pointed to their glasses on his way to the door.

The tea towel she'd been polishing with was wadded between Lily's clenched hands. 'I'll be waiting, Tony,' she told him and, for the first time he remembered, there were tears in her eyes.

Getting to the parish hall on foot only took minutes.

Uncomfortable minutes.

Tony's father strode along with his chin thrust forward, his hair a white halo in the sharp reflected light, and a silent attitude that didn't invite conversation. Not that they were likely to say much with Lamb there.

Too many vehicles for comfort crammed the sides of the road outside the hall. Tony didn't like the van with an aerial, or two others with locking compartments on the sides.

Lamb sprinted ahead. James Harrison kept pace with Tony running up the front steps and inside.

More trestle tables had been put into service and two officers worked over a map on the hanging boards. Each time an instruction was called out by one of a group gathered around a computer screen, several wearing headsets and mouth-pieces, one of the two drew another line on the map.

The place was freezing and all the officers wore their greatcoats. The smell of old coffee permeated the air and sandwich wrappers overflowed two bins.

Lamb went to take up a place beside O'Reilly, and a man Tony recognized as Madden from an earlier encounter. Several constables concentrated on another screen. Lamb talked close beside his boss's ear.

'Has something else happened?' Tony said. He made straight for O'Reilly and Lamb's group.

The group fell silent, but continued to watch the screen.

'Was Alex still at the Black Dog when Will Cummings left?' O'Reilly asked.

Tony swallowed. 'Yes. He'd already left when I got there. Is this significant?'

'We wouldn't be talking about it if it wasn't,' Lamb snapped, and got a quelling glance from his boss.

'Come and look at this,' O'Reilly said.

Tony's father went with him to stand behind the computer. The men and women moved to make room for them. 'What are we looking at?' his dad wanted to know.

On the screen, a grainy video moved in a loop, repeating over and over again. A man walked from a building, paused to look in every direction and opened a folder file to check the contents, which looked to be scant.

'Watch him walk,' Lamb said. 'Look at his face, or what you can see of it. Is he familiar?'

Crouching, Tony gripped the edge of the table and stared closely at the screen. 'Any hints? What am I looking at?'

'That's the library on Brunswick Road. In Gloucester,' O'Reilly said. 'We've been tracing the obituary that was pinned – or darted – to Alex's kitchen table.'

Tony turned to look at O'Reilly, 'And?'

'We think that man is leaving with the photo-copy of that obituary. It's from a magazine called *Our Kind*.'

Incredulous, Tony turned back to the screen. 'You mean that could be the man who was in Lime Tree Lodge?'

Grunts were the only answers he got. His dad leaned over his shoulder. The hand he rested beside Tony's turned white-knuckled. 'Can you freeze the picture on the man and make him closer?'

'Already done,' O'Reilly said, hitting a key. 'We had it isolated and they got rid of as much pixilation as they could.'

The close up was still blurred. A man in a woolen hat. Stocky. Angry.

'Doctor Harrison?' O'Reilly said, touching that white-knuckled hand. 'Tony, is it him?'

'Oh, yeah. It's Will Cummings,' James Harrison said before Tony could answer.

'Getting Cummings, and fast, is a priority, but we need to make sure Alex is in a safe place,' O'Reilly said. 'Are you sure you don't know where she might be, Tony?'

Protesting incoherently, Cathy Cummings was led in by Constable Smith, who looked more than gloomy at his task. He held Cathy's upper arm as she tried to twist away.

'Not back here,' O'Reilly said and pointed to a chair in front of the table. 'Hello, Mrs Cummings. Take a seat.'

'I want to go home,' she said quietly. 'Please can I go home. I can't help you with anything.'

'She hasn't so far, boss,' Smith said unhappily. 'Doesn't know anything about anything.'

O'Reilly smiled kindly at the woman. 'We meet again, Cathy. Twice in one day. You were upset at the Derwinters.'

Her expression changed, turned hard and angry. 'Leonard said my boy meant nothing to him. Nothing to *them.* If it had been his boy who died in that river it would have meant something. Graham was a lovely little boy. Cornelius Derwinter tried to make it as right as he could but then . . .' She looked startled and closed her mouth.

'It's all right,' O'Reilly said. 'Terrible thing, to lose your child.'

'You can't blame Will for feeling the way he does. The Black Dog has been his reason to get up in the morning. Cornelius couldn't have meant the money to stop coming for us. He wanted us there. It was Leonard and Heather who interfered – but it was all going to be all right in the end if Alex would—' Again the frightened, bewildered look.

'Constable Smith is going to take you into the station, Cathy,' O'Reilly said. 'He'll make sure you get to say your piece with a solicitor there. Always good to have a solicitor to guide you.'

'I didn't want anything to happen to Alex,' Cathy muttered. 'She's kind, always was. If only she'd given up and gone away again.' She let Smith guide her away.

Tony met his father's eyes. 'Alex got a call from St Mary's Hospital in London. Supposedly Reverend Restrick is asking for her and Mrs Restrick had a nurse make a call to Alex. She's on her way there now.'

By the time O'Reilly was on his feet he had car keys in one hand. 'Do you know exactly what route she'd take?' he asked Tony.

'Yes.' The shortest was obvious.

'Do we have solid coordinates for her mobile yet?' Lamb roared. 'They've had long enough.'

'Should do anytime now, Sarg,' one of the line-drawers at the boards said.

Tony looked at the man over his shoulder. They were in crisis mode here and seriously searching for Alex.

'Reverend Restrick is still in a coma,' O'Reilly said, jogging for the door with Lamb behind him. 'Absolutely no visitors. He's had two surgeries to relieve the pressure on his brain. His wife can stand by his bed for five minutes at a time. If there had been any change in his condition, I'd know. There's round-the-clock security on him. No one would call Alex and tell her to visit – no one who didn't have another reason for wanting her on her own and away from here.'

They dashed down the steps outside.

'You should have told us about the call Alex got right off,' Lamb said through his teeth. 'We've wasted time.'

'I'm coming,' Tony's father said. 'There are things you've got to know but we can't hang around talking. I've been a fool. I didn't think . . . Will . . . I just didn't think it of him.'

'We're both coming,' Tony said. He opened the back door of O'Reilly's Volvo and got in. 'Why not have me call her when you think the time's right? If there's someone with her who shouldn't be, a call from the police could be dangerous.'

'Why do you think we're working on her location?' Lamb said. 'You don't have to ring a mobile to find out where it is – if you're lucky.'

256

They were triangulating or whatever they did. Using phone towers to try to find Alex. 'You really think Will could be with her, don't you?'

'He might be,' O'Reilly said, starting the car and swinging it in a tight circle before spitting snow and gravel from beneath racing wheels. 'Now he's our number one suspect for planting that obituary at Alex's, it's likely.'

'Would he kill Edward because he blamed him for the accident that killed little Graham Cummings?' Tony said. 'If Edward went to the pub the night he died, Will might have recognized him and flipped out. Then, when Brother Percy showed up, he could have been afraid he'd let the cat out of the bag about Edward's identity and the game would be over. I'm very sure he didn't want that – I just can't work out why. Not definitely.'

'Cathy probably called Will after she was at the Derwinters' this morning,' Lamb said. 'He's already on the edge – make that over the edge. Hearing his boy's death had been dismissed like that would be enough to finish it. I think he's been trying to frighten Alex into leaving the village. Cathy backed that one up, sure.'

'Leaving the pub he thinks should still be his, you mean,' James Harrison said.

Thirty-Six

'There's an extra mug in the cubby,' Alex told Will. 'Flask is by your feet. It's pretty good

257

coffee. My mother made it.' She took a now tepid sip from her own cup. It was strong and wet and that was all. She didn't care much.

'Not for me,' Will said. He'd unhitched the shoulder harness from his seatbelt and leaned forward, staring through the window as if he could make the journey go faster. 'Bloody road works don't help anything,' he muttered. 'These sods'll still be leaning on the same shovels in the same spots come next Christmas. Lazy bastards.' His demeanor had flipped.

'You're in a nice mood,' she said, hoping to calm him down. She didn't fancy the drive to London in the company of an angry man. 'We're all tired of the bad weather and inconvenience. Winter gets to be too long, doesn't it?'

'A lot of things get to be too long.' He turned sideways in his seat, facing away from her. 'You must have had enough of everything in Folly by now. I'm surprised you haven't already gone back to your art permanently. I thought you'd be gone long ago. You moved on to get away from the village when you went off to school.'

'And I came back because it's home and there was nothing tying me anywhere else – not any more.'

His foul temper bothered her. She felt trapped but there was nothing she could do to change his mood until he was ready to relax.

'Underhill was your home, not Folly,' he said. 'You and Lil. That's where you're from.'

She thought about what he'd said. 'Could you top up my coffee, please, Will?' she said, buying time while she tried to work out what was bothering him.

'Your wish is my command,' Will said, and at least he was careful not to slop hot coffee from the flask. 'You like giving the orders. Fell right into being the boss lady like a pig sliding in shit.'

'If you don't want to pour it, I'll pull off and do it myself. I'm used to being on my own.'

He'd already dealt with the coffee and was tightening down the lid on the flask. 'Ah, you're no different from anyone else. You like being a big fish in a little pond.'

She accepted the cup and took a slow, considering sip, screwing up her eyes against the steam. 'Are you trying to make a point, Will? It's not like you to say nasty things. Are you trying to goad me, or what?'

He leaned against the back of the seat and crossed his arms. 'You don't think much about how other people feel, do you?'

'Yes, I do,' she snapped back, tempted to pull over. But she couldn't bring herself to tell him to get out in awful weather, with no transportation and the traffic works barriers and signs lining the verge leaving nowhere safe to walk. 'Tell me what put a bee in your bonnet, Will. You know I care a lot about you and Cathy. One of the reasons I bought the Black Dog was because I knew you'd be great managers, and because I didn't want you to leave. You love the place.'

'And you wanted Lil to—'

'Lily,' Alex interrupted. 'My mother goes by Lily and always has.'

'Lil's a good barmaid's name,' he said, and she felt rather than saw him sneer. 'And that's what Cathy and me called her. We gave her a job when no one else was keen to take a young woman with a history like hers.'

'That's enough.' Alex's cheeks burned. She felt sick to her stomach and shaky. 'You don't know my mother's real history and even if it was what you're suggesting, who would care? Now or then? She's good at whatever she decides to do. Anyone with a suitable job would have hired her. Would you like me to find a bus stop for you?'

Breath whistled through his teeth. 'I'm in a lousy mood, is all. Cathy's mooning around over the life she should have had. Came from money, y'know.'

'So I heard. She seems happy to me – at least, most of the time. With everything in the village so upside down I think it's been hard for her. She's a quiet person.'

'You don't know anything about her, but no matter. You could be right. We'll turn off before long. We won't get all this messing about on the back roads.'

He leaned forward again, gripped the dashboard.

Alex glanced toward him. He seemed to be watching for whatever turn off he wanted.

Her mobile rang. She picked it up from between the seats and answered. 'It's Tony,' a wonderfully familiar voice said.

'Hi Tony.' She gathered her thoughts for how she could signal that something might be wrong here. 'I've got—'

Will's right hand clamped her shoulder painfully. He shook his head, pointed to himself and mouthed, *I'm not here.* His face was red and sweaty.

'Hi, Tony,' she said. Her dry mouth made her cough.

'What's up?' he said, quite softly, as if he wondered if she had company.

'The roads are pretty rotten but I'm taking it slowly. Road works everywhere. Why they don't try to get this stuff finished before winter, I'll never know.'

'Where's your sense of adventure?' he said, but there was something forced about it. 'I wanted to make sure you're OK, Alex.'

Will passed a forefinger across his throat, indicating for her to get off the phone. To her horror, he pinched the sensitive muscle in the top of her shoulder and she almost hissed in a sharp breath.

'Yes,' she said into the phone, completely flat.

Tony fell silent. She heard the sound of an engine and knew he must be in his Land Rover.

'You shouldn't drive and talk on the phone,' Alex said. 'Sorry, I forgot you have hands-free and I know I ought to get it. But I've learned to improvise. If traffic's heavy I can have both hands on the wheel and talk at the same time.' It was the closest she could get to telling him what she intended to do.

'Is someone with you?'

She didn't answer.

'OK. Please stay calm, sweetheart. I'll get you.'

'Sounds like fun. I'd better concentrate. I'll see you later.' It wasn't easy to keep fear out of her eyes and off her face when she looked at Will, but she managed and tucked the mobile into the door armrest without turning it off. 'Nice to have someone care about you. It's been a long time.'

'You ought to be careful around young Harrison.' Will laughed, an unpleasant sound. 'It's a shame not to control the few things you can do something about.'

'What does that mean?'

'There's more to our vet than most people think. That's all I'm saying. Not that it matters.'

'Will, what's wrong? Whatever it is, I'll try to help you.'

He narrowed his eyes at her and she felt his hatred. Why would he hate her?

'You're nothing,' he said. 'Nothing better than me, anyway. Maybe not as good. Think about that. You come from nothing but you managed to get your hands on things that don't belong to you. I'm going to change that. Take a right here.'

'Here?' He'd indicated something no bigger than a lane. 'What's it called?' she asked loudly.

'Doesn't matter. Do what I say – it'll be a shortcut for us.'

'I don't think so, Will. It's going off in the wrong direction.'

'Do as I say.'

A pine cone hit the windscreen and she swerved, flinching.

'Concentrate. When we get where we're going I'll tell you a story. You're never going to believe it.' He laughed and the sound made her sweat.

She started the right turn. 'Look, there's a llama farm up here,' she cried, laughing and coughing at the same time. She cleared her throat and all but screamed, 'Who has a llama farm? Have you ever been to a llama farm?' as if it were the funniest thing she'd ever seen.

Thirty-Seven

The four men in the Volvo didn't need a warning to remain silent. Tony had put his hand over the mobile and the others read horror in his face. Lamb took out a notebook and pen and began to write, then put a note in front of O'Reilly, who nodded.

He showed the note to the other two. 'We've got to hang on to Alex but get off the speaker from our end. I can do that and listen.'

Silently, Tony gave the man his phone. Lamb slid on a headset and attached a wire to the mobile. He made some adjustments and said, 'Now I can hear them but they wouldn't hear us. We're off at this end.'

'Where are they?' O'Reilly drove fast, while Tony prayed they wouldn't have to deal with a zealous police stop. 'Can't use a light or siren,' O'Reilly added, as if he read Tony's mind.

'They can't be far from Bourton-on-the-Water but Will told her to turn off.'

'Turn off where, man?' O'Reilly said. 'They're headed for the A40.'

The rare sound of car horns blared all around them. A path had begun to open as vehicles swerved out of the way.

'Alex is shrieking about something,' Lamb said. 'Laughing?'

Tony's stomach turned over. 'Is she still shouting about a llama farm?'

263

'Yeah . . . No, not any more. She doesn't know where they are . . . He keeps telling her to just drive.'

'She was trying to let you know where she was,' James Harrison said. Like Tony, he leaned forward to grip the seat in front of him. 'Llama farm? You know anyone with llamas? Treat any?'

'Will's losing it,' Lamb said, looking at Tony. 'He hates her.'

'I don't care what—'

Lamb's upheld hand shut Tony up.

'According to him, if she'd kept her nose out of it he'd have been all right. The money had started coming again. *It was more than I ever hoped for*. I'm quoting Will here. That silly bugger Leonard found where that piece of filth, Cornelius Derwinter, kept an account he used to keep current with what he owed me.'

'*Owed* him,' James Harrison scoffed.

'Psht!' Lamb's hand went up again. 'The fool had started paying up again – took him a bit but he got the picture in the end. Either he paid me or I let everyone know about his sainted father. That slag of a wife of his, snooty bitch, she was on my side whether she wanted to be or not. She wasn't having her crown tarnished. It was beautiful. If bloody Edward hadn't come back from the dead, showing up at the Black Dog and wanting to do his holier-than-thou revelation of the truth so he could throw forgiveness around, we wouldn't be here now – as long as you took the hint you weren't wanted and cleared out. Uppity cow.'

'Code,' O'Reilly said, driving between two

lorries with flapping canvas sides. 'Sounds like code.'

'I want to get my hands on him,' Tony said, and didn't even close his eyes against being turned into a lorry sandwich on a non-existent lane. 'No more doubt it was Edward.'

'Think about llamas,' his father shouted. 'And listen to me. Graham Cummings wasn't Graham Cummings. He was Cornelius Derwinter's boy.'

'For God's sake, Dad. Are you serious?'

'Never more serious. I always wondered if Will had anything to do with Edward being sent away. A sort of payoff because Cornelius had his two sons and had even taken away the one Will thought was his. I heard Will try to say Edward pushed the little boy but he wasn't like that. It would never have happened – and he was almost catatonic by the time I got to the river. And nowhere near where Graham had fallen.'

'Shit,' O'Reilly muttered. 'That's what this was all about. Will being cuckolded and turning it to his own advantage. Perpetual payoff. What kind of a man does that? If he'd killed Cornelius I might have got it, but all this?'

'Listen,' Tony's dad said. 'Will wasn't to know what could happen if he left a young wife alone in a cottage up on the Derwinter estate. Cornelius had a reputation. After his wife died . . . well, with or without Cathy's willing participation, she became pregnant but nothing was said. That's how I pieced it all together. Cathy as good as admitted it to me at one point. It was obvious Will never knew until the accident, and given that there was never any sign of another pregnancy with him and Cathy, it could be he's sterile. That drives some men mad. It wasn't until the lad hit his head and drowned that it came out, and then it was only by chance I overheard what I did. When I got there Cornelius Derwinter had the boy's body in his arms and he was crying over him. I heard him say, 'My son, my son.' Will heard it, too. I'm sure he didn't know before that. But it was obvious he got it then. He looked at me and I saw it in his eyes. It was never mentioned again. Next we knew, Will and Cathy were in the Black Dog – it belonged to Cornelius, like most things around here.'

Signs for the villages of Upper and Lower Slaughter came up on the left.

'Llama farm!' Tony yelled. 'I've seen it. Back there. We've gone past the bloody thing.'

'Oh, fuck!' O'Reilly checked his rear- and side-view mirrors. 'Hold on. Use the light, Bill. Can't risk the siren.'

Lamb lowered his window and slapped a light up top. O'Reilly leaned on the horn. Oncoming traffic in the other lane reacted slowly, a van driver hitting his brakes, then speeding up again. Two cars after him did the same thing.

A motorcycle tried to get off the road and hit an orange and yellow barricade, sending splintered wood and metal flying and workers leaping for a ditch.

'Pay attention, you stupid gits!' Lamb yelled. 'Something's changing in Alex's car, boss. He's yelling at her so loud I can't hear a word. He's threatening her, I can tell that much.'

266

Thirty-Eight

'Fucking bitch,' Will bellowed at Alex. 'Give that to me.' He reached across her for the phone.

She punched at him. 'Stop it. I'll go off the road.'

'We're going off the road anyway. Give that to me.'

Punching him again, crying out, Alex veered to the left, hit a broken branch loaded with snow. The load cascaded in front of her and she drove blind, the wipers pressing a film of instantly frozen snow against the windscreen.

Will slugged her across the jaw, snapped her head around and grabbed at the phone again.

He slammed a hand over hers on the wheel and tried to ram a foot down on her boot to press the brake. His jacket slid up and a piece of steel handle gleamed in his back pocket. A knife.

She was dead. She knew she was dead.

With her left hand, she managed to close her fingers around her coffee mug. The drink wasn't scalding but it was hot enough when it splattered into his eyes.

Will screamed and went for his knife. The blade, curved, evilly pointed and double-edged, ridged on one side, shot out.

A bloody gash opened across Alex's knuckles.

She didn't pause.

Her seatbelt responded to a single jab with a

thumb and she was out of the Land Rover in one motion, snatching the phone on the way.

She had no time. No time to save herself. Fighting, batting at laden branches, sliding down a bank, tripping over hidden tangles of under-growth, Alex threw herself away from the vehicle.

Losing him was the only escape she could think of. If she ran along the road she would be clearly in his sight. They hadn't passed another car on this rutted way that was barely more than a lane. On the open she'd be an easy target.

With every stumbling step, every painful, wracking breath she took, a space on her back, between her shoulder blades, prickled and burned. The hunting knife, switch blade, whatever the horrible thing was, could hit there and sink in, go through her entire body like a hot wire through butter.

A spatter of scarlet drops sprayed the snow.

Her hand. He would see the blood and follow, like a trail of murderous breadcrumbs.

With a couple of tugs, the scarf around her neck came loose and she wrapped it around her fist, held the injured hand up while she stumbled on. One foot after another sank into the soft drifts.

It was like climbing through crusted meringue. Slow, slow, slow, and her thighs already ached from the rush of adrenaline and the cold she met with each move.

The incline threw her forward, struggling to keep her balance, wading. More trees awaited her at the bottom of the steep bank and she pushed through the first cross-hatched twigs and limbs, flinching at the barrage of wet sticks that struck her face.

Her heart beat harder but easier. She might have lost him. Not a sound came from behind her. The coffee could have done more harm than she hoped. Closer and closer together, the trees rose from uneven ground she couldn't see. Rocks caught at her feet and thorns tore through her jeans to scratch her legs.

She heard sounds now, but they came from her breath and her rasping throat.

If she was calm, she could move silently through all this.

Alex swung around, searched behind her. His feet wouldn't make more noise in the snow than hers did and the snapping, cracking cacophony around her head was no different from what was happening to him.

He was back there, Will, getting closer because he was stronger.

He would hear if she vomited. Alex forced herself to stand still in a small copse of skinny ash trunks and sucked air deeply through her mouth until the sickness passed enough for her to think. And she listened.

Nothing.

Tears sprang, stinging her eyes. Please let her have lost him. She had no idea where she was. She could walk into anything as long as she moved blind like this.

But she had to go on.

A shattering crack sounded. Not close, but back there. It could just be the weight of snow breaking a branch,

The next barrage of breaking limbs took only seconds to reach her. She had the lead on him but she hadn't lost Will.

Here and there, where the woods had shielded the ground, she saw dark patches and ran from one to another, dashed on until she burst, abruptly, into an open space – on the edge of another snow-camouflaged ravine.

Alex changed direction and ran left, along the rim of the gully. She ran until more trees scattered the slope, and launched forward, using branches to hold on to and control her downhill charge.

She fell, cannoned head-first and rolled, arms flailing.

Winded, she found her feet and staggered on, hugging her aching middle.

The next fall landed her in a throbbing heap inside a hollowed ditch overhung with the edge of a bank where runoff had caused the earth to break away.

Alex pressed a hand over her mouth. Black flecks burst before her eyes. Passing out wasn't an option. Driving in her heels, she pushed backward into the hollow until she was completely under a ledge.

Not a ledge but earth and debris caved into the mouth of an old culvert with an icy coat over the opening where dripping water had frozen. Dimly, Alex saw a shiver of light through the blue-white veil and spread a hand on a knobby, hard surface.

The light would come from the other end of the culvert.

If she could get inside – it was as big in

diameter as she was tall – there was a chance Will would never find her. If he did, there were two entrances, which also meant two exits, and she was more agile than he was.

Alex listened intently. Her hand throbbed, deep and hard, but it was too cold for the blood to drip from the scarf.

Ice spiked her eyelashes and coated much of her face. Every move felt like a decision but when she looked at that shimmer on the ice curtain, a rush of hope gave her strength.

She chose what looked more like a piece of broken concrete than a rock and smacked it against the ice.

The noise was dulled but still she drew her neck down into the collar of her coat and waited.

Should she accept Will, his knife, and no hope out here? Or risk the noise to get into a culvert where she might have a chance?

Alex battered at the ice and swallowed a sob when it cracked and a hole opened the size of a fist. The beating of her heart in her throat shortened her breath, but she hacked faster and the hole grew bigger.

A jagged slice of ice broke away. The smaller, the less obvious the opening she made, the better. She didn't hesitate to shove a booted foot through the space and squeeze inside. The freeze deadened an odor of rot but she still gagged, held her nose and breathed through her mouth. And she prayed the smell of death came from nothing more horrifying than rodents.

Thirty-Nine

Not one of them could have expected an a-hole driving a combination mega lorry and construction-sized cement mixer to opt for committing mass murder – even though he would die pulling it off.

O'Reilly had managed a hair-raising but successful one-eighty through oncoming traffic and they'd ended up heading in the right direction . . . before the mammoth mixer turned suicidal.

From the back seat, craned forward to see between O'Reilly and Lamb, Tony felt his mouth open but the only noise he heard was the wild, grinding howl of the mud-covered monster lurching across the path of the Volvo no more than a hundred and fifty yards ahead.

'Back up,' Lamb yelled. 'Back up!'

He was, Tony realized, shouting to the lorry driver, not O'Reilly. The colors of other vehicles spun around them, running together before his eyes. A steady blare of horns drummed amid the shrieking of tires that weren't grabbing anything but ice.

O'Reilly cranked the steering wheel left, as hard left as it would go, and the Volvo shuddered, slid, found some traction and leaped inches from the road to slam into a bank. They roared upward, O'Reilly pumping the brakes and fighting for control.

They stopped.

Tony fell backward against the seat. His father didn't make a sound. In the front seat, Lamb filled any lull with colorful language mostly unintelligible to Tony.

He started to open his door.

'Stay where you are,' O'Reilly snapped. 'We need to move. Now.'

Miraculously, the Volvo made a smooth descent to the roadway – only to be confronted by the maniac equipment driver who waved his arms in front of them until they stopped.

'Not now,' O'Reilly hissed. He told Lamb to, 'Give the fool a card and warn him off.'

They were already moving again when Lamb rolled down the window and a scrawny man covered with cement dust from the top of his Mohawk to the steel caps of his Doc Martens grabbed the open rim and stuck his head inside the car.

'Shite,' said O'Reilly the Irishman, braking again. 'Take our number and call it in, son. We'll deal with you later. And get out of our way.'

The man pointed back to his cab and yelled, 'The police are for emergencies, right? My missus is dying in there.'

Forty

Cradling her left hand, Alex molded her body tighter to the curve of the culvert. When her lungs burned, she remembered to breathe. Listening so hard her ears popped, even the sound of air shifting in and out of her body was too loud.

There was nowhere else to go. Not any more. Here she would stay until help arrived – how could it? – or Will came. If help came, it would be Tony or the police and they would come, shouting and running and sliding. If Will came, it would be like a snake, looking for a silent way to wherever she was, the knife in his hand.

And if it got dark, if the icy veils at either end of the culvert turned from hazy blue-white to black, would she have the strength, the courage to crawl out and try to find her way, or would the cold and the weakness she felt seeping into her have left her to slip away in this huge, stinking pipe?

Whispering reached her.

Alex held her breath again and listened, tried to make out voices, or a voice.

The light changed. At the end furthest from where she'd climbed in here, the end where the ice was unbroken and looked thicker, a black rim showed like the thinnest crescent moon painted in silhouette.

She sighed, slumped a little . . . until the whispering came again, and the black crescent became a half moon, slipped to obscure the lower half of the opening, then covered it completely in a final shushing crescendo of the whisper.

Sweat broke out on her face, cold sweat, and between her shoulder blades. When she blinked it didn't stop the burning in her eyes. If Will came in the same way she had, her plan was to escape the other way. But she knew what had

274

happened. Snow and ice and probably rocks had fallen like an avalanche to block the second opening.

The waves of tremors started in her knees. If she didn't hold on, she'd slide into the muck that rose around her ankles. Panic didn't respect her needs. Now she needed to cling to some shreds of reason, not pass out from a lack of air.

With her mouth pressed beneath the cuff of her right sleeve, Alex blew. She blew and blew and sucked in, and blew, trying to imagine inflating her parka. Somewhere there was a character that blew up, or looked puffy, something made of rubber . . . or pastry. A doughy, pastry creature, white like the world and blowing up with each push of air. A laugh came out as a hiccup and she pressed a forearm over her mouth.

The Land Rover. Someone would see it beside the road and at least wonder. They'd call it in? The police would come. They could be coming now, clambering all over the area looking for her and they'd know it was her from checking the license plate.

They could miss this altogether . . . unless she made a lot of noise.

And guided Will straight to her. He could be out there – right above or somewhere near the culvert.

Or he could have known he was finished and driven the Land Rover away to try an escape.

The opening into the culvert, the one she'd used, smashed all the way. A scream stuck in Alex's throat while she watched glittering shards of ice burst inward. Step, by backward step, she moved slowly away. *Say something. Call out.* She looked over her shoulder at the blocked end. If it wasn't heavy snow she might still break a way out.

'Bitch! I've got you now.' Will's voice echoed, hoarse and terrible, along the pipe.

Alex turned, slipped and dragged herself to the darkened ice and fought to break a way through. She scrabbled and grabbed a rough rock and hacked at the surface. It didn't give. The water from uphill must have been heavier during brief thaws and the result was an impenetrable wall.

'That greedy fool Restrick had his uses in the end,' Will said, standing still to watch her fight. 'He knew Cornelius Derwinter was paying me not to let on how he raped my wife, and how the kid wasn't mine, y'know? And the price for that holy bastard's silence was donations to mend the bloody church roof. Can you imagine that? The church roof? Me? It was your fault in the end about the other *monk* or whatever he was. If you hadn't pushed him on Restrick, I wouldn't have known where to go to get rid of him.'

Alex put her hands over her ears but heard him just as clearly.

'That one begged for his life at the end. God-fearing but begging for his life. Some tripe about having the wrong cincture. He didn't know anything about anything, just wanted to give Brother Dominic back his cincture and get his own. What's a cincture – you tell me that?'

'Will.' Her voice sounded hollow and rusted.

'And afterward, Restrick wanted out. He wanted

to go to the police and tell them what he knew – how he'd left the front door of the rectory open for me to go and talk to Brother Percy. Restrick should be dead and he will be. First you, then him, and I'm away free.'

She wanted to yell that he was mad, that everyone knew what he was and what he'd done by now, but all she dare do was wait and be quiet.

From the pocket of his coat, Will drew the knife and flicked out the blade. The noise it made was like an explosion in the enclosed space.

He started toward her, slowly. 'Why didn't you just go? Once you saw the Black Dog was doing OK again, why didn't you see you weren't needed and get out? You weren't wanted as a kid and you're not wanted now but you've ruined everything. Did you like finding the piece about your precious baby? She was lucky, she got out early. You were supposed to go away then. You were supposed to go when I fixed the electrics for the motion sensors. Nobody remembers anything around here. It was old man Derwinter who had me take the electrical classes. I'm good at it.

'Everything would have worked out. Leonard started the money again. I was getting everything back. But first it was that Edward crawling in to talk about mercy and forgiveness, then you wouldn't leave any of it alone.'

Adrenaline shot through Alex. Never taking her eyes off him, she crouched to claw up stones. She threw them at him, one after another and filled her hands with more. If she could throw darts, and she still could if she wanted to, she could throw rocks – accurately.

Will yelled and threw a forearm over his brow. And she bombarded him with more and more debris, even hitting him with the slimy carcass of a rat. Will screamed that time.

He was too close now and she threw with arms that ached.

The knife, streaking at her, showed silver for an instant. It flipped over and landed, blade into watery mud in front of her feet.

Alex snatched it up and held it in front of her. She weighted it, aimed it. Hitting him would be easy from where she stood.

With his hands spread, palms toward her, Will began walking again. 'Give it to me,' he said.

He rushed her.

Dropping the knife, Alex took the rock she still held in her left hand and aimed it for the space between his eyes. She put her whole body weight behind it and heard the squelching impact. Will had tried to turn his face aside and the missile crashed into his eye, shattered the socket.

His head snapped back, he staggered, and crumpled into the mud.

Forty-One

The sight of her, falling with every other step, scrambling uphill, her face streaked with dirt and blood and with ice caked in her hair and on her clothing, hit Tony with enough relief to all but wind him.

O'Reilly reached Alex first with Lamb close behind. She stopped trying to walk and let them hold her up.

Tony slowed down. He began to feel warmer inside – and more jumbled and besieged by emotions than he could have imagined.

He was only yards from her and he smiled. 'You gave me such a scare,' he managed to say, wanting to be the one supporting her, wrapping her in his arms.

That wasn't something he had a right to do, but in time perhaps . . . If friendship was ever there in the first place, it might grow back. He'd have to be patient; not his strong suit.

Uniformed officers ran past him and were sent on toward the open end of the culvert from which Alex had appeared. Lamb left to follow them.

'I don't think I've killed him,' Alex said, looking at his face. 'I didn't want to kill him.'

'Will's in there?' Sickened, Tony stared at the opening she'd climbed out of. 'You were in there with him?'

'He had a knife.' Her voice broke. 'He murdered Edward and Percy – and he was the one who attacked Reverend Restrick.'

He could almost feel her shock settling in. 'She doesn't have to talk about this now, right, Inspector? She can tell it all when she's warm and dry.'

Medics carrying gear, including a stretcher, hurried by them.

'Alex says the keys are in the Land Rover,' O'Reilly said. 'Will you drive it to pick up your dad and get it back to Folly-on-Weir, then?'

Tony took another step toward Alex and the detective. He was being dismissed. 'Is that what you'd like, Alex?'

She didn't answer or even seem to hear.

'My dad went to help a woman in labor.' All he saw in Alex was confusion. 'In a cement-mixer truck. I need to find him now.'

When she still didn't say anything, he turned uphill and started to climb. He couldn't feel his hands or feet – or much else.

'Tony!' Alex's shout started level and got higher. 'Tony?'

He faced her. 'I'll bring your Land Rover back. Where shall I take it?'

'To Corner Cottage,' she said, looking at O'Reilly who nodded, yes. 'That's where I'll be, then. Can you come in? Will I see you?'

He gave her two thumbs up and carried on up the hill.

From somewhere, warmth washed into him.